Praise for Jessica Clare

"[A] steamy holiday confection that equally delivers heart-warming laughs and heart-melting sighs." —*Booklist*

"This Christmas contemporary is a glorious treat. There's enough chemistry to melt snow, the story's flow is as smooth as ice, and readers will have a jolly good time taking the journey with this adorable couple."

—*Publishers Weekly* (starred review)

"Great storytelling . . . delightful reading. . . . It's fun and oh-so-hot." —*Kirkus Reviews*

"[Clare is] a romance writing prodigy."

—Heroes and Heartbreakers

"Blazing hot." —*USA Today*

A Cowboy Under the Mistletoe

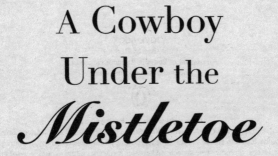

JESSICA CLARE

JOVE
New York

A JOVE BOOK
Published by Berkley
An imprint of Penguin Random House LLC
penguinrandomhouse.com

Copyright © 2019 by Jessica Clare
Excerpt from *The Cowboy Meets His Match* copyright © 2019 by Jessica Clare
Penguin Random House supports copyright. Copyright fuels creativity, encourages
diverse voices, promotes free speech, and creates a vibrant culture. Thank you for buying
an authorized edition of this book and for complying with copyright laws by not
reproducing, scanning, or distributing any part of it in any form without permission.
You are supporting writers and allowing Penguin Random House to continue to
publish books for every reader.

A JOVE BOOK, BERKLEY, and the BERKLEY & B colophon
are registered trademarks of Penguin Random House LLC.

ISBN: 9781984804006

First Edition: October 2019

Printed in the United States of America
1 3 5 7 9 10 8 6 4 2

Cover art and design by Sarah Oberrender
Book design by George Towne

For Kristine

CHAPTER ONE

He had arrived.

Jason Clements drove his small pickup truck down the long gravel driveway that led to the Price Ranch, which was to be his new home and place of work. He didn't stare at the farmhouse for too long, but instead focused on the scenery. Wyoming was very wide-open, he saw, and he liked that. There were mountains in the distance, but here surrounding the ranch it was very flat. He found that comforting.

No place for snipers to hide.

He liked the look of the place, with its pristine snowy ground, the frosted trees, the crisp scent of the air, and the white-capped mountains in the distance. That all seemed mighty nice.

Then he saw the herd of cattle. His mouth went dry at the sight of so many of the big animals. That sure seemed like a lot of livestock. And he was going to be a cowboy?

Maybe this was a bad idea.

Then again, he didn't have a lot of options left. He parked his truck in the driveway, thinking. He'd worked as an auto mechanic last, until a car in the parking lot backfired and he hit the deck, sweating. His coworkers had stared at him so hard that when he could stand, he'd brushed himself off and walked out the door. He'd never gone back. The job before that was truck driving, but he'd hated the long hours in the enclosed cab and the constant stops at motels. He never felt safe. Before that? It was a string of utterly forgettable jobs, all sabotaged in one way or another because he couldn't forget the past.

In a tight moment, his brain still thought he was in Afghanistan, in that ambush. And that usually ruined everything for him.

But this place was open and spacious, and there weren't a lot of overhanging buildings with second floors or high ledges or anything that made him uneasy. It was just a tiny ranch in the middle of nowhere . . . and what looked like hundreds of cattle.

Hundreds of cattle that he was supposed to know something about.

Even as he stared at the herd, a cowboy walked over to his vehicle. He'd come out of the sprawling ranch house and approached, dressed in a puffy vest over a red-checkered flannel shirt, jeans, and boots. He definitely looked like more of a cowboy than Jason ever would.

Jason was here, though. He'd driven all day and all night to come here. Might as well go through with the charade.

The cowboy nodded at Jason as he exited the vehicle. "You must be Jordy's cousin."

"That's me. Jason Clements." He stuck his hand out for the other man to shake.

"Taller than I thought you'd be." The cowboy grabbed it

and gave him a hard, firm handshake. "I'm Eli. Jordy's a good kid."

Jordy was nearly twenty-five, only five years younger than Jason, but he still had an innocence about him that Jason hoped the navy wouldn't drum out of him. "He is."

"Anyone he recommends is good in my book," Eli said. "We'll be glad to have you. Come to the house. I'll show you around."

And that was that. Some of Jason's tension eased, and he followed Eli as the cowboy crunched through the snow and walked toward the house. His heart sank as a dog rushed out to meet Eli, tail wagging. It looked nothing like his German shepherd, Truck, but the sight still filled him with an ache that hadn't left since his dog had died last year. Truck would have loved all this wide-open space.

As they walked up to the covered porch, a woman with dark, long curls came to the door. She had a baby in her arms and beamed a smile in his direction. "You must be Jason. I'm Cass, Eli's wife and the housekeeper here." She took one of the baby's chubby hands. "And this is Travis."

"Nice to meet you both," he said. Jordy had warned him about all the babies. It seemed two of the three cowboys had just gotten married and had children, so he could expect lots of diaper talk. He didn't mind, not really. As long as they left him alone and his thoughts stayed clear, he was fine with as much diaper talk as the next person. So he smiled at her, but that smile faded when more dogs crowded the doorway around their legs.

He'd forgotten to ask about dogs. It made sense that there were dogs, of course. The few YouTube videos he'd watched about ranching to prep for his job showed that there were cattle dogs that helped out, rounding up strays and chasing off predators. It hadn't really occurred to Jason that there'd be so many at the Price Ranch, though, and that each one would feel like a knife in his gut.

He missed his service dog something awful. Truck had been more than just a companion while he readjusted to civilian life, he'd been a lifesaver. He'd known when Jason was about to panic, and had steered him out of areas that might have triggered his PTSD. Without Truck at his side this past year, he felt lost. At first, he hadn't wanted to replace his dead friend, but after several triggered events and lost jobs, he'd made inquiries about a new service dog.

Truck had been gifted to him by a charity when he'd first been diagnosed with PTSD. Getting a second dog wasn't so easy, though. Turned out they cost tens of thousands of dollars, and the wait was more than a year. He'd just have to suffer through on his own until he could afford one. Which was another reason why he needed this job.

He rubbed his mouth and did his best not to look at the tails wagging with delight at the sight of him. Instead, he focused on what Eli was saying.

They all lived in the sprawling ranch house, it seemed. As he went inside, he took careful note of his surroundings. The house had a log cabin feel to it despite the size, with rustic decor and woven rugs. There was an enormous plaid couch in the main room, and several sitting chairs. A huge Christmas tree took up the far corner of the room across from the fireplace, and stockings were hung over the large fireplace. Christmas carols played softly in the background. It seemed very domestic and charming, but he still scanned it twice to make sure there were no hidden corners as far as he could see, no shadowy places where an enemy could hide.

Habit.

As they entered the living area, he met another woman with bright red hair named Annie, who had a baby as well, and more dogs at her feet. Her husband, Dustin, was out moving the herd, and Jason was told that another cowboy, Old Clyde, had been here for the past forty years, but he'd recently gotten married to his sweetheart in town, Hannah, and had moved into Painted Barrel proper to help her with the inn. It'd just be him and Eli and Dustin ranching over the winter, and they'd get a greenhorn or two to help over calving season.

He nodded and pretended to look like he knew what they were talking about. All the while, the bright smiles of the women and the dogs underfoot were eating away at his bravado. He avoided looking at any of them, hoping they wouldn't see the lies on his face.

"So, where did you ranch before?" Eli asked him.

Damn, it was the question he knew would come up, but he still wasn't ready. "Quarter Circle in Kansas," Jason said, making up a lie. He'd passed by the place as he'd driven, and it seemed as good a place as any. Truth was, he'd never ranched a day in his life, but when Jordy had called and said he was joining the navy and asked if he knew anyone that wanted a ranching job, Jason had jumped at it.

He might have lied a little about his experience.

Or, okay, a lot.

The lie didn't seem to be setting them off yet, though. Eli grunted, arms crossed as he nodded. "Can't remember. How many head did they have?"

Of cattle? Jason thought for a moment about what would be a good answer. "Thousand." That sounded like a decent number. How many cattle did a productive ranch have, after all?

When Eli's brows rose, he knew he'd messed up. "This should be easy for you, then," was all he said. "We run about four hundred."

"Great," Jason said, and he felt like a fraud.

Eli pointed at Jason's leg. "Noticed you have a bit of a limp. That going to be a problem?"

This was more comfortable territory, oddly enough. Jason rubbed his thigh. "I took five bullets in Afghanistan in an ambush. One tore my ACL pretty bad. The limp doesn't mean it's not working, though." He smiled to put them at ease.

"Oh my goodness," Annie breathed, holding her baby closer. "What an ordeal. Thank you for your service, though."

He nodded, doing his best not to look at the dogs that crowded nearby, eager for attention. "My old injury won't be a problem, I assure you. I'll work as hard as I can."

"I'm sure you will," Eli said. He gestured at the Christmas tree in the corner of the room. "With the holidays coming up, we're going to be short-staffed. Annie and Dustin are leaving in about a week to go stay with family in LA, and Old Clyde's gonna be visiting his daughters. That means it'll just be me and Cass here on the ranch . . . and you, unless you've got plans."

"No plans," Jason said. His parents and brothers were back east, but they knew he was working. He'd send cards and make a few calls for the holiday, but right now a job and making money was more important than a holiday with family.

Plus, he'd been so messed up in the head lately that he didn't much feel like celebrating.

"All right, well." Eli clapped his hands and rubbed them together. "Enough chitchat. I'll show you to your rooms, and then we can saddle up and I'll show you around the ranch."

Saddle . . . up?

Right now? Start working? He was a military man, had done dozens of combat trainings, seen war-torn countries and nearly lost his life in the process. He'd seen some shit go down. He'd made difficult choices.

But right now? He was breaking out in a cold sweat at the thought of riding a horse.

"I can't right now," Jason blurted, pretending he didn't see the surprised looks on the women's faces, or the cool, shuttered regard in Eli's face. "I have some stuff I have to take care of in town. I need until Monday."

Eli was silent, studying him under the brim of his cowboy hat.

"Oh, I'm sure Monday's fine," Cass said, and immediately handed her baby over to her husband. "Why don't I show you your quarters, and when you come back on Monday, I'll have the linens freshened for you."

"Thank you." He wanted to leave right that moment, right now, but he somehow politely managed to follow Cass through the house as she pointed out the basement storage, the kitchen they all shared, the main living area (already covered in Christmas paraphernalia) he'd already seen, the den, and of course the bedrooms. His was a single bed with a quilt, an old wooden dresser, a small television parked atop it, and an adjacent bathroom. "It's great," he managed to tell her. "But I should get going."

"Monday, then?" she said, her voice kind.

"Monday." He nodded at her and then headed for the front of the house. He nodded at Eli, too, who just watched him without expression. "You have my number if anything pops up. I'll be back Monday first thing in the morning."

"All right, then," Eli finally said.

And Jason somehow managed to leave the house and all the dogs and all the Christmas carols behind. He stepped back outside into the brisk, open air and sucked in a deep breath.

He had until Monday to figure out what the hell he was going to do, because he wasn't sure he could do this.

Cass was silent as the tall, lean man turned and fled their ranch house as if it were on fire. She said nothing until his truck pulled out of the driveway and headed back toward town. Then she turned and looked at her husband, who had been equally quiet. He held their son, letting the baby pat a hand on his chin over and over, but the look on Eli's face was carefully blank.

She knew her husband, though. And she knew that when he was trying to hide what he was thinking, it was when he was feeling the most. "That's not a good sign, is it?"

Eli just snorted and gave the baby a jiggle. "Thousand head of cattle, my ass."

She bit her lip. "Jordy said he had experience. But the way he was looking around . . ."

"If that man knows how to saddle a horse, I'll eat my hat." Eli grabbed one of the baby's hands and pretended to eat it, much to Travis's delight. The baby giggled with happiness, and some of Cass's worry trickled away. She smiled as Eli spoke again, this time in a cooing voice aimed at their son. "He's not a cowboy, is he, Travis? No, sir, he is not. Not like Daddy."

Annie came to her side, a worried look on her face. "Did you see how he looked at the dogs?"

"No, why?" Cass was curious.

"Just . . . it was strange. He would look at one and then try to look anywhere but at them. And he'd start sweating." As an animal trainer, Annie was always fixated on the well-being of the ranch's many dogs. "There's a story there."

"He's a combat veteran. I'm sure there's lots of stories,"

Cass said soothingly. "And I remember Jordy was brand-new and you took him under your wing, Eli."

"He didn't lie about it, though," Eli told her flatly.

"No, he didn't, but Jordy also said his cousin was a good man and trustworthy. And I believe him. Jordy's young but he's good with people." Cass crossed her arms over her chest. She wasn't entirely sure why she was defending the newcomer—Jason—so much. Perhaps it was because she didn't want to see her husband overwork himself during the winter trying to do the labor of three cowboys. Or maybe it was because Jason Clements had seemed so very . . . alone. Like he was trying hard to find a place in the world and failing.

"We'll trust Jordy," Eli agreed, handing her back the baby and then pressing a kiss to her brow. "Jason can still have the job. But I'll be watching him closely all the same."

CHAPTER TWO

There was no holiday Sage Cooper loved more than Christmas. It always seemed to bring out the best in everyone. People donated to strangers. They made gifts for one another. They sang songs full of joy and went to parties and spent money they didn't have just to see a child's face light up on Christmas. It was the holiday that brought people together the most. She loved it and loved the spirit of community.

Maybe that's why she was trying so hard with this particular Christmas—because it'd be her last one with the Painted Barrel community.

She was going to do her best to make everyone in town enjoy the season to the fullest. Of course, she hadn't counted on all of the Christmas decorations for the town's future holiday fest coming in sheets instead of punched out. It was too late to order new ones, so there she was, sitting on her stool behind the counter on her day off and punching snowflake after snowflake out of cardboard.

Someone had to do it, after all.

She didn't really mind. It wasn't like she had family to go home to, or anyone to buy Christmas presents for. Which was depressing if you stopped to think about it, so she chased the thought out of her mind and went back to dutifully punching snowflakes.

"I should have known I'd find you here," called out a cheery voice. "You do realize it's Saturday?"

Sage looked up, beaming a smile at her childhood friend (and onetime crush) Greg Wallace. "Oh, I know. But this has to get done and I don't mind it."

"You never do." Greg sauntered up to the counter in the small office. He picked up a snowflake, studied it, then tossed it back down. "Cute."

"Thanks. Where's Becca?"

He grinned at her. Once upon a time, that grin made her heart flutter with longing. She'd had the biggest, nastiest crush on Greg ever since she could remember. Her earliest memories of him were in fourth grade, when his braces came off and he beamed a huge, white smile at her. Maybe that was when it started, but it got really bad her senior year of high school, and she'd pretty much been head over heels for him all her adult life. He had pale blond hair and a nice face, but the thing she liked most about him was his personality. She'd dreamed of marrying him. She'd written their paired names in notebooks and composed teenage love letters to him, positive that someday he'd notice her.

Instead, he'd dated every girl in Painted Barrel but her, and was now engaged to Becca Loftis, the only beautician in their tiny town and the sweetest angel of a human being ever. So how could she be sad about that? She was friends with Becca, friends with Greg, and she was truly happy for them.

And if Greg and Becca had been engaged for more than

five years and Sage occasionally had the thought that maybe he didn't want to marry Becca, well, that was just wishful thinking. She'd gotten over her crush.

It didn't mean that she wasn't happy to see Greg, though.

He shrugged and picked up another snowflake, leaning over her counter. "Working on a Saturday morning. Someone had a beauty emergency, and Becca squeezed her in even though we have plans." He rolled his eyes. "What are you up to?"

"This." Sage gestured at the snowflakes spread out in front of her. "The holiday festival is next week, and I can't wait until the final moment to have everything ready. I'm handling the decorations and flyers today, and then Monday through Wednesday is finalizing food, cleaning the conference room, and then lining up last-minute fixes." She plucked the snowflake out of his hands before he could bend all the corners. "Don't touch."

"I see we're all festive." He eyed her stuffed antlers headband and her light-up reindeer sweater. "I have no idea where you find that stuff, but it's hideous."

She just laughed. She knew it was hideous, but it was attention getting and a conversation starter, and lately Sage had been so lonely that she'd take any conversation she could get. "You know me. I love Christmas. How's the wedding coming?"

Greg and Becca were finally going to walk down the aisle two weeks from today.

"Great," Greg said, beaming at her. "You're going to the rehearsal dinner?"

"I wouldn't miss it."

"You bringing a plus-one?" Before she could answer, he chuckled. "Wait, I forgot who I'm talking to. This is Sage Cooper. She never dates!"

Her smile froze on her face. "Right. It'll just be me."

She was sure that Greg hadn't meant to hurt her feelings, but gosh, that comment left a mark. It was well-known around Painted Barrel that she never dated. None of the local boys had ever been interested in Sage. She was the dimpled, cheery little sister to all instead of the gorgeous one they chased after. She went to softball games and played paintball with the rest of them. She went hunting with the guys. She was the first kid to have a PlayStation back when she was growing up, and everyone hung out at her house. She'd always been friends with all the guys, but never more.

And now at twenty-nine, that hadn't changed. Even her dating profiles on the four different apps she'd signed up on got no hits. She was man-repellent. They saw her name and ran.

It was yet another reason to move.

"Nothing wrong with coming alone," Greg teased her, that winning smile on his face. "I'll tell everyone you're still pining after me."

She laughed, because it wasn't in her nature to pine, and she really, truly was happy for him and Becca. "You do that."

Greg chuckled. He watched as she expertly punched another snowflake and then gave her a curious look. "I forgot, this is your last Christmas here in town, huh?"

"Last one," she agreed with a cheerful note in her voice. "I'm selling Dad's ranch in the spring. Most of the livestock are gone, and there's just cleaning things up to prepare for a move."

"Where to?"

She honestly had no idea. Somewhere with a larger dating pool than Painted Barrel, Wyoming—population 200 or so. Sage shrugged. "Casper, maybe. Or maybe someplace east. I've always wanted to see New York City."

Greg blanched in horror. "Why? You'd miss the mountains and the fresh air." He leaned forward on her desk. "You'd miss me."

That flirt. She knew he meant nothing by it, so she just gave him a wry smile. "I *would* miss you. I'd miss all my friends."

"Best friends," he corrected, grinning at her. "Me and Becca both would miss you."

Annnd yet another reason to move. Sage only smiled absently at him and went back to work on her decorations. "What are you doing?"

"Oh, just came by to have some mail metered and stuffed." He shrugged and pulled out a thick stack. "More marketing pamphlets, you know?"

She did. He was doing his best to make his real estate business launch, but there wasn't a lot of housing turnover at this end of Wyoming. She'd helped him with his pamphlets before. "I'm here working late. Just leave them with me."

He gave her a grateful look and pushed them across the counter. "You know I appreciate you, Sage."

"Oh, I know," she replied cheerfully. But he didn't love her. And she was tired of just being everyone's friend, so she was leaving in the spring, absolutely.

Greg stayed and chatted for a while, but it was clear he was just killing time while Becca worked late. Once the tiny hairdresser popped her head in the door, Greg gave the counter a cheery thump and then pointed at Sage. "So you'll get those in the mail for me?"

"I will, but it's Saturday. By the time they get picked up it'll be Monday."

"The mail's running in Casper, I heard. Holiday hours. You think you could take them there before the end of the day so they can be in everyone's mailboxes first thing on

Monday instead of later in the week?" He gave her a pleading look. "I'd do it myself, but me and Becca have to work on wedding stuff."

Drive all the way to Casper today? She hesitated, but at the look he gave her, she sighed and nodded. "If I head in that direction, I'll take them." And she immediately switched to the pamphlets, since she'd need to prioritize them if she was taking them to Casper later today before the post office there closed.

Greg winked at her and then rushed out the door, murmuring an apology to his fiancée.

And then Sage was alone with her snowflakes and Greg's work. She gazed down at a copy of one pamphlet, which was bragging about how he'd sold a nearby farm, and inwardly winced at a typo on the cover. Maybe if she printed up some black stickers, she could cover that extra apostrophe without anyone noticing.

Greg was lucky he had a friend like her.

The thought made Sage feel incredibly lonely, though, and she picked up her phone and scrolled through her dating apps. No real hits, just the weird messages she got from old men wanting to exchange nudes. No, thank you. She flipped through app after app, but no, Sage Cooper was just as much man-repellent as she ever was.

With a sigh, she tossed her phone back down on the counter and picked up Greg's paperwork. It'd be different in New York City. Probably.

It was December, and Jason was sweating.

He walked along the snowy sidewalk in Painted Barrel, focusing on the quaint buildings that lined the main street of town.

It had been six years since Afghanistan. He could have sworn he was getting better. But because it was a blustery winter and the town was small, it was quiet out.

Too quiet.

No one came out of the souvenir shop across the street, or went into the hotel. The gas station at the far end of the street, the only one in town, was empty. The lights were on, and he could see the clerk reading a magazine behind the counter. Painted Barrel boasted a bar that doubled as the town's only restaurant, but because it was midafternoon, it was closed. No one was around. It was like the entire town was deserted, despite the festive wreaths that hung on the doors.

His sweating grew more intense. Jason could feel his heart speeding up, and adrenaline rushed over his body. The sky overhead was bright blue despite the fresh layer of snow on the ground, and it felt . . . open. Too open.

Open was bad.

It reminded him of that day that everything happened, when he was visiting a village just outside of Kabul. When a gunman opened fire, killing his buddy and shooting him five times and nearly taking his life.

Ever since then, quiet spaces bothered him. Small towns bothered him, too.

Kinda dumb for you to take a job as a cowboy, then. He could hear Kirk's voice in his head, even though Kirk was dead these last six years. And heck, maybe it was dumb, but Jason really thought he could learn to handle this over time. Even after his PTSD service dog, Truck, passed away, he kept hoping things would change. That he'd have a break-through and wake up "normal" again.

Guess not.

His sweating increased and the self-preservation instincts kicked in. He needed to find someplace to hide.

Anywhere, really. Just needed to get out of the open, and fast. Panting, Jason raced down the sidewalk and tried the first door he came to. Locked. With a low growl of frustration, he sprang to the second one, and when it opened, he flung himself inside.

A wall of heat hit him, and he skidded on the tile floor, his wet boots unable to find traction. Jason slammed into the wall and stayed there for a moment, trying to calm down. He sunk down low, the urge to crouch and hide overwhelming.

To take cover.

Someone cleared their throat. "Hi, can I help you?"

Jason closed his eyes. He didn't know where he was at the moment, but he was pretty sure he'd just made a spectacle of himself. And since Painted Barrel was a small town—population about two handfuls—it was sure to be on everyone's lips in less than a day. That was bad. The last thing he needed was his new employer finding out that Jason suffered from PTSD.

Great. Just great.

"Are you . . . here to return a library book?" The voice was kind, quiet. Soft.

He cracked an eye open, willing his racing pulse to slow down. "I need a moment."

"Take all the time you need," the woman said. "Let me know if I can get you anything."

And that was it. She said nothing else.

Huh. That wasn't the normal reaction he got when he lost it. People panicked when he did, assuming that because a nearly seven-foot-tall man was freaking out that there was something to freak out over. Because of his height, Jason wasn't real good at blending in with the crowd, so when he lost control, everyone noticed.

He was rather thankful that the woman left him alone. He leaned back against the wall and tried to focus, to ground himself in reality. No one was shooting at him. There were no snipers in nearby windows. It was quiet not because people were waiting to attack, but because it was just quiet.

So he focused on coping mechanisms, wishing again that Truck's warm, comforting presence was at his side. He forced himself to pay attention to his surroundings. Wood paneling on the walls. Serviceable metal-armed chairs—two of them—across from him. The room itself was small, and off to one side there was a shelf of books that all looked as if they were twenty years old and hard used. There was a computer in a corner, with an uncomfortable-looking chair parked in front of it, and a solitary counter. Behind the counter were rows of what looked like metal mailbox cubbies and a woman.

A woman in a very ugly Christmas sweater and a headband with stuffed reindeer horns.

She smiled at him, noticing his attention. "Take your time. You're not the first person to come in here sweating at the thought of paying your bills." And she winked, as if that weren't the most ridiculous thing ever to say.

He laughed, the sound nervous. "I didn't come in for a bill."

"Library fine, then?" She arched a brow at him.

Jason found himself laughing again. He took off his baseball cap—wet and cold with dampness—and ran a hand through his military-short hair. "Is that where I am? The library?"

"You are in the municipal building of Painted Barrel, Wyoming," she told him in a voice that was somewhat proud, somewhat wry. "We handle the water bills. And the mail. And the library." She gestured at the sad shelf of books. "And animal control, but I have to warn you that if you've got anything bigger than a stray dog, I'm going to need help bringing him in."

He stared at the woman in surprise, noticing her appearance—well, beyond the ugly sweater and antlers—for the first time. She was about his age, maybe a few years younger. Pretty, golden-brown hair that hung like a curtain past her shoulders. Round face. Dimples. Gorgeous eyes, gorgeous smile, and a welcome expression.

He liked her immediately, more so because she hadn't acted like he was crazy. "Are you the mayor?"

"I am a municipal clerk," she admitted, moving to one side and picking up a coffeepot. She poured some coffee into a ceramic mug and then came from behind the counter and approached him, holding it out. As she approached, he noticed that while her sweater was ugly and boxy, her legs were thick but shapely and she had a great, round bottom. She didn't look like the kind of girls he normally dated, but he liked that she was different. She didn't look like someone that wanted to go out to the club and drink the night away—she looked like someone that'd be happy curling up on the couch with you.

And he liked that most of all.

"What's your name, municipal clerk?"

"Sage, like the herb," she announced, crouching next to him and offering the coffee. "If you don't like caffeine, I can make a pot of decaf."

He took the mug and gulped half of it down before he could think about it. He was feeling more normal with every moment that passed, and Sage-like-the-herb was a great distraction. She was pretty, she was sweet, and she apparently had a sense of humor. "You offer everyone coffee when they come in to pay the bills?"

"In the winter, I have to spike it with something once people hear just how bad the heating bill is." She winked at him and then got to her feet. "Kidding. I don't offer to everyone. You just looked like you needed something to drink." She tilted her head, studying him. "And you must be . . . Jason Clements, right? Jordy's cousin?"

Jason stiffened, all the pleasure rushing out of him. "Why, because I came in here with my head all messed up?" His tone was abrasive, accusing. "Is that the rumor around town?"

Her big, brown eyes widened. "No," she said softly. "Because you didn't know who I was. Painted Barrel's kind of small. We don't get a lot of newcomers that wander in, especially in winter. One bad snow and the passes close, so we know all of the new people that come around. Jordy said his cousin was coming here to ranch and that you were tall." Her smile returned, but it was hesitant, tight around the edges.

He felt like an ass. "Sorry. I'm a little distracted today." He'd slept in his car last night and he was definitely feeling it this morning.

"It's okay."

"And I'm a jerk."

One of the dimples returned. "You said it, not me."

He found himself smiling again. "I, ah . . . have a bit of a phobia about being outdoors when it's real quiet." Jason hated to admit it, but he didn't want her looking at him strangely. He wanted to keep her smiling. "Sometimes it sneaks up on me."

To his surprise, she nodded and went back to stand

behind the counter. "I had an uncle who was agoraphobic. I recognized the look."

She did? She wasn't judging? He ran a hand over his mouth and then drank the rest of the coffee. Most times when people heard he had PTSD from the war, they acted like he was utterly crazy and about to snap, or they gave him pathetic, pitying looks and treated him like a drooling idiot. He hated both reactions.

Jason found himself getting to his feet, and he returned the coffee cup on the counter. "I appreciate the understanding. I haven't told many people about that."

The woman—Sage—flashed him another dimpled smile and picked up a stack of mail, sorting Christmas catalogs into piles. "This is a no-judgment zone. Well," she amended, tilting her head and making the reindeer antlers cock, "unless you came here to use the library computer to look up porn like the high school kids do. Then I'm going to judge you."

He snorted. "No, ma'am."

"Miss," she clarified, and to his surprise, she turned bright red in the cheeks. "It's miss. I'm not married."

"Ah." He didn't know what to say. She looked distinctly uncomfortable, her face as red as the reindeer nose on her sweater. She was pretty, and charmingly sweet, but it was clear his head was still a damn mess. Asking her out would be a bad idea. Besides, she probably had a boyfriend in a town as small as this. He cleared his throat. "I guess it's a good thing I'm here at the library."

"Oh?" She tucked a strand of long, silky hair behind her ear, and he tried not to look at how cute—or small—that delicate ear was. "You need a book?"

"Yeah. On ranching. Something like *Ranching for Dummies* would be great."

Her pretty brown brows furrowed, and her mouth pursed. He noticed that she had real full, pink lips that would be perfect for kissing, and then he got mad at himself for noticing that. For a man not interested in dating, he sure was liking everything he saw about Sage. "I'm sorry, did you say a book on ranching?"

"I did."

"I . . . thought you were a cowboy? Working out at the Price Ranch?"

He managed a rueful smile. "Hence you see my dilemma. I need to know a lot, and real quick before anyone finds out I don't know what I'm doing."

CHAPTER THREE

S age blinked at the tall, sweaty man standing in front of her. She must not have heard him correctly. "You want to learn ranching from a book?"

He rubbed his hair and then had a chagrined look on his face when his hand came away sweaty. "Yeah," he said, distracted by the sheen on his hand. "Like I said, I don't know what I'm doing and I'm going to get fired before I get my first paycheck." Jason wiped his hand on his jeans and then looked up at her, dark eyes wary. "If you don't have a book, it's fine."

"This is the library," Sage chirped, putting on a chipper mood. "Of course we have books. I just . . . don't know if you'll find what you need. Ranching's a more practical-type job than something that can be written out in a user manual. It's all about doing whatever is needed on the ranch that day." She went to the nonfiction shelves (both of them) and skimmed through the books there, looking for something that would fit his needs. "I have books on gardening, and canning, and oh, one on goat husbandry." She pulled it off the shelf and held it out to him.

Jason nodded, dusting off his pants with a nervous gesture. He took the book from her and gave it a wry look. "I think they have cattle. Is it the same?"

Oh dear. "Uhhhh." Sage gave him a forced smile. "Not really?"

He grimaced. "What about a book on riding horses?"

She bit her lip. "No."

"How to run farm equipment?"

She shook her head.

Jason rubbed a hand along his jaw. "Well . . . what do you have here?"

Sage turned and picked up a thick book off one of the shelves. "We have Harry Potter! While I can't imagine it'll teach you much about farming, it's very enjoyable."

He stared at her as if she were crazy.

"That was a joke." She bit her lip again. "Sorry."

"It's okay. I'm just . . . struggling right now. I've gotten myself into a bit of a jam." He was sweating again, she realized. The poor man was terribly nervous and unsettled. He kept glancing at the window, as if he expected to be jumped. Perhaps this wasn't agoraphobia after all. He was defensive about things, too. There was a story there, but she didn't know what it was.

All Sage knew was that he was a person in trouble and needed her help. And she was nothing if not the helpful sort. "Have you ever been on a ranch in the past?" She hugged *Harry Potter and the Order of the Phoenix* (her favorite in the series) to her chest. "Or had any sort of outdoors type of job? Camping? Fishing? Anything?"

"I was in the navy for six years. Master-at-arms. I can tell you down to the nuts and bolts how often a base posts patrols and what kind of official protection visitors should have at a foreign base, but I don't know shit about ranching." He grimaced as the cuss word left his mouth. "Sorry."

"That's all right. Shit!" she exclaimed and then blushed because she sounded like an idiot when, really, she was just trying to make him feel better. "I don't mind a bit of damn cussing."

His mouth quirked a little, as if he were going to smile. "You're not very good at it."

Her nose wrinkled. "No, I guess I need a little work on it. Maybe I'll pick some up if you stay around, dammit."

Jason chuckled, and a slow smile spread across his lean face, and oh, her heart did the craziest little flip. Despite the sweating and the weird situation, Jason Clements, newbie to Painted Barrel, was handsome. He was tall and wiry, and his cheekbones were blade sharp. His eyes were piercing, and his dark hair was cropped extremely short—naval regulation, maybe? But his smile was utterly breathtaking.

And he was *smiling* at her. Even though she was being goofy and weird and wearing ridiculous reindeer antlers, he was smiling at *her*. Sage Cooper.

Man-repellent.

It was a heady feeling. In that moment, she wanted to help him and get more of those smiles. Whatever was causing his stress, she wanted to help him fix it. Sage genuinely loved helping people, but she had a different goal in mind when she looked at Jason. She just wanted him to smile again.

"You really don't know how to ranch?" she asked.

He pursed his lips and shook his head.

"Why did you lie?" It didn't seem like a job anyone would take on the spur of the moment. There were easier jobs out there than ranching, and they probably paid a heck of a lot more.

Sage watched, fascinated, as his jaw clenched. "Reasons."

Meaning that he had a secret. Well, that was all right. She'd always thought of herself as an open book, but things had changed over the last year. After all, weren't her dating app profiles a secret? A humiliating, awful secret that Greg would laugh and laugh about if he knew . . . and then tell Becca? Who would then tell everyone in Painted Barrel?

Yeah, Sage knew all about keeping things secret to protect yourself.

"I won't ask," she told him. "But I can help you."

Jason looked at her with a frown and then dawning realization. "You can get me some books?"

"Well, not exactly." She hugged *Order of the Phoenix* tighter to her chest, as if to bolster herself. "But I do have a ranch."

His eyes flared with interest, and the breath stole from her lungs. Oh, were his eyes gray? She liked that. She liked that a lot. "You do?"

"Everyone here does. There's not much around Painted Barrel but ranches, you know?"

He gestured at the mail desk, where Greg's pamphlets were spread. "But I thought you . . ."

"Municipal clerk. I know. I am." She went to tuck a lock of hair behind her ear, flustered, and ended up smacking her reindeer horns. "My father was the mayor of this town before he passed, and he got me a job as a municipal clerk when I was a teenager. And I sort of stayed on and have done it ever since. But yeah, my father has a ranch, and now that he's gone, it's mine. I've sold all of the cattle but two, and just one horse. You can come over to my place and practice until you get comfortable, if you like."

He stared at her, stunned. "You'd do that for me?"

She beamed at him. "Of course. Why wouldn't I?"

"Because most people don't do things out of the goodness of their hearts. Not anymore." He rubbed his jaw again. "Can I pay you?"

Sage waved a hand, dismissing the thought. Once she sold all her father's acreage, she'd have more money than she knew what to do with. "Don't be silly."

But he gave her another intense look, leaning in. His height was . . . amazing. She gazed up at him and felt as if he were the tallest—and handsomest—man she'd ever seen. Oh, her new crush was *baaaad*. "I'd feel better if I didn't owe you," he murmured.

An idea occurred to her, and she clutched the book tighter. Did she dare? Should she ask? Her mouth worked silently, and then before she could think better of it, she blurted, "I do need a date."

A . . . date?

Jason stared at the woman in front of him. He'd just met her five minutes ago, sweating and on the verge of a panic attack, and she was asking him out? She was cute, he'd admit, but she also had terrible timing. "You want to go out with me?"

Her cheeks flushed bright red, and he noticed her dimples creased her cheeks as she smiled. Damn, but she had cute dimples. "Well, not a *date* date, but I need a plus-one for a friend's rehearsal dinner on Wednesday. He's getting married a week from Saturday, so I guess I need a date for that, too. It's kind of a joke with everyone that Sage Cooper never has a boyfriend and I want to prove them wrong." She glanced down at the thick book in her arms and fidgeted.

Really? He was surprised. While she wasn't traditionally pretty, those dimples were everything, and she had big, soft brown eyes that drew him in. He'd have dated her if he'd met her in a bar. Of course, that was back before Afghanistan, when he wasn't a damn mess in his head. Right now he wasn't sure if he should date anyone, fake or not. "I might not be an ideal date," he admitted, rubbing his sweating palms. "Why not get a real one?"

Sage looked up at him, those big eyes full of rueful amusement. "They're hard to come by out here. The only hit I ever got on a dating app—any dating app—was a cousin. We're not quite as populated as, say, Casper."

And here he'd thought Casper was small, too. This place was tinier than tiny. "Yeah, but I'm a stranger."

"Only a little. You're Jordy's cousin, and Jordy's good people." She beamed at him as if that solved everything. "And it wouldn't be a real date. I mean, it's not a real rehearsal dinner, either. Becca's birthday fell between her wedding day and Christmas and she wanted to have a legit party, so this is more of a birthday shindig disguised as a rehearsal dinner. It's all kind of complicated." She bit her lip. "Anyhow, you just have to show up and eat dinner with me, and then we'll leave fast, I promise. It's just that everyone in town thinks I'm pining after the groom, and it'd be a lot more comfortable for me if I had someone with me to stop that rumor."

She was clutching the book in front of her so hard that he was sure she was going to bend the edges of the hardcover.

"I see."

"It's okay," she said quickly, turning away and spinning on her heel. She went back to the bookshelf, returned Harry Potter, and started skimming the covers. "I'm sorry I asked. It was weird of me. Maybe we can find something that can help you out—"

"No, it's okay," Jason said quickly. "I need help before Monday. I'll be your date. How fast can you show me the basics?"

She turned back to him with wide eyes. "Really? You're sure?"

No, he wasn't sure, but she was sweet and innocent, and he was in a hell of a bind of his own making. By Monday, he had to at least look like he knew what he was doing. "I told the people at the Price Ranch—"

"Eli and Cass?" she interrupted, proving she really did know everyone around here. "Or Dustin and Annie?"

"Eli," he confirmed, and continued. "I told him that I had stuff I needed to get done and wouldn't be able to start working until Monday. I have until then to get a clue about ranching."

She didn't look intimidated by that. "We should be able to cover the basics, sure." There was a determined look in her eye. "When did you want to start?"

"When do you get off work?"

"Oh. I'm not actually working." She glanced back at the desk that was heaped with mail. "Well, I'm not supposed to be working, anyhow. I'm off the clock, but I thought I'd come in and do some of the decorations, and Greg asked me to take some pamphlets to Casper . . ." She thought for a moment and then shook her head. "But those can wait. This is more important, and one day isn't going to matter for those pamphlets. Much." Sage beamed at him. "I'll shut things down and get my purse. You got a car? Want to follow me out there?"

Just like that? She was that trusting? He knew that living out in the country was different than the city, but he was still surprised. "I have a truck."

"Great. I'll take a picture of your plates and send it to my boss, and then we'll go." She gave him another dimpled smile.

And he found himself smiling back. Maybe Sage wasn't as wide-eyed as he thought. She was trusting, yes, but smart, too.

And she was going to help him. Jason didn't know what he'd done to deserve such luck, but he'd take it and grab it with both hands.

When he pulled up behind her Jeep, for a moment, Jason thought they were lost. Or she was stopping to drop off something, because this place could not possibly be hers. The ranch in front of them was utterly sprawling. He'd thought the Price Ranch was big, with its large, rustic house and rolling fields, but what was before him put that place to shame. The enormous two-story house looked like a ski lodge, the peaked roof covered in snow and a split-rail fence lining the road up to the house itself. Everything was coated in a layer of pristine snow, and behind the house, the mountains rose high. Off to one side, he saw an equally enormous barn and a rounded row of baled hay.

All of this place for just one person? Didn't she say she wasn't married? Puzzled, Jason kept following her, not entirely convinced she wasn't going to turn around at some point. They'd driven on a few back roads out of town, this place so remote even his GPS wasn't showing much. But sure enough, she pulled up to the house and the garage door went up. She drove her Jeep inside, and he parked out front in the enormous circle drive. As he did, she bounded out to meet him, her stuffed antlers bouncing.

"Hope you didn't mind the ride," Sage said perkily. Everything about her seemed to be perky and upbeat, and he found himself responding to it in kind. Just being around her sunny attitude made him feel like smiling. When was the last time that had happened?

He gestured at the house. "This is yours?"

"It is now. Like I said, my father died and now it's just me until I manage to sell things." She hugged her jacket against herself and gazed up at the house, her expression growing wistful. "It's my home, but it's also a lot of place for just one person, and far too much ranch."

"Why wait to sell?" he asked, curious.

She gestured at the front door of the house, and he followed her. As he did, he noticed that all the windows were dark and the massive fireplace was cold. It was to be expected, of course, but did look a bit lonely from that aspect. Sage was the only life for what felt like miles around. Even the rolling fields that spread out for as far as the eye could see were empty.

"Winter's a bad time for selling," she explained to him as he trailed behind her. "Especially the holidays. No one wants to think about moving or taking on a new ranch during this time frame. They just want to snuggle up by the fire with family." She tossed him a wry smile over her shoulder. "So I'm going to wait until spring."

"Ah." He didn't know what else to say. It made sense, but it also had to be hard being out here by herself, with no one else around. She was such a chatty, personable woman that he couldn't imagine her alone in a place like this.

As they walked inside, he was staggered anew at the place. Antler chandeliers hung from the twenty-foot-high ceiling, and heavy wood furniture filled the place. Aztec rugs dominated the wood floor, and everywhere he looked, the furnishings screamed money and western themes. Two large sofas were placed across from each other with a glass table between them, and a large flat-screen television was hung over the sprawling stone fireplace, just adding to the feel of the whole "ski lodge" vibe. It was a great home, but it also didn't match the dimpled woman with reindeer antlers and an ugly sweater who stood next to him.

For one, there were no Christmas decorations, and that surprised him. The Price Ranch had been wall-to-wall holiday decor, and given Sage's outfit, he'd have thought she'd be the type to do the same. "Nice place."

"Thanks. You want a cup of coffee? Something to warm you up before we head out to the barn?"

"Sure." He followed her as she walked into the kitchen, and this area showed signs of life at least. There were a few dirty dishes in the sink and the world's tiniest lit tree on a dining table in the eat-in kitchen. The Saltillo tile looked bold against the rustic pine cabinetry, and he wasn't sure, but the handles of the cabinets looked like horseshoes. Man, they really loved their western motifs out here. Jason leaned against one of the counters and watched as she pulled out two Christmas mugs and started the coffeepot. The sight made him smile, oddly enough. "I was wondering if you had more holiday stuff tucked away. You didn't seem like the type to have such a bare living room in December, especially not after that sweater." He gestured at the light-up reindeer.

Sage turned, leaned against the opposite counter while the coffee dripped into the pot, and grinned at him. "I love Christmas. Adore it. But there's no reason to decorate everything when it's just me out here. Even the cleaning lady only comes once a month now, and that's just to dust everything. I concentrated all of my Christmas cheer in the direction of the office and the town itself. All those wreaths on the mailboxes and light posts? The garlands? I did those. And I'm working on preparations for the town Christmas party next week, too."

"You need a date for that as well?"

Her eyes went wide. "You'd do that for me?"

Jason shrugged. "I don't have plans, and I'm gonna feel like I owe you big-time if you can help me get on my feet with this whole ranching thing."

Her expression softened, and those dark, liquid eyes looked so deep that he was entranced. "I would love that," she whispered. "Even if it's just for pretend. So everyone doesn't look at me like I'm pathetic."

"You're not pathetic. It's hard to meet people when you're trying." Heck, he'd tried real hard to get another job, and it was like the moment people smelled desperation, they backed away. He could relate to her search for a date in the same way. "I'm still not entirely sure why you're helping me, but I'm grateful."

"Why wouldn't I help you?" Sage gave him another gentle smile and then poured two cups of black coffee. "I don't have any plans for the weekend other than driving Greg's mail to Casper, but what he doesn't know won't hurt him."

"Greg? Coworker?"

"No, just a friend. The one getting married." She smiled into her cup. "You want cream and sugar?"

He shook his head and took a gulp of the coffee. Strong as hell, but she was drinking it plain and he would, too. He'd have thought she was the type to fuss up her coffee, but she drank it just as dark as he did. Interesting. There were things about Sage that made him curious, and it had been a long time since he'd been curious about a woman. She was just being friendly, though. He couldn't forget that he'd shown up on her office doorstep sweating and in a

36 JESSICA CLARE

panic. No woman would be attracted to that, even one as cheery as Sage. Disgusted with himself for being such a mess, he gulped down the rest of the scalding coffee and then set his mug down. "I guess I'm ready to get started if you are."

CHAPTER FOUR

Jason's mood was unreadable as she led him out to her barn. Once it was full of horses and livestock, back when her father's ranch was a working one and the small adjacent cabins had working cowboys that lived in them. Now it was just her, and it was a lonely place. Most of the barn was completely empty, and only two stalls were currently in use, both of them with old, rangy cattle that no one would be interested in except maybe the slaughterhouse.

"Say hello to Ethel and Lucy," she told him as they paused outside the two stalls. "The last two cattle of the Flat C Ranch." She pointed at her father's old brand, with a slanted, encircled "C." Just the sight of it made her ache, because it reminded her of her father, his big, boisterous smile and oversize hat, and the way he'd hugged her close and led her through this barn a million times as a child. The ache of loss never went away, she was learning. She was just getting better at living with it.

"These are the cows you kept?" he asked, glancing over at her.

She nodded. "Our cattle were beef cattle, so you learned not to get too attached. But when I was a kid, I bottle-fed a baby that was sick, and that baby learned to follow me around because she thought she'd get fed. We joked that Lucy was more like a dog than a cow, and my father always found an excuse not to sell her, because he knew it'd break my heart." She smiled at the memory. "Ethel was my high school 4-H project, and we never sold her for the same reason. Now they're both so old that they'd be immediately sent to the slaughterhouse, so I kept them here. I'm going to put a clause in the ranch sale that they're both allowed to live out the rest of their natural lives here. I can't bear for them to be killed just because I've moved on." She glanced over at him. "You're not supposed to be sentimental with ranching, but it's something I've struggled with."

"I get that." Jason glanced over at her, and that reluctant smile that made her heart flutter was back. Distracted, she smiled back at him, and then when he glanced at Lucy's pen, she remembered why they were here. Right. Cattle.

"Okay! So," she began, flustered. It was embarrassing to get so distracted. He was just a nice man who really needed to learn ranching. That was all. She had to stop mooning over him, no matter how endearing his smiles were. "I figured we'd start out with the most important thing—handling cattle. You stay right where you are and don't move, and I'll get Lucy in place." When he nodded, she opened the stall door and then moved toward Lucy at an angle, murmuring a greeting. "Hello there, my sweet Lucy. Look at how pretty you are. Aren't you just the prettiest little side of beef? Yes, you are. You're my sweet girl, aren't you?" As she cooed at the animal, she carefully moved into the flight zone and extended her hands slowly, so the cow would head forward. She did, and then when Lucy was out of the stall and in the middle of the big barn, nosing through the loose hay on the floor, Sage moved over to Jason's side.

He was rubbing his jaw and doing his best not to grin as he glanced over at her. "Do I have to use the baby voice?"

She chuckled. "It's a bad habit of mine, I know. I'm attached to Lucy and Ethel, but no, you don't have to use a baby voice. You do want to talk to them, though." She tapped the sides of her face. "Their eyes are spread wide apart, right? So they have a massive blind spot behind them, and you never want to approach from behind. You never want to startle a cow, either, because one nervous cow will make another nervous, and then you have a whole herd of nervous, and that's just bad news all around."

Jason nodded, his expression grave. He'd leaned in, as if he could soak in every word she told him. He was really tall, she noticed again, and she got flustered once more.

Right, cattle. *Focus, Sage.* "Do you know anything about a cow's point of balance?" At his blank look, she went on. "Flight zone? Pressure zone? Do you know what a bull looks like versus a cow?" When he shook his head again, she tried to fight back a sinking feeling. He really didn't know anything at all about ranching or animals.

This . . . was going to be more than she thought.

Okay, then. She could do this. Beaming him another confident smile, she went to work. She talked as she approached Lucy again, and gave Jason a quick anatomy lesson—not about hooves or withers, but about where a cow's point of balance was and where to stand in the flight zone to make the cattle move where you wanted them to. It was as natural as breathing to her, but she'd also been around cattle all her life. She could tell it was a lot for Jason to remember, and after a while, she felt guilty for all the instructions she was spouting at him. Make sure to walk tall when approaching the cattle. Give a new mother space. Never go directly at a cow. If the head's lowered, that's a bad sign. Watch the tail to see placement. Avoid bulls. Stand here but not there. Look strong but not aggressive. On and on it went until she could practically see his frustration bubbling. He was sweating. More than that, he was distracted. He kept eyeing the empty stalls and looking around as if the barn bothered him. She couldn't figure it out, but his agitation was affecting the cattle, and both Lucy and Ethel were starting to stamp their feet.

When his first attempt at herding ended up driving Lucy directly for her, he swore under his breath and swiped a hand over his sweating brow.

"Maybe we should stop for now," Sage suggested delicately as he began to pace.

"No. I'm going to get this right. I am." He raked a hand through his sweaty hair. "I just . . . I need to do something first."

She watched, a little mystified, as he walked away from her and headed to the far end of the barn. For a moment, she thought he was leaving, but when he swung the stall door open and scanned the interior and then moved to the next and did the exact same thing, she knew it was something else. He was . . . looking for something. But what?

This wasn't agoraphobia after all.

Curious, Sage watched him as he moved around the barn. She herded Lucy off to the side so he could continue uninterrupted, and by the time he was done, he'd checked the entire place out, top to bottom. He'd even gone up the ladder to the hayloft, kicked the hay around, and then come back down.

Of course, all of this was making Lucy incredibly nervous, so Sage guided her back into her stall and gave her fresh feed, rubbed her ears, and then turned and looked at Jason, who'd finally finished his rounds of . . . whatever it was he was doing.

His face was flushed and he was still sweating, but more than that, he looked utterly miserable. Her heart squeezed with sympathy. She waited for him to explain what he'd been doing, so she could understand.

She didn't get an explanation, though. "I should probably go," was all he said.

"No."

He looked surprised. "No?"

Whatever it was that he was going through, leaving wouldn't help. It wasn't agoraphobia, but it was definitely something, and she wasn't so awful of a person to send him home when it was clear he needed to get out of his head for a bit. "I could use some more coffee," she said, and extended her hand toward him. "And dinner. Should we go wash up? I've made enough for two."

Jason hesitated a moment and then put his hand in hers. It was clammy, but she just gave it a comforting squeeze and then led him toward the house. He was completely silent, but Sage didn't press him. She knew he needed time to figure out whatever was going through his head. Instead, she released his hand the moment she went inside and then told him all about the taco casserole she'd made and how she'd been eating it for two days already and could he please eat a ton of it so she wouldn't have to eat it all week? She kept up a stream of lively chatter as they washed up and kept it going as she heated the casserole in the microwave, plated it, and then poured two more cups of coffee and set the dining table. They ate in silence for a few moments, and

Sage peeked up to study him. He wasn't sweating any longer, which was a good sign. The corners of his mouth were turned down as if he were disgusted at something—himself? But his color was normal, and he was eating with vigor. So there was that.

"Can I ask you something?" She kept her tone light and took another bite of her food. She was going to push him, and she knew that was probably a bad idea, but she had to know what was going on if she was going to help him.

He gave her a wary look and pushed his plate away.

Sage put a hand up. "I'm not asking to judge. I just need to figure out what we're working with so I know how to help you. I can tell you all kinds of embarrassing things about me to use as blackmail material so you won't feel like I'm going to blab your secrets all over town."

He stared down at his near-empty plate, then looked up at her. Wariness—and exhaustion—was all over his handsome face. "Like?"

She thought for a moment, turning her fork on a casserole noodle. "Like . . . you know how I said everyone thought I had a crush on the guy getting married next week? I really did." She paused. "For like . . . ten years." Her cheeks were getting hot at the thought. Not because of unrequited feelings, but just because she'd mooned after Greg like an idiot and he'd gone and gotten engaged to someone else. "It's a real fuck," she said, deciding a cuss word would be placed nicely at the end of that statement.

There was no answer, and she looked up from her fork to see that Jason's mouth was beginning to quirk in that smile again. Suddenly, she felt all hot and flustered for entirely different reasons.

This . . . almost felt like a date. It was dinner, right? Cozy. Just the two of them.

Oh my lord, she really was crazy and desperate, wasn't she? Maybe the others in town were right. The thought was a depressing one.

"You're really not good at cussing," Jason said dryly.

"I'm really not." She nodded. "That wasn't natural?"

"Not in the slightest." But he was smiling at her, and oh, he was so handsome that it made her regret all those years crushing on Greg Wallace when she could have had someone like Jason smiling at her.

He kept smiling at her without speaking, and she squirmed in her seat, flustered at the attention. This wasn't a date. He wasn't her boyfriend, and she needed to stop being so lonely and desperate that she was seeing things that weren't there. Jason just wanted a tutor in ranching.

Right. She needed to focus.

Sage cleared her throat. "I need to know what it is about the barn that makes you nervous if we're going to proceed. You said it was open spaces that bothered you, but the barn is definitely not open. And I know the Price Ranch has a barn. You're not going to be able to avoid them, but maybe if you tell me what the deal is, I can help you work through it."

His Adam's apple bobbed, and she watched his throat work. He stared at her for a moment, then at a picture on the wall of her with her father and three of the ranch's cowboys from back when she was a kid. She was sitting atop a horse while her father held the reins, all pigtails and dimples and childhood chubbiness . . . and sometimes she felt like the adult Sage was as dorkily invisible as that child. Gosh, and she was wearing a reindeer sweater. She touched her head and, yup, sure enough, she was still wearing antlers.

No wonder he smiled when he looked at her. She didn't look pretty or sexy.

She looked like a festive idiot.

"It's not agoraphobia," he said flatly, dragging her attention back to the situation at hand.

"I guessed as much."

He hesitated for a long moment, staring at the picture (but she suspected not really seeing it), and finally said, "It's not open spaces, either. Not really. It's . . . a lot of things. Spots where snipers can hide. Ambush zones. Unsafe spaces where someone can hide with a gun or leap out at you and attack."

That hadn't been what she was expecting, but it made sense. She nodded and took another bite of her food, silently encouraging him to continue speaking.

It was as if the words were glue in his throat. They came out slowly, as if they didn't want to come out at all. "I was in Afghanistan. Navy, so I shouldn't have really seen much combat. But I was in security, and one outpost I was at was attacked. It was . . . bad." He was silent for a long, long time.

She chewed and chewed, but the food tasted like sawdust in her mouth. She kept chewing because it was impossible to swallow, but she had to do something.

"I . . . Sometimes the memories catch up with me," he finished.

"Of course," was all that she said. What could she say that would make it any better? Nothing. Nothing at all.

"It's been a problem with a few of my last employers. I've been fired or just quit. Kinda hard to hold down a job when you're busy checking the perimeter instead of manning your workstation." His mouth flexed, as if he was trying to smile, to make a joke, but the rest of him wouldn't play along.

"I would never say anything to anyone," Sage promised.

"You have my secret; I have yours." She reached across the table impulsively and touched his hand. "If it helps, Wyoming is very safe. Painted Barrel has only had one real 'crime' since I started working for the mayor, and it was a couple of kids breaking into the hardware store to huff paint. It's very quiet here."

The look on his face was wry. "It's not about being safe. I know that here"—he thumped his heart. "But this part doesn't know." And he tapped a finger on his temple. "I'm sure it sounds silly to you—"

"It doesn't," Sage told him quickly. "I had an uncle that was an agoraphobic, remember? Don't worry. I know it's in your head and you can't shut it off. I don't think it's silly at all. I just want to help you."

He seemed to relax a little at that. Jason touched his thumb to her hand and then pulled his away. "Just talking to you helps, you know. Knowing the area helps, too. And knowing what I'm doing when I show up for my job Monday will help, as well."

"Then I'll show you the entire ranch after dinner," she told him easily. "I don't have plans."

"No hot Saturday-night date?"

She pointed her fork at herself. "Sage Cooper, man-repellent."

He shook his head, a hint of a smile on his face again. "I don't get that. Men around here must be blind . . . or they don't like reindeer." He gestured at her sweater.

Was that a compliment? Or was he just being nice? She blushed. "I don't wear this all the time."

"'Course not." He nodded at the door. "I'd like to try again with the animals after dinner. Once I've calmed down. If that's all right with you."

"You bet—"

Sage's phone rang, the Trans-Siberian Orchestra blasting through the kitchen.

She grimaced and jumped to her feet. "Let me grab that. You keep eating." She was too flustered to eat another bite. *Men around here must be blind?* Really? She didn't know what to think. She crossed the room and picked up her phone from where it was sitting on the counter.

Greg.

Uh-oh. With a stab of guilt, she remembered the stack of real estate pamphlets sitting on her desk back at the office, the ones she'd promised to drive to Casper. "Hey, Greg," she said cheerily as she answered. "What's up?"

"Sage! Glad I caught you." Greg's voice was as cheerful as her own. She glanced over at the table and noticed that Jason had put his fork down and a hint of a frown was playing around his mouth. "Did you get those pamphlets out to Casper? Just wanted to check."

"Hmm? Oh yes! Sure did." Heavens, but she was a terrible liar. She wrinkled her nose, grimacing at how false it sounded. "They're all on their way." Or they would be as soon as she got to the office bright and early on Monday and hid them under the rest of the outgoing mail.

"Great! You're a lifesaver. That wasn't why I called, though."

"No?" Was this just friendly chatter, then? He wanted to hear her voice? Talk about the wedding plans? She was confused.

"Yeah, I wanted to ask you . . . you know those peppermint brownie cookies you make? The ones with the crushed candy canes on top?"

He was calling her about cookies? "Yes?"

"You think you could make me a batch? I've been thinking

about them all day, and no one bakes quite like you do. I could pick them up first thing on Monday."

"Oh, let me see if I have the ingredients." She went to her fridge. Eggs, milk, butter . . . She wasn't sure if she had candy canes to crush, but she supposed she could drive to the corner store and see if they had any left. "I'm sure I can whip something up."

"That'd be awesome. You're the best, Sage."

For once, his flattery didn't make her giddy with excitement. "It's just . . . does it have to be Monday? I'm really busy this weekend." She didn't look over at Jason, because she knew he was watching her, and this one-sided conversation probably sounded odd.

"You are?" He laughed. "Doing what?"

"Helping a friend."

"Who?"

"No one you know."

"You have friends I don't know? Come on, Sage."

"I'll see when I can get them done for you, but it might not be this weekend," she said again, firmly. "Did you need anything else?"

"I guess not." A pause. "I really appreciate you, Sage. You're always there for me."

And now she felt guilty. Greg was probably as crazy busy as she was—if not busier, with his wedding coming up. She couldn't imagine what his schedule was like. "Of course. What are friends for? I'll make those cookies for you as soon as I can and text you when they're ready, okay?" They mumbled goodbyes, and then she ended the call, setting the phone back down on the counter.

Jason was watching her, his arms crossed over his chest.

"You want some more taco casserole?" she asked,

pushing off the counter and moving toward the table. "There's plenty."

"I'm good. Who was that?"

"It was my friend, Greg."

"The groom?" When she nodded, his brows went down. "If you don't mind me asking, why's he calling you?"

She opened her mouth and then closed it again. Why had he called her? "Because he wanted cookies, I think. I've made them for him before."

He grunted. "Can't he get his fiancée to do it?"

That was a great question. "He's always asked me before and I never minded. Maybe that's why he's asking now."

Jason looked openly skeptical. "You're too nice. Hell, you shouldn't even be helping me."

"Why not?"

"Because no one else would bother."

"I think you're wrong," Sage told him softly. It never hurt to be kind, and Jason was in desperate need of some kindness right about now. "Besides, what else am I going to do?" She gestured wide at the house. "I'm bored and lonely. It's either this"—she motioned between him and her—"or go back to the municipal office and work on more decorations for the Christmas party."

"You don't have girlfriends to hang out with on a Saturday night?"

She huffed a laugh. "They're all married and having kids. The only reason they'd want to hear from me is if I volunteer to babysit." That brought a hint of a smile to his face, and she spoke again. "Before you can ask, no, no hot dates, either. I have four different dating profiles, and none of them have gotten a hit."

"Other than your cousin."

"Other than my cousin." And she gave a horrified giggle, because in a way, it was funny.

Jason chuckled, too. "All right. Well, maybe I can look at your dating profiles. Give you a few tips from a guy's perspective. It's the least I can do in exchange for your help. I already know more about cattle than I ever thought I'd need."

"It's my pleasure."

"You sure I can't pay you?"

Her heart stopped. Was he trying to get out of being her date to Greg's wedding? Oh, she'd be absolutely crushed if he was. In the same way, though, she'd understand. His PTSD might mean it would be too much for him to undertake. "If you don't want to be my date for the wedding, you don't have to. I'll still help you."

"That wasn't what I meant." Jason frowned at her. "I just don't want to take advantage of you. I'll still be your date."

Her voice was shy. "You're sure?"

The big man smiled at her. "I'm sure. What should I wear?"

"Just your best boots and a button-down shirt. It's not formal."

"Mmm. Guess I need boots." He glanced down at his sneakers.

Sage had to grin at that. "You're going to need them anyhow. The first time one of the cattle steps on your feet, you're going to wish for good steel-toe boots."

"Fair enough." He got to his feet. "So . . . can we try the cow wrangling again?"

"Absolutely."

CHAPTER FIVE

Because she now knew that Jason struggled with unfamiliar places, Sage got one of the ATVs out of the barn and drove him around the property so he could learn it and pause to check out anything that made him nervous. That took some time, and it was cold out, but Jason was visibly relaxing as they went over the property, and in her eyes it was worth it. They checked over the barn one more time, and when he was satisfied, they went back to the cattle.

"Sorry," he said to her as she let Lucy out of her pen again. "I know it's a lot of trouble."

"It's no trouble at all," Sage told him, and meant it. People needed different things in their life, and there was no shame in this. She wouldn't judge him. "You ready to try again?"

"I am." He nodded, and this time there was a lot more ease in his body. When he moved forward slowly, arms spread to guide Lucy back to her pen, Sage felt a burst of pride. He'd remembered what she'd told him earlier, even though she'd thrown a lot at him. He'd get this down, and by Monday, he'd know enough that they'd be impressed.

She knew the people at the Price Ranch. They were good people, and Eli was kind even if he was very gruff. As long as Jason wasn't a danger to the herd or anyone else working there, he'd do fine. He just needed to know enough to keep everyone safe.

So they practiced with Lucy a few more times, and when Sage was satisfied with his progress, she let Ethel out of her pen and let the cows spread out before having Jason herd them both together and back into their pens. They were old cattle, and slow, and she reminded him that he'd likely be dealing with cattle in their prime, and later on cattle with calves to defend, but he was doing fantastic.

They practiced over and over again, until she was yawning and the air in the barn grew so crisp she could see her breath.

After his most recent round of cattle directing, Jason closed the stall door to Ethel's pen and then glanced at his watch. "Damn, it's late." He looked up at her. "How late is that hotel in town open until?"

Uh-oh. A quick glance at her phone showed her it was two in the morning. "Hannah only keeps it open until eight at night. You're staying there?"

"That was the plan, at least until Monday." He shrugged. "I'll go drive my truck back to town and sleep in the cab again. It's not a big deal."

"Well, that's just nonsense. I have this big, empty house, and you need to be here at dawn to help with the feeding." She made her tone teasing.

His look was sober. "Sage, I know you're a nice person, but we only just met today. You sure you're going to be safe in this house with me alone? I wouldn't want to make you uncomfortable."

She'd already thought about that sort of thing, but her bedroom door locked on the inside, because they'd always had cowboys coming through the house growing up, and her father was protective. In addition, she had a heavy dresser she could park in front of it. As a woman alone, she always thought about these sorts of things, no matter the situation. But Jason felt safe. "It doesn't make sense for you to drive to town, sleep in your car, and then come back here in three hours, Jason. And if you wanted to hurt me, don't you think you could have done so a dozen times already? It's pretty obvious I'm the only one out here."

He shook his head, displeased. "You're too trusting."

Maybe so, but she instinctively knew that Jason wouldn't hurt her. He had that same protective air about him that her father had—heck, even now, he was still trying to protect her. It showed he was a decent person. "You do realize a creep wouldn't offer to leave?"

"I . . . guess?" He raked a hand through his short hair. "Still doesn't feel right."

"There's a guest room. Or if you'd rather, you can sleep in one of the cowboy cottages." She gestured at the row of four small houses lined up a short distance away from the barn. "But if you do, you need to be ready to go at five in the morning. I'll make breakfast, and then we'll get started."

He didn't move, clearly hesitant. "You said yourself this is a small town and people gossip. Won't they gossip about me being out here all weekend?"

Oh, they would. They definitely would. Sage didn't care, though. In a way, it was nice. Finally, Sage Cooper was going to give people in town something to talk about other than how pathetic she was. She put on a bright smile. "It'll just lend credence to our dating story and you'll really seem like my boyfriend at Greg's wedding."

"If you're sure?" He gestured at his truck. "I can sleep out there—"

"Is your car so comfortable that you're dying to sleep in it?" With one last exasperated look at him, she took his arm and steered him toward the front of the barn. "Come on. Let me show you to your room so we can get what little sleep we can tonight."

His mouth quirked with another one of those hesitant smiles. "Yes, ma'am."

She made him sleep in the main house, because the heat was off in the cabins and they were downright frigid. The guest room was all the way on the other end of the house and on the bottom floor, but she still locked her door and pushed the dresser in front, just in case. Then she took a hot, soothing shower and thought long and hard about Jason and his situation.

Eli Pickett was the head cowboy at the Price Ranch, and he'd know right away that Jason was lying about his experience. No one knew more about ranching than Eli, and he'd pick up on how green Jason was in an instant. But they'd also taken Jordy under their wing and taught him everything he knew, and Jordy had been legendary for how terrible he'd been when he'd started. She figured as long as Jason was competent to a certain extent, and worked hard, he'd be able to keep his job. If it ended up being a problem, she'd show up at the ranch with Christmas cookies for Annie and Cass and put a bug in their ears about how good a person Jason was, because Sage liked to try to fix things for everyone.

Cookies. Shoot.

Somewhere this weekend she had to try to make cookies for Greg. She could always make them Monday, or

Tuesday, but this entire week promised to be busy, and she'd feel like she was letting him down if she didn't deliver as promised.

Strange how she was going to let down someone else's fiancé.

And Jason hadn't approved of any of it. Maybe he was right. Maybe she was a pushover, but had he ever been so desperately lonely that he'd bend over backward for people just so he was on someone's radar? Probably not. As a teenager, she'd always had friends and her father. She knew everyone in town through him, and she was involved in everything Painted Barrel, even at a young age. Heck, the postman had let her practice her driving on his mail route. Even if she hadn't had a boyfriend or gone away to college, she'd never felt lonely. She'd always felt included. She'd had her never-ending crush on Greg to comfort her romantic side and a father that doted on her.

But then her father had gotten sick and had to retire, and when it became clear he wasn't going to get any better, the cattle were slowly sold off and the ranch hands given severance payments. Along with a hospice nurse, she took care of her father until the bitter end.

And then it was just her. And since Greg's long engagement suddenly moved forward with a wedding date and became "real," she had nothing to fill her heart. Nothing to look forward to. It was hard. For a long time she wasn't sure how to cope, and she struggled. Eventually, she just threw herself into work, but it wasn't the same. Loving your job was great and all, but when people went home at five, you were no longer on their radar. There were a lot of lonely hours to fill, and Sage realized that if she stayed in Painted Barrel, no matter how much she loved the place, she'd end up alone and utterly forgotten.

Which was why she had to move. She had to start over somewhere new, become someone a little more exciting than Sage Cooper, man-repellent. Or she'd be miserable forever.

Sage toweled off and then crawled into bed, but she wasn't tired. In fact, she was buzzing. Today had a lot of ups and downs, but it was also the most excitement she'd had in a long time, and she couldn't stop thinking about Jason. There was something so sad and lost about him, but still strong and protective when it came to her. She wanted to help him, not just with the ranching aspects, but with everything.

Pulling out her phone, she opened her browser and began to read up about PTSD and war trauma.

Sunday morning, Jason was up just as early as Sage was, and she was pleased that she didn't have to hunt him down to begin the day. They fed the cattle—or rather, he did and she talked him through the types of feed and how much water and how often—and then they let the cattle out in the closest pasture. He'd never ridden a horse, and she didn't have one, so they put a saddle on one of the stall dividers in the empty barn, and he practiced getting atop it and getting off, and how to buckle everything.

They had lunch and went over how to run most of the farm equipment, and Sage talked the entire day, trying to cover every possible scenario he'd run into. They spooled hay even though it wasn't needed. She pulled out calving equipment and went over it and all the things that could happen, and what to expect, even though it wasn't calving season. And then, of course, there was more feeding to be done, and settling the cows for the night since there wasn't a herd for them to huddle up against. She explained the differences between how her old cattle were treated compared to the big, healthy herd they'd have at the Price Ranch. Over dinner, she told him all about Dustin and Eli, and their wives, and everything she knew about their personalities.

"You think I'm ready?" he asked her at the end of the day, when they were sharing a final cup of coffee and relaxing by the fire.

Sage looked over at him in surprise. This was the first uncertainty he'd shown all day. He'd been hardworking and utterly devoted to his task, trying his best to pick up everything she showed him the first time so he wouldn't have to be shown again. Jason had been the picture of focus.

"I honestly don't know," she answered him, and it was the truth. "I think all this will help, but there's bound to be scenarios that will come up that neither you nor I thought of. Every ranch handles things differently, too, so keep that in mind as well. But you know how to take care of a cow and how to move it. You know how to put on a saddle. You know how to use a lot of the ranch equipment. You're already leagues ahead of where you were, and I think you'll be just fine. Eli's a tough man but he's not a monster. Just work hard and you'll be fine."

He nodded, his expression thoughtful. He stared at the fire for a moment and then looked over at her. "You wasted your whole weekend working with me, didn't you?"

She blushed to hear his words. "I wouldn't call it a waste."

"What would you call it?"

"Helping a friend?"

"Well, I'm glad I met you, Sage Cooper."

"I'm glad I met you, too, Jason . . ." She paused, waiting. "I forgot your last name."

He chuckled. "Jason Clements."

"Jason Clements," she echoed, beaming at him. "I don't care that this weekend was a lot of work. I had fun."

"Me too, oddly enough." And he smiled at her and her heart skipped a beat.

CHAPTER SIX

At Sage's insistence, he spent Sunday night at her house again but woke up an hour before dawn. He made his bed, packed up his things, and then brewed a pot of coffee in the kitchen. He found some paper and left a note next to the coffeepot, knowing she was sure to see it there.

Sage,
You've been an amazing hostess and friend. I can't thank you enough for your patience and understanding. Wish me luck today because word on the street is that the Price Ranch has real horses.

Jason

PS—Here's my number. Text me the details of the party and when I should pick you up for our date.

He read the note twice, then headed out to the barn to feed her two old cattle. It was deathly quiet in the early morning predawn, the only sound that of Lucy's and Ethel's hooves. He put feed in their buckets and fresh water down like she'd shown him, and even though he was familiar with the barn, the hairs on the back of his neck pricked like they did when he went on alert. It would be so easy for someone to sneak up on him . . .

But no. Sage had sworn to him that this was a safe place. That no one would trespass.

Then again, they'd sworn they were safe at the outpost in Afghanistan, and he ended up with five bullets in him. His bad leg throbbed, and even though he needed to get on the road and head out for his first day on the job, he went to the far end of the barn and checked the first stall.

And then the next one.

And the next. Because he had to. Because Sage was sleeping innocently up in her house, and he couldn't leave unless he knew she was safe.

An hour later, he finally got into his truck and headed toward the Price Ranch, that pit of dread in his stomach growing by the moment. It was just nerves, he told himself even as his hands sweat on the steering wheel. Nerves about being new to a job.

It had nothing to do with Afghanistan.

Nothing at all.

Nothing.

If he kept telling himself that, maybe he'd even start to believe it.

He didn't want to disappoint Sage, though. Not when she'd worked so hard all weekend to give him a crash course on what she knew. So for her, he kept driving toward his destination even when he wanted to turn around and head right back to North Carolina, where his family was. Sage had been a real trooper all day and all night, never taking a break, never losing her patience with him and his constant need to survey the area or his ignorance when it came to the basics. She was calm, sweet, and funny. He'd never met someone so generous with their time. Who else would take a stranger off the street and spend the entire weekend with him—or her—just to try to help with a new job? Very few people, but Sage seemed to genuinely want to help him. He felt like he'd made a real friend this weekend, and he couldn't put into words just how much he appreciated her.

So he'd just have to do his best at the job today. If he didn't get fired by sunset, it'd be a win.

As he drove, he tried to remind himself of everything she'd gone over with him. Instead, he just kept picturing her dimples and the way her entire face lit up when she thought something was funny. She radiated happiness . . . and yet she was lonely.

If he wasn't such a mess, he'd have asked her out. But she didn't deserve to be stuck with a disaster like him. She was just being nice, anyhow. Her heart was set on that idiot that was getting married. Just as well. The timing wasn't right for him, either.

The sun was coming up, and since it was winter, that meant he was late. Jason pulled up to the Price Ranch house and parked his truck. The front door immediately opened, two dogs racing out toward him as he got out and grabbed his bag. A man stood in the doorway and raised a hand in greeting. It was a different cowboy, he noticed as he walked toward the door. "You must be Jason. I'm Dustin. Come on in."

There was an enormous, dark-haired dog at his side, tail wagging, and for a heartbreaking moment, it looked like Truck. But as he got into the house and the lighting changed, he saw this one was shaggier, the coloring slightly different. Not a German shepherd.

Not Truck.

He forced himself to stop staring at the dog and nodded at Dustin. "Nice to meet you."

Dustin gave him a friendly smile and slapped his leg. "Don't let Moose bother you. He's big but he's a marshmallow." The dog trotted over to him, pushing his face against Dustin's hand in a way that reminded Jason of Truck once more, and that sense of isolation hit him even harder than before.

Think of Sage, he reminded himself. She'd want you to do good today. And he thought of her dimples. Those dimples were going to be a good luck charm for him, he decided. He stuck his hand out to Dustin, and the cowboy shook it. "Jason."

"Everyone's eating. You're welcome to join us."

"I'm fine," he told him. He couldn't eat a damn thing anyhow. His stomach was full of acid. "Didn't mean to interrupt."

"Not at all."

In the kitchen, a baby cried, and then Eli came out a moment later with his infant son in his arms. He paused and gave Jason a hard look. "You ready to start work now? Or you got somewhere else you need to be?"

He bristled at Eli's flat tone, but he reminded himself of what Sage had told him. That Eli was brusque but fair. He took his job seriously and expected everyone else to. He'd give Jason a hard time at first. For all her dimpled smiles, Sage was good at reading people. So he didn't rise to the bait. "Everything's taken care of," he said boldly, as if what he'd done in town was extra important. "I just need to set my bag down."

Dustin waved him in. "You remember where your room was? Eli's gonna be a moment changing that dirty diaper anyhow." He grinned. "Come on, it's this way."

Jason let Dustin lead him in, trying to be as cool and calm as anyone would expect from an ex-military man. As they passed each closed door, though, his senses pinged.

Not today, he told himself. *I don't need this bullshit today. Focus on the job at hand.*

He managed to remain calm as he set his bag down. Dustin was saying something, but he couldn't hear it over the roar of blood in his ears. When he turned around, the cowboy was looking at him expectantly. Had he been asked a question? He honestly didn't know. He licked dry lips and decided to go with the stalling tactic he and Sage had come up with yesterday. "I know it's my first day," he began. "But every ranch is different, and I'd be a lot more comfortable if we could do a tour of the ranch first. I'd like to get a sense of how things are laid out, see all the buildings, the land boundaries, see the herd, get a feel for everything before I get my hands dirty."

It sounded like an excuse to him, but Dustin only nodded and clapped him on the shoulder. "We can do that. I'll take you out in the Gator while Eli saddles up. We can meet up with him later. Sound good to you, Eli?" He yelled through the house.

"Go," Eli called back.

Dustin grinned at him, clapped his shoulder again, and told him, "Lemme kiss my wife and we'll be on our way. You can change if you need to."

Jason glanced down at his clothes. He wore a long-sleeved T-shirt and jeans and sneakers. Not typical cowboy gear, but the cows wouldn't care, would they? Maybe Dustin was referring to the weather. After a moment's hesitation, he grabbed his favorite baseball cap and threw on a light jacket, then went to head outside.

Or he tried to. He paused in the hallway, at the line of closed doors, and his heart hammered in his chest. They're just doors, he reminded himself. Bedrooms.

It doesn't mean that someone's waiting to ambush you. They're just doors.

Tension surging through his body, he forced himself to walk slowly down the hall as if he were a normal person. As if doors didn't make him break out into a cold sweat.

At the end of the hallway, a small, white dog with a flat snout sat and watched him. As Jason approached, the dog tilted his head, dark eyes curious, and he looked so out of place in contrast to the rest of the ranch dogs that Jason immediately relaxed at the sight of him. He found himself smiling at the little fella. For some reason, he felt safe at the sight of what was obviously a pet. There were babies here, he reminded himself. They wouldn't put them in danger.

There was no ambush waiting around every corner. There wasn't. It was all in his head, and sometimes his head was still stuck back in Afghanistan.

He thought of Sage's encouraging smile as she'd worked with him all weekend, and he somehow managed. She was counting on him, he felt. Not because she had a stake in his success today, but because he needed to make her proud. So he would.

Jason somehow managed to keep his cool all morning long. Dustin took him out in a ranch vehicle called a Gator, which was like a rugged golf cart with a flatbed in the back for hauling things. To Jason's dismay, three of the dogs had piled in the back and gone with them, but he found that he could tune them out. Mostly. He was too focused on his surroundings to pay much attention to the dogs. Dustin drove the Gator all along the property lines, telling him that the ranch covered thousands of acres. He pointed out the split-rail fencing that divided their property from the Swinging C, their "neighbor" up the mountain. But mostly, it was wide-open space, and the farther they got from the ranch house, the more Jason began to sweat.

It was just a tour of the area. It was remote. There were no inhabitants but the cattle that wandered in the snow, pawing their hooves at the occasional clump of grass and skittering away when the Gator got too near. Dustin whistled as he drove and kept up a steady stream of conversation, and if he noticed Jason's silence, he didn't say anything. Eventually, the Gator headed back toward the ranch, and then Dustin gave him a tour of the barn, which was much fuller than Sage's. It was brimming with livestock, from sick cattle to horses to a few more dogs that were lounging in the barn. There were even chickens in an outdoor pen. Next to the barn was another large building, this one exclusively for housing the rolls of baled hay that would feed the cattle, along with the "cake" supplements that they were given. According to Sage, you "caked" cattle more in the winter because it helped them thermoregulate. That was something he knew now, at least.

Eli was in the barn. He wore one of his ever-present cowboy hats and was mucking a stall, pitchfork in hand. The sight of it made the hairs on Jason's neck rise, and a shiver went down his arms.

It's not a weapon, he reminded himself. *It's not. This isn't a war zone.*

Eli gave him a dismissive look and cocked his head at Jason. "You ready to work or you going to stall for time again?"

For some reason, that brought him back to ground. He found himself breathing easier. "I'm done stalling, thanks."

Dustin laughed.

Eli just snorted. He rested the pitchfork against the wall and gestured at the stalls across from him, where the horses whickered and ate with gusto. "Saddle up, then. Let's go fix the rails in the south pasture. Looks like they took a beating overnight."

"All right." Jason knew this was a test. Eli didn't move to show him where the saddles were, or how to saddle a horse. He knew he wouldn't. This was supposed to be rudimentary rancher stuff, but Jason had only ever saddled a stupid stall divider in the barn.

But he thought of Sage's dimples and how they would appear with pride as she smiled when he got through today. So he closed his eyes, took a deep breath, and opened them again. It was just a barn. He was in a safe place.

He walked forward and looked for the tack room.

S omehow, Jason made it through the day.

It might have been one of the longest days of his life, though. He'd managed to saddle a horse, and he'd even ridden the damn thing based off of Sage's instructions. Not well, of course, but he'd ridden it. He'd done everything Eli had asked him to do. He'd unspooled hay on the spooler and spread it in the pasture. He'd helped repair fence posts. He'd mucked stalls and managed not to get kicked.

And with every moment that passed, his mind had screamed at him more and more. That he wasn't safe. That every time he turned around, he'd see someone waiting to ambush them. He knew it was just his PTSD, but that didn't mean it didn't wear at him.

By the time they called it a day, the sun was down and it was getting late. He didn't want to be the first one in, though. He had to be the last one in or they'd think he was lazy. Eli watched him like a hawk, and he could tell from the look in the other man's eyes that he didn't trust Jason. Jason didn't give up, though. He just worked harder, and whatever they put in front of him, he did.

He was glad to be done with the day. He followed the other two as they trooped into the mudroom and stripped off their layers. His sneakers were soaked from all the snow he'd walked through, and he needed to get those boots like Sage had suggested.

Sage.

The moment she entered his mind, he wanted to see her, desperately. He needed to talk to someone that would look at him with approval, someone that would tell him that he'd done a good job. Someone that would know how hard it was for him to get through this day.

So he didn't take his shoes off. He hesitated in the mudroom, thinking.

"Smells like chili," Dustin said cheerily. "My favorite." He looked over at Jason. "Hope you've worked up an appetite."

"Actually, I think I'm gonna skip dinner," Jason said.

Both Eli and Dustin turned to look at him. "You get meals and board, you know," Dustin said. Eli just glared.

"I know. I just have a friend in town I want to go visit."

"Who?" Eli asked.

Did it matter? But he knew they knew Sage, and it sounded like she was on good terms with them and everyone else around Painted Barrel, so it couldn't hurt to drop her name. "Sage Cooper."

Dustin looked surprised. "I didn't know you knew Sage."

"Yeah, met her a couple of days ago." They didn't have to know that he'd spent all weekend with her learning ranching basics. The more he thought about it, the more he wanted to see her, too. He needed to get away from this place and the feeling that he was somehow messing things up even when he was trying his damndest to do things right.

A woman popped her head through the door to the mud-room. "Did I hear you say you were heading to town to visit Sage?" Cass asked. "I made Christmas cookies and ended up making too many. Can you take some to her since you're on your way?"

"Sure." In a way, Jason was relieved. Now he had an excuse to leave, and Eli couldn't say anything about it. "I'll be back before it's too late at night," he told them.

"We start at five in the morning," Eli said. "Don't stay out all night."

Dustin just looked at Eli oddly. "He's visiting Sage, not barhopping. She won't let him stay out too late."

Eli grunted agreement.

Jason shrugged his jacket back on, and a moment later, Cass was there with a plastic-wrapped paper plate loaded down with colorful cookies. "I appreciate it," she told Jason with a smile. "She always makes us cookies, and I thought I'd return the favor this year."

"Thanks." He took the plate, managed a smile, and then headed back out of the mudroom before anyone else could say anything.

Once he was outside, the crushing sensation in his lungs eased a bit . . . only to be replaced by the same jittery nerves at the quiet. He hated his brain. He hated that no matter the scenario, he couldn't relax. With a groan, he closed his eyes and took a deep breath, steeling himself like so many years of therapy had taught him. Years of therapy didn't matter when your brain wouldn't shut up, though.

He opened his eyes again and looked around. Everything in the darkness seemed normal, and there was fresh, powdery snow falling on the ground. It was calm. Quiet.

Unlike his mind.

Eli kissed his wife as she handed him a bowl of chili, and he sat down in his usual chair. Travis was in his high chair, waving his arms with excitement, and Eli couldn't help but grin at his boy. Seeing the slobbery, toothless smile brightened his mood after such a long day.

"Well?" Cass asked as she sat down with him at the table. Dustin grabbed a bowl for himself and headed to the living room, where his wife was nursing their baby. Cass looked at Eli eagerly, her eyes full of hope. "How did it go?"

"He's a total greenhorn," Eli said in a flat voice. "Rode the horse like he had a pole up his you know what."

Her expression fell. "Oh no. Really?"

"Really. It's the strangest thing. He knows the mechanics of how things work, but it's clear he has no experience. He put the saddle on Buster, and when the horse pranced sideways, I thought Jason was going to fall over in surprise." He shook his head. "Either he lied to Jordy, or Jordy lied to us. I've been around enough men that know ranching, and I can tell you right now, that man does not know ranching. Plus, he's odd."

"Odd like how?" His wife propped her chin up on a fist and leaned forward, her disappointment evident. She wanted him to have help around the ranch, he knew, so he wouldn't have to work so hard. She missed him when he was out from dark to dark. Truth be told, he missed her, too. This would be a disappointment for everyone.

Eli gave her a disgusted look. "Well, for starters, he wore sneakers on a damn horse."

She giggled. "Okay, that's definitely a greenhorn move."

"I know. I almost wished Buster would have nipped him in the ankle. He'd have boots lickety-split." He took a heaping mouthful of the chili and ate. Cass still wasn't a great cook, but one thing she did extremely well was chili, and tonight's was tasty. He shot her a pleased look and a wink of approval that made her blush. He liked that he could still make her blush, even though they were no longer newly-weds. "And he was sweating."

"He was sweating?" she echoed, confused. "Because it was hard work?"

"I don't know if that was it." Eli shook his head and shoved another bite into his mouth before answering. "He was a hard worker; don't get me wrong. Anything we showed him, he did. Never complained, never had to tell him anything twice. But he twitched and was sweating and looked nervous as hell all day long." He sighed. "I really don't know what to think."

Cass bit her lip. "You don't think it's drugs, do you?"

"Maybe. Ain't a lot of things to explain it."

His wife looked concerned. "And he's mixed up with Sage? She's so sweet and innocent. I don't know if I like that." She sat up, drumming her fingers on the table as Eli ate. "You know, after he left on Friday, I called Hannah over at the inn to see if he was staying there. Since he'd run out of here so quickly, right?" She gave a small shake of her head. "He wasn't. But he claims he met Sage a couple of days ago."

"Mmmhmm." Sage was a nice girl, but it was none of his business if she made bad dating decisions.

"I don't like this, honey," Cass told him, a worried look on her face. She reached across the table and touched his hand. "I don't want him to take advantage of her if he is a cokehead."

"We don't know if he is," Eli explained. "I don't know many cokeheads, but he worked hard today. Harder than Jordy ever did. He's no stranger to hard work, and I can't fault him for that. I didn't have to chase him or explain myself. I didn't even have to tell him not to scare the cattle. He's a greenhorn, but he ain't completely stupid. I just can't figure him out." And he shrugged, as if that was that.

"Hmm. Okay."

Suspicious at his wife's quick acquiescence, Eli looked up from his dinner. "That's it?"

Cass gave him what she likely thought was a sneaky glance—except he knew his wife, and knew that she wasn't very good at such things. "I think I'll go into town tomorrow and talk to Sage. Fish for some information."

He bit back a groan. "Don't make this into a bigger mess than it is, sweetheart. He gets a week for me to figure him out. If he doesn't work out, Jordy or no Jordy, we can send him packing."

"But then you'll be working alone over Christmas and I'll barely see you." Her face fell. "Or Dustin and Annie will have to cancel their trip to Los Angeles."

It wasn't ideal, any way you looked at it. "We could call Jordy, see what's up," he suggested.

"But if he's the one that lied about Jason's past experience . . ." She trailed off.

"Right." They wouldn't know if he was telling the truth or not.

Cass leaned over and patted his hand. "Don't you worry

about a thing, babe. I'm going to drop by the post office tomorrow and chat with Sage. Maybe I'll be able to figure out what's going on."

And she had a determined gleam in her eye that told him arguing was futile.

CHAPTER SEVEN

Jason couldn't decide if it was smarter to drive straight to Sage's ranch or if he should stop by town. It was getting late—almost seven at night—and the snow was blowing, but he remembered what she'd said about the big house and how lonely it was, and how she practically lived at work just to have something to do. On a hunch, he drove down Painted Barrel's main street, and sure enough, the Old West–looking building that doubled as the municipal office had a light on. When he parked his truck out front, he could see Sage behind the counter, wearing those reindeer antlers again. Today, she also seemed to be wearing a necklace of Christmas lights, and they flashed merrily against her neck.

He sat in the truck for a moment. Should he bother her? Or should he leave her alone? Would she think he was an idiot if he showed up all sweaty and messed up in the head?

But then he thought of her dimples when she smiled, and the memory of that made him get out of his vehicle. He crossed the deserted sidewalk quickly and looked around. The streets were empty, and that made his senses tingle. His mind recalled one time before in Afghanistan when the streets were empty and they should have been filled with people . . .

Before he knew what he was doing, Jason found himself pulling frantically on the glass door. It was locked, so he hammered a hand on the glass, making the entire frame shake.

Sage looked up in alarm, her eyes wide, and when she saw him, she rushed out from behind the counter and raced to his side. "Jason, my goodness, are you all right?"

He pushed inside, careful not to touch her, and then shut the door behind him. With wild eyes, he gazed down the street, but it remained empty and still, no matter how long he stared at it. After a long, long minute, his shoulders relaxed, just a little, and he turned toward her. "Sorry."

Her eyes were wide and startled, but she only nodded. "You're limping. Come sit down."

Was he? His bad leg must have been acting up. "I'm all right."

"I'll be the judge of that." Sage moved behind the counter, and it took everything he had not to check behind it. She pushed a rolling office chair out into the middle of the floor and pointed at it, indicating he should sit. He did, and she bustled past him to close the blinds on the windows. He watched her as she moved, noticing that she was wearing another hideous Christmas sweater—this one of a stuffed Christmas train that moved across the hem of the bright red cable-knit sweater—and that the hem itself brushed against what was a very fine, rounded posterior.

Well, now.

He rubbed at his mouth as she turned back toward him,

worry in her gaze. Here she was, probably wondering what was going on, and he was ogling her. Man, he was a jerk.

"Can I get you something to drink? Coffee? Tea?"

Jason frowned up at her. "I figured you'd want an explanation as to why I'm showing up on your doorstep again."

"You're pale and sweating. Something's troubling you. You don't have to talk about it if you don't want to. We can just hang out." And she gave him a gentle smile. "Coffee?"

"Sounds good. 'Preciate it." She moved back behind the counter again, and this time he carefully did not look at her rounded, bouncy bottom. That wouldn't be right of him. "I see you're wearing another Christmas sweater," he rasped, his throat dry. "That one's uglier than the last one."

Her laughter filled the quiet office, and hearing it was like a warm blanket. His nerves settled, just a little. "You want to hear a crazy confession?"

"Sure."

"I have a closet full of ugly sweaters. My dad used to buy them for me all the time because he wanted to see how ugly he could get them before I wouldn't wear them." She turned and winked at him. "But I like a challenge."

"Your dad sounds like a good man."

She nodded, her head bent as she poured the coffee. "He was. I miss him every day."

"Your mother?"

"Died when I was two. Pneumonia." She picked up the mugs and moved toward him. "I don't have any memories of her, just my father." The smile she offered him was a little tremulous, and when he took the mug, she crossed an arm over her front and sipped her coffee, falling silent.

Should he talk? He didn't know. He drank his coffee in silence as well, aware of the throb of his bad leg, like a pulsing wound. He was very mindful of how sweaty he was, his clothing sticking to his skin and his short hair damp against his scalp. Hell, he was a real mess.

But she knew that. "Today sucked."

"I didn't think it'd be fun." Her smile returned, just a little. "But you got through it. Still have a job?"

"As far as I know."

"What'd they have you do?"

"Ride a horse." When she gave a little grimace and then nodded, he added, "I didn't fall off, though."

"That's great!"

"And we fixed a lot of posts and fencing."

She nodded. "Some days, cattle ranching feels like just fixing things that the cows break. Every day will be different, though, and Eli should be able to direct you through most of it. He knows his stuff."

"He doesn't like me."

"He doesn't like anyone but Cass. Not at first. If you haven't been fired, though, that's a great sign." Her dimples came out, her smile wide on her round face as she beamed at him. "I knew you could do it."

And just like that, a lot of the awful tension eased out of him. Jason leaned back in the chair, and it rolled a few feet to the side. "God, and I was a mess the entire time. You should have seen it, Sage. It was twenty degrees out, snowflakes everywhere, and I was sweating like a pig because I was so damn anxious at how quiet it was. It was throwing me off, and the more I tried to tell myself that everything was fine, the more my brain wouldn't shut up. I swear I jumped at every sound, and I checked the barn six times before I mucked out the stalls. I'm exhausted." He paused, staring down at the mug in his hands. "I don't know if I can do it."

"But you did do it," she told him quietly. Her voice was full of confidence and pride, as if he'd done something special instead of flop-sweated his way through the day. "And every day, you'll keep doing it. And every day, it'll get a bit more familiar and easier. You'll get used to the quiet, and you'll get used to the job."

Being around her was calming his frayed nerves. Her smiles were soothing, as was her unshakable faith in him. Jason was growing addicted to the sight of her dimpled smile. There was something just so utterly . . . joyous about it. "You should be irritated with me, you know."

"Why?"

"Because you killed yourself all weekend to train me as much as you could, and I still ended up a wreck." He tapped his foot on the linoleum floor, all nervous energy.

She shook her head. "You didn't get fired within an hour, so I count this all a win. I think you did fantastic. You already got through the hardest day."

Jason sighed, rubbing his neck. It was sweaty, too. Damn it all, but he really was a mess. "Every day is hard, Sage. Every day. I'm just so tired sometimes."

"Maybe you need a service dog?" she suggested in a gentle voice. When he looked up, her cheeks were pink, as if she were embarrassed. "I was doing some reading about post-traumatic stress disorder. Having a service dog can really help, or so I've heard. They're there to pull you out of your head when you start to go to a dark place."

A stab of pain knifed through his heart. No, a service dog wouldn't let him be the mess he was right now. The bad moments still hit now and then, but with Truck at his side, he'd known the animal would never let him down. He knew Truck would be on the lookout for him, and when Truck nudged his hand in that anxious way, he knew to stop what he was doing and focus on grounding exercises. Hell, he couldn't count the number of times Truck had woken him from his sleep, knowing that he was having nightmares. Truck had been more than a service dog—Truck had been his best friend, his guide, and his rock.

And he was gone. The pain of his loss still hit him fresh every day, even harder than the buddies he'd lost in Afghanistan.

"I had a dog," he found himself saying, and then, to his surprise, Jason found himself telling Sage all about his service dog. He hadn't talked about Truck since he'd left the vet's office that horrible day with his arms empty and his heart hollowed out like an apple without a core. He told Sage about what a mess he was when he'd first gotten back from Afghanistan, and when he'd first met Truck, the calm German shepherd hadn't seemed like the solution. But it only took a day or two for Truck to take over his life, and then they were inseparable and he'd felt normal again. Like he could function like everyone else that wandered happily around this Earth.

And then last spring, Truck had collapsed during their routine morning jog, and Jason had rushed him to the vet, frantic. Truck had an enlarged heart that had given out, and there was nothing to do except watch him slip away. A piece of Jason had died that day, too.

It seemed like he'd been spiraling out of control ever since.

"I know a lot of people say they're just dogs, but he was everything to me," Jason told her in a hoarse voice. He stared down at his coffee cup, not wanting to see the pity in her eyes. "He was my best friend, my partner, and my confidant. I miss his doggy breath and his wagging tail and the way he'd stare at me when I ate peanut butter like I was betraying him to even take a bite without sharing it . . ." He shook his head, his throat clogged. When he could speak again, he continued. "More than that, I knew when he was around that things would be normal. He was trained to distract me when my head got to be too much."

Sage was silent.

When he looked up, Jason was surprised to see the sheen of tears in her eyes, her hand at her throat. Why was he surprised, though? Sage was sensitive and kind . . . and she knew what it was to grieve a major loss. "I'm so sorry, Jason."

Hearing her say that made him feel a little better, oddly enough. Platitudes couldn't bring Truck back, but it showed that she wasn't dismissing him as some idiot that couldn't get over the death of his dog. "I was a mess right after he died. I lost my job, forgot to pay my bills, and basically lived every day in a puddle of my own sweat." He grimaced at his current sweaty state. "I didn't want to get another dog, not so soon after Truck, but I was going crazy so I had to try. Everyone I approached either told me it'd be tens of thousands of dollars and over a year wait." He spread his free hand. "So I'm trying to earn some money."

"Oh, Jason. Is there anything I can do to help?" Her expression was full of sympathy.

He shifted in the chair, clearing his throat. "Can we . . . not talk about Truck anymore? It's hard for me."

"Of course."

"And you're already helping. Though I wouldn't mind learning how to ride a horse without bruising my ass." He shifted in the chair again, and the stupid thing rolled a little closer to the door.

She giggled. "That happens to everyone. Just remember

to loosen up and move with him or you're going to bruise the heck out of your backside." Then Sage bit her lip and averted her eyes, her face turning bright red.

"What?" His curiosity chased away the sadness threatening to overwhelm him. "What is it?" He would have been nervous, except those dimples were out and her cheeks were bright red. Anytime he saw those dimples, he knew things were fine. "Have I got something hanging from my nose?"

Her nervous laughter filled the air. "You, ah, rolled right under the mistletoe."

Jason looked up.

Sure enough, holiday decorations hung from the yellowed ceiling tiles of the municipal office. Happy snowflakes dangled on bits of string, and glittery red garland crisscrossed and looped over the ceiling in a garish checkerboard pattern. There was a clustered ball of leaves above him, tied off with a red ribbon, and sure enough, it had to be mistletoe.

What a romantic—if odd—gesture to put in a post office/municipal office. But that was Sage, he supposed. Romantic and dreamy even when life seemed determined to try and beat it out of her. He glanced over in her direction, and she had averted her eyes, biting her lip. The dimples were still there, but she looked so awkward that he didn't even joke about kissing her.

He wouldn't do that to her. She was just being nice to him. She still had her heart set on that dumbass Greg. "Right. Sorry." He scooted the chair over a few feet and drank the last of his coffee. "Can I have another round?"

She rushed forward and grabbed the mug from him.

Jason grimaced to himself—he'd made her uncomfortable.

He didn't deserve her friendship. He especially didn't deserve to be thinking about what would have happened if he'd moved back under the mistletoe. He got to his feet, heading away from the mistletoe and stretching his leg. "So, ah, did you make Greg his cookies?"

"What? Oh. No." She shook her head as she poured another cup of coffee. "He stopped by this morning to see if I had and was disappointed. Gave me a bit of a guilt trip, so I promised I'd do them tonight." Sage gave him a wry look. "I know he can be a bit of a user sometimes, but he's been my friend for so long, and I didn't have anything else to do, so I figured I might as well."

"If you need cookies, Cass made extra and told me to bring them to you." He gestured back at his truck, out in the parking lot. "I can go get them."

Sage returned to his side and handed him a refilled cup. "Cass is sweet. She's always thinking of me." Her dimples flashed. "But I don't know if that's a good idea. She's still learning a lot about cooking. And I don't mind, really. I don't have anything else to do." Before he could comment, she snapped her fingers. "Oh! And that reminds me—I brought you a present." She set her mug down and then raced behind the counter again.

A present? Really? He was stunned. When did she have time to go out and get him something? And . . . why? But when she set the pair of cowboy boots on the counter, his jaw dropped. They were finely tooled leather, looked expensive, and made him acutely aware of just how soggy his own shoes were. "You got me boots?"

"Well, every cowboy should have a good pair of boots." She picked one up by the heel and held it out to him. "And they were actually my father's. He never had a chance to wear them, because they were going to be a Christmas present. I want you to have them, though."

Her father's? Jason watched Sage, the sad look in her eyes, and shook his head.

She ignored his hesitation, turning one boot over. "They're a size thirteen, and I hope that's all right. My father had big feet, but you're tall so it might work out. If they're too small, we can have them stretched, and if they're too big, Jimmy over at the souvenir shop can put in some inserts that will help until you get your own pair—"

"Sage," he murmured, taking the boot gently from her and setting it back down on the counter. "I'm not taking your father's boots."

"But I want you to have them," she protested, nudging it back toward him. "You'll trash your sneakers, and the horses might bite your ankles. Plus, they're just going to waste sitting in a closet. Please take them, Jason. If he can't have them, I want them to go to you."

He looked at the boots and then back at her. "Why are you such a good person?"

She shook her head, the smile returning to her lips as she came back around the counter. Once she was in front of him, she picked up the boots and offered them to him again. "Perhaps I'm just trying to help out another good person."

She was so damn sweet. As she looked up and gave him another dimpled smile, he fought back the sudden urge to cross the distance between them and kiss her. To tilt that pretty face up and watch her hair spill down her back, her dark eyes getting heated with arousal as he leaned in and brushed his lips over hers. God, he wanted that. He wanted to drag her back under the mistletoe and see how she reacted if he kissed the heck out of her.

But . . . she was just being friendly. She was lonely and bored, and he was just a project to her, like Greg's cookies. He was a wreck of a person, and she was just being nice.

"I don't deserve your friendship," he told her, wishing that it was more than just that. That she'd look at him with real interest instead of sympathy.

"Sure you do," Sage told him with another gorgeously dimpled smile. "You're going to be my date, remember? This is a give-and-take relationship. Friendship." She corrected herself quickly, and her cheeks pinked again. "And trust me, I'm going to appreciate that date far more than you can ever know."

"Because you want to make him jealous?"

"No. Well . . . maybe. Am I a bad person if I say I wouldn't mind it?"

He laughed. "Not at all."

She pushed the boots toward him again, and this time, he took them. "Have you eaten dinner? I'm just about to finish up here and then go make cookies at home, but I'd love some company."

Now that he wasn't out of his mind with anxiety, he realized he was rather hungry. Exhausted, yes, but hungry, too. "I could eat. I kinda left the ranch pretty quickly once the day was done. I needed to get away."

"Come on, then," she said, and picked up her keys. "I make a mean dinner omelet."

He spent the rest of the evening with Sage, enjoying her happy chatter and, surprisingly, telling her all about his day and how he'd handled things. Her dinner omelet was great, just as she'd said, and he helped her make cookies for Greg just to pass the time, even though he secretly wanted to shove a stray hair or two in them just for kicks. They gnawed on Cass's cookies, and because Sage thought of everyone, she made another batch of her peppermint brownie cookies and plated them for him to take back to Cass as a thank-you.

It was late when he left, promising to text her the next day to keep her abreast of how things were going. He was relaxed, too. Surprisingly so. Sage's presence was calming to him, and she never let him sink into his thoughts so deeply that they started to go wild on him. He wasn't sure if she was doing that on purpose, but whatever the reason, he was grateful for it. The calm stayed with him until he pulled up to the Price Ranch and parked his truck. He got out, and immediately, the quiet gave him goose bumps. It was just something he'd have to get used to this far out of the city, he reminded himself. It didn't mean there was a problem. The layer of snow on the ground muffled everything, too.

But it was still hard to cross the short distance to the front door and open it. He saw a few of the dogs piled near the Christmas tree on their beds, and they raised their heads when he entered but didn't get up. He went into the kitchen with Sage's cookies and set them carefully on the counter. Somewhere in the house, he could hear a TV playing, the only sound to break up the quiet. He'd had a good evening. He should have headed to bed.

Instead, Jason couldn't stop thinking about the silence outside. How still everything was. How both Cass and Annie had young children and were likely curled up sleeping, oblivious to any danger that might be outside. And because he knew it was going to bother him, he opened the back door and headed toward the barn. He was going to check over everything one more time and then head to bed. One of the dogs followed him out—one that looked like a blue-eyed collie. It padded behind him quietly, and whenever he turned back to look at it, the dog sat down and wagged its tail. It was as if it wanted to figure out what he was doing . . . or just wanted to keep him company.

For some reason, the little guy's presence wasn't irritating. It was kind of nice. Like it wasn't just him against the world tonight. With his new friend at his heels, Jason checked the stalls, and every nook and cranny in the barn. He circled the perimeter of it and then went completely around the house, just in case. He checked near the cars parked in the carport. When he was done, he headed back toward the house . . . and was surprised to see Dustin rubbing his eyes, standing on the porch in slippers and flannel pajamas. "Everything okay, man?"

"Just thought I'd heard something," he lied. "Wanted to check it out."

"Could be raccoons or coyotes. We see a fair number of both around here. You want me to get dressed and help you look?"

"Nah, I looked over everything and didn't see anything strange," Jason said, heading inside. "And your dog didn't go on alert for anything."

Dustin dropped to a squat and reached for the collie, who went to him happily. "Bandit's a good boy. He'd tell you if there was a critter out there."

"There was nothing," he said again, and headed inside. Because there never was anything. It was always in his mind, always, except for the one time in Afghanistan that had scarred his mind ever since. He went to his room and undressed, took a quick shower, got under the covers, and stared at the ceiling. Even though he was utterly exhausted and it was growing late, he couldn't close his eyes to go to sleep.

Even after all these years, Jason was still afraid that every time he went to sleep, he'd see all the things he tried so desperately hard to forget in the daytime.

CHAPTER EIGHT

S age hummed as she sorted through the outgoing mail,
readying it for the driver. She loved seeing all the different Christmas cards that came in, but her hands were
covered in glitter by the time she was done, and no
amount of washing got every speck. She'd probably end up
with some of it on her face, and then Jason would laugh at
her. The thought made her smile, and for a moment,
she briefly considered putting a few flakes on the end of
her nose deliberately, just because Jason needed to smile
more.

Her poor, rookie cowboy. The greenhorniest of greenhorns with the saddest eyes.

Thinking about him made her get out her phone, and
he'd promised last night that he'd text her throughout the
day. She hoped that if he was sending her messages, that it
could be a good distraction for whatever he was going
through, and if he had questions, she could discreetly help

without making the other cowboys aware that he was getting assistance.

But since she hadn't heard from him, she jumped the gun and sent him a picture of her torso.

SAGE: U like? It's the Grinch, done Mona Lisa style. And the Grinch's face is fuzzy, no less.

It took a few minutes for the reply to come in, but she expected that.

JASON: God, that is ugly.

JASON: It's an affront to my eyeballs.

JASON: I'm laughing so hard.

Oh good. That was exactly her intent. She chuckled to herself as she typed out another response.

SAGE: I wore it just for you!

JASON: You shouldn't have. I mean that.

JASON: I showed it to one of the horses and it screamed in terror.

Now she was the one giggling.

SAGE: I hope you're not texting from horseback. That's dangerous! Comparable to texting while driving, but the horses probably have bigger teeth than your truck.

JASON: Nope.

He sent her a photo of the inside of a stall, along with a gloved hand holding a pitchfork.

JASON: I'm on mucking duty.

JASON: I think Eli hates me. He gave me a few dirty looks today and suggested I clean out the barn. I'm here by myself while they're moving the cattle.

Her heart squeezed. She was sure Eli didn't hate him. Eli was a nice man. He was quiet, but he'd always been very kind to her. He doted on his wife and his baby son, but she also knew he was fiercely proud of being a cowboy and rancher, and had no time for other people's nonsense. He probably didn't know what to make of Jason and his post-traumatic stress disorder, especially since Jason hadn't told anyone but her.

SAGE: Cleaning stalls is just a big part of the job, I'm afraid.

SAGE: I don't think it means he hates you. Maybe he just didn't have the time for chitchat today?

JASON: He noticed me triple-checking the barn and stared at me for a while.

Sage winced.

SAGE: How is it going today?

JASON: About the same as yesterday.

JASON: Texts are helping tho. Please keep talking to me.

Oh, she would. She'd text him all day long if that was what he needed. She'd pull every ugly sweater out of her closet and put on a virtual fashion show if it would keep him out of the dark places in his mind. So she texted him a mindless, innocent question.

SAGE: Have you finished your Christmas shopping? I have to buy some office gifts and some presents for the food pantry a few towns over, but I really don't have many people to shop for. It's a shame—I love giving presents.

JASON: As evidenced by my new kicks. Thank you, by the way. They fit perfectly with a pair of thick socks.

SAGE: Fantastic! I'm so glad. My dad would be pleased, too. No sense in letting them go to waste.

JASON: You're too nice, Sage. Anyone ever tell you that?

SAGE: Most people forget I'm alive. :) Unless they have to pay the water bill.

JASON: Then they're morons.

She didn't know what to think of that response. He was

so flattering to her, but she was just being a nice person, wasn't she? Wouldn't anyone try to help someone like him?

It didn't hurt that he was tall and handsome beyond her wildest dreams. Even now, just thinking of his smile made her heart flutter. How he looked at her with such an intense gaze. He was probably the only person in town that truly, truly saw her. He didn't think she was just Sage, another town fixture and about as interesting as a lamppost. He talked to her. Listened to her.

He thought Greg was crazy for ignoring her.

She bit her lip, smiling to herself.

Just then, the bell on the door clanged even as her phone buzzed with another text. For the first time in a long time, she was irked at the sight of Greg. She knew he'd only come by to check if she'd made his cookies, and his insistence was starting to irritate her. Couldn't he make his own cookies? Didn't he realize she didn't sit around waiting to fulfill all his needs?

Then she realized that he didn't know that, because she'd always leapt at the chance to help out in the past. Gosh, she was a dummy sometimes. "Hey, Greg." She pushed her phone into her pocket, hoping this wouldn't be a long visit. "I have those cookies for you and the mail." She grabbed the tray and put it on the counter, along with his stack of catalogs. "Tell Becca I said hi."

He paused at the counter, frowning down at the stack of cookies. But his words were kind. "You always think of me, don't you, Sage?"

That was an odd thing to say. She didn't point out that he'd nagged her about the dang cookies for the last two days. "I'm your friend," was all she replied.

Greg toyed with the plastic wrap on the edge of the tray, not leaving, and she tried not to be impatient as her phone buzzed with yet another text from Jason. She really, really wanted to check her screen, but she'd just have to wait until Greg left, because she didn't want to field any questions.

But he didn't leave. He sighed heavily—twice—and then looked at her, frustration on his face. "What do you think of bachelor parties?"

She blinked. "Are you inviting me? Because I'm not sure I'd be comfortable—"

"No, no. I'm not having a bachelor party." His tone took on a bitter edge. "Becca doesn't like the idea. And I think she's being ridiculous."

Oh. Sage opened her mouth wordlessly, then snapped it shut again. Becca was extremely sweet, but she definitely wore the pants in her relationship with Greg. Sage didn't realize that he'd minded. Somehow she felt like this question was a trap. If she told him that she agreed with him, she worried he'd use it as ammo against Becca in an argument. But if she agreed with Becca, she was a bad friend to him. "I see."

"It's my wedding, too, you know?" Greg sighed again and leaned on the counter. "I just can't believe she's being so stubborn about this."

"Perhaps she has strong feelings about it." Diplomacy was a good tactic.

"I should have just married you. You'd have let me have a bachelor party, I bet." He gave her a winsome smile.

Stunned, she blinked at him for a moment. He should have just *married* her? He was in love with Becca! They'd never even dated! How was that possibly on the table?

"Thanks for making my cookies," Greg said, oblivious to her shock. He took one out and bit into it. "Finally."

"I've been busy," she said automatically, still reeling from the first part of their conversation. What on earth was eating at him? Her phone buzzed again, and as Greg leaned on the counter, it was clear he was here to hang out, so she excused herself and moved away a few steps. "I need to check my phone."

She practically galloped to the back of the room and pulled her phone out, turning her back to Greg so he wouldn't see her expression while she checked her messages.

JASON: No Christmas shopping. And I think this horse must be Eli's. He hates me.

JASON: Oh man, and this next stall smells. I think Eli planned this.

JASON: Oh god. Not to be gross, but can horses get diarrhea? What the hell do I do?

A horrified giggle escaped her as she imagined poor Jason dealing with a sick horse.

"Sage?"

She whipped around to look at Greg. "Huh?"

He'd straightened and was frowning at her like she'd done something wrong. "Something funny?"

"Oh no. Just, ah, a friend texting me." She shoved her phone into her back jeans pocket, mentally hoping Jason wouldn't think she was ignoring him. "He's my plus-one to your rehearsal dinner tomorrow night, actually."

Greg gave her a shocked look. "You have a date? Who?"

Why did he look so floored? Feeling defensive, she lifted her chin. "Just a friend."

"The friend you spent the weekend with? Or last night? Someone said you left here with a guy."

Gosh, news really did travel fast in a small town. Was that why Greg was lurking at the counter today? He wanted to gossip about her actually having a social life?

"You're blushing," Greg pointed out. The look on his face was unreadable, but she could have sworn he almost looked displeased.

"Just a friend," she repeated quickly. "You'll like him when you meet him, I promise."

"Huh." He shrugged. "I'm glad you found a date." Except he didn't sound all that glad. He sounded irked. What, did he expect her to wait around in case he changed his mind? Please. The moment she'd heard he'd gotten engaged, she'd been thrilled for him and her crush had dissipated like a soap bubble. Greg was nice and cute, but it just wasn't meant to be, and she wasn't one to dwell on the past.

Seemed like Greg was one to dwell on it, though.

The door to the post office/municipal office opened again, sleigh bells clanging, and in walked Cass, her baby bundled in a fuzzy red outfit. Here was someone that liked Christmas as much as Sage, at least.

She beamed at Cass. "Hello, stranger!" Maybe now Greg would leave. Normally, she loved the company during slow times of the day, but Greg was just being downright weird.

"Hey there! I love your sweater!" Cass giggled, her nose red from the cold as she stepped inside. Her arms were full of Travis, and Sage immediately moved forward and put her hands out so she could hold the baby. He was the cutest, most roly-poly little thing with the fattest cheeks.

"I'll talk to you later, Sage," Greg said, rapping his knuckles on the counter in goodbye. He picked up his tray of cookies, nodded at Cass, and headed out even as Sage moved to Cass and took Travis in her arms.

"See you at the dinner," Sage said absently, and cooed at

Travis. "Aren't you the cutest! You look like one of Santa's little helpers!"

Cass chuckled, smiling at the two of them. "That is outfit number two, believe it or not. Outfit number one had a horrible accident before I could even leave the house. It's definitely gonna be a laundry day." She smiled and gestured at two envelopes that she'd pulled out of her diaper bag. "Can I leave these with you?"

"Of course! This is the post office. Regular delivery okay?"

"That's fine. They're just Christmas cards, and I know I'm late sending them out, but it's the thought that counts." She studied Sage. "How are you? Enjoying this mild weather?"

"It beats the blizzard from two years ago," Sage said with a wink, because everyone knew the story of how Cass had crashed her car in that very blizzard while heading to her parents' cabin in the mountains, only to be rescued by Eli. They'd been snowed in together and fallen in love.

It was the most romantic thing, Sage thought. Well, except for the car crash and blizzard. Two years later to the day, they were married and had a sweet baby.

Cass chuckled absently. "I guess it does. You have Christmas plans? Going to visit family?"

"Not this year," Sage said, her heart aching. Christmas had always been a special time with her dad. "Just gonna lie low and probably man the desks on the holidays in case anyone needs anything. Or maybe I'll go to the big grocery store in Casper and buy groceries for families that need it." Something that would give her the warm fuzzies and remind her of all the good things in the world.

"You have a good heart," Cass told her, and then her face fell. "Can we . . . talk?"

Sage's phone buzzed again, and she forced herself to concentrate on the baby in her arms and Cass's worried frown. "What is it?"

Cass averted her eyes and traced a finger on the beaten-up postal counter. "It's about the new guy at our ranch. Jason. I heard you know him? That you two are friends?"

Oh no. This wasn't a friendly visit. This was Cass coming to get information. Sage had reassured Jason that his job would be secure if he hadn't gotten fired on the first day, but this was day two, and Cass was coming to fish for info? Not a good sign. "I met him on Saturday, and we've spent some time together. He's a really nice man. Very kind. He came over for dinner last night."

"So you two are dating?"

"Just friends," Sage said, and she could feel a blush heating her cheeks. It sounded ridiculous to protest, but she wasn't going to tell Cass the real reason Jason had been hanging out. He'd asked her to keep his secrets, and she would.

"Ah." Cass chewed on her lip. "Here's the thing, Sage." Her voice was gentle. "We're a little . . . concerned. We were told he was an experienced ranch hand when he came out, but he can barely keep his seat on a horse. He says he knows more than he does. What's worse is that he's making us all very nervous, so I need to know what's going on."

"Nervous?" Sage had expected to hear the inexperience thing. You couldn't hide it no matter how hard you tried, but she'd hoped that he'd have enough tools in his toolbox to pick up quickly and it would be a nonissue. Making them nervous was something else entirely. "Why does he make you nervous? He's a sweet man." The baby grabbed a fistful of Sage's hair, and she tugged it back out of his slobbery hand. Jason was tall, sure, but he had the most lovely smile and kind eyes. She didn't see how he could make anyone nervous.

But Cass looked upset. Her lips pulled down in an unhappy frown, and she reached over and fussed with one of Travis's sleeves. "He does some weird stuff. Like, late last night, Dustin found him walking the perimeter of the house. He said he circled around it three times and went to the barn, then came back and went around the house one more time."

Oh no.

"And he's sweating all the time. And nervous. Like, I've never seen anyone sweat so much. He just seems twitchy and distracted. We're worried he's on something and it won't be safe to have him near the babies."

This was terrible. She could understand Cass's fear—with two small children living out at the ranch and Jason being a stranger? Her worry made sense, and poor Jason had been struggling the last few days. She thought of how her father would have reacted to find one of the new ranch hands walking around the house over and over again late at night. Her father probably would have fired him immediately, because he'd have been worried for Sage's safety. Being a parent meant you had to be cautious about who was around your child, and Jason would be living at the ranch with them.

She understood, she really did. She just didn't know what to do. "He's not on something," she told Cass, confident she could share as much as that. "It's not drugs."

"But it is something?" Cass asked, her expression worried.

"It's . . . not my secret to tell," Sage said. "I'm sorry. I'm not trying to be mysterious; it's just that I promised him he could confide in me, and I can't break that promise."

"It could be the difference between him getting let go tomorrow and staying on for the entire winter, Sage." Cass's expression was full of frustration. "It's going to be just me and Eli over Christmas, and the baby. That means extra work for my husband, and if Jason is trouble, it could put Eli in danger. I can't have that. You understand, don't you?"

"I promised I wouldn't tell," Sage said, pleading. "Please understand."

"I'm trying."

Sage knew Cass, and knew that she wouldn't be threatening unless things were dire. This wasn't a shakedown for information, Sage realized, but a last-ditch effort to understand Jason and help him keep his job.

Oh, she was screwed either way, wasn't she? If she told Cass Jason's secrets, he'd keep his job, but she'd have lost his trust. And if she didn't, he'd get fired. "You're putting me in a bad spot, Cass."

"I know, but I have my husband and my baby at the ranch to think about, Sage. You know I wouldn't be here if it wasn't important." She took her baby back from Sage's arms. "Please. Help me help him, okay?"

With a heavy sigh, Sage said, "He has post-traumatic stress disorder from his time in Afghanistan." She closed her eyes, feeling like the worst kind of traitor. Jason would never forgive her if he found out. "He goes around the building because he's checking the perimeter. He sweats because he's nervous and his PTSD flares up in certain situations."

When she opened her eyes, Cass's mouth was hanging open. "Oh. I wasn't expecting to hear that." She juggled Travis in her arms. "That poor man."

"He's a good guy," she promised Cass. "And he's no danger to the children at all. He's just having a hard time since his service dog died."

"Oh." Cass's eyes were soft. "Is he as new as we think?"

Sage said nothing.

"Well, silence is a pretty obvious answer, you know. If he was experienced, you'd be rushing to tell me about it," Cass pointed out.

"I've said enough," Sage said, flushing. "Just be . . . kind and understanding, all right?"

Cass nodded, her expression distracted. "Well, that changes things. I'll talk with Eli."

"And no loud, sudden noises, all right?"

"Sure." Cass smiled at her and then headed for the door, but her expression was distracted. Her thoughts were obviously on the problem at hand and she'd clearly forgotten about Sage's presence already.

Sage hoped she'd made the right decision. It didn't feel like it, but how much worse would Jason have felt if he'd been immediately fired? He'd emphasized to Sage just how much he needed this job. He'd worked so hard, too, to learn as much as he could in advance.

And . . . if he'd been fired, he'd probably have left town right away. How awful a person was she that that was part of her incentive to tell his secret? Because she wanted him around.

CHAPTER NINE

Sage stewed on revealing Jason's secret for the rest of the day. Jason didn't come over that night, but he'd texted her on and off all evening, and she hoped he was in a better place than he was the night before. She hadn't seen Cass again, or heard from her. Greg, either, really. It had been a quiet day at the office, and she'd worked on her decorations for the town's Christmas party since she was the decorating committee as well as, well, everything else. Her prizes for the raffles had come in, and she spent most of the day wrapping them in festive paper and stuffing the stockings that would be given to every child that came to the party. She'd paid for those out of her pocket, but Sage didn't mind. She loved seeing the little faces light up when they got their Christmas goodies.

Then it was time to get ready for the rehearsal dinner. Sage drove home, nervous, fed the cattle and petted their noses for a few minutes so they wouldn't feel neglected, and then went inside to get ready. It was a casual dinner, since most of the people invited were ranchers and didn't have time for the fuss of getting fancied up, so she put on jeans and boots, and then, because she was seeing Jason, she found one of her ugliest sweaters—one her father had called "Christmas checkerboard" thanks to its eye-watering green and red repeating squares. She put on a pair of jingle bell earrings and brushed her hair until it was a smooth waterfall down her back, and she fussed with her makeup over and over again, trying to perfect a smoky eye. It just made her look like she had a black eye, though, so she gave up, wiped everything clean, and went for a simpler look—mascara.

Her phone buzzed with an incoming text just as she finished swiping the wand over her lashes one last time.

JASON: I'm outside, doing a sweep of the perimeter.

SAGE: OMW

She moved to the front door and waited for him to come there and knock so she wouldn't startle him. She opened the door, smiling, because he looked gorgeous. He'd worn a white button-down shirt with long sleeves, the collar barely open at the neck. His long legs were encased in dark jeans, and he wore the boots she'd given him. He was freshly shaven, and his hair was neatly combed. More than that, he looked like he'd had a good night's sleep, and she hoped that was a positive sign.

"Hi, Jason."

He stared at her sweater, rubbing his jaw. "That is . . . something."

"You like it?"

"Am I a jerk if I say no?"

She chuckled. "No, you're honest. It's another one of my father's ugly sweater gifts. It's meant to be blinding."

"Damn, he could pick 'em." He shook his head. "You gonna wear that to the rehearsal dinner?"

Sage glanced down at the checkerboard pattern. She knew there was a thing where you weren't really supposed to glam up so much at a wedding that you outshone the bride, but she was pretty sure this didn't qualify in that category. "You think it's too loud?"

He shook his head and touched the door, heading inside and slipping past her. "You said you wanted to make him jealous, right? That ain't gonna do it."

Oh. Truth be told, she hadn't been thinking about Greg at all. Her thoughts had been purely on Jason and what would make him smile. She wanted to hear his chuckle. She wanted to see his eyes light up when he looked at her. "I guess. What should I wear, then?"

"Can I see your closet? I'll help you pick. We'll find something that'll make him sweat a little."

"Sounds good." She led him upstairs and then gestured at her closet. "I have to warn you, though, I'm very much a sweater and jeans sort of girl. I don't have a lot of dressy wear."

"You don't need it. We just want something that makes him think about what he's missing out on."

"I'm not very good at revenge," she admitted as he poked through her sweaters. Thank goodness she'd closed her panty drawers earlier, because he was standing about two feet away from her collection of undies and bras, and that would have made her squirm.

"You're too nice," he agreed, and while he flipped through her closet, she studied him. He wasn't sweating tonight, and the hunted look was gone from his eyes. Maybe having a distraction tonight in the form of the party was helping him stay grounded? If so, that was good, because she was the one that was darn nervous. "Everyone's going to think we're dating," she pointed out to him. "I hope that's all right."

He glanced over his shoulder and grinned at her, and her heart flipped. "I thought that was the point of this."

"I mean, it is. But even if it's not, just having company tonight so I'm not sitting alone is fantastic." Gosh, she was feeling flustered now that it was time to execute her plan. Would everyone be able to see right through her for the phony she was? They would take one look at how gorgeous he was and wonder what the heck he was doing with a blah person like Sage. She doubted they'd buy the whole "dating" thing. Heck, not even she believed that someone as good-looking as him would be interested in someone like her.

"Sage, I am going to hang all over you tonight and make everyone there positively jealous of how loving we are, all right?"

Oh my goodness, her cheeks felt scorching hot. "All right."

"Which means no goofy sweaters. We need to show them how pretty you are."

Was it possible to pass out from blushing too much? she wondered. He finally pulled out a plain black sweater, her softest one, and held it out to her. "Here, wear this."

"Black? To a wedding rehearsal?"

"You said it was casual, right? No one will care." He gave her an easy grin. "And no reindeer antlers, all right?"

With a chuckle, she headed into her bathroom to quickly change. The moment she pulled the sweater on, she felt different. It was a good call, she realized. The sweater was a thin, clingy tunic that showed off her figure and made her eyes look luminous. Or so she thought. It was definitely a different look from ugly sweater–ville. With one last vain fluff of her hair, she headed out of the bathroom and went to rejoin Jason. "Better?"

He rubbed his mouth. "Damn. Much."

Okay, that was an amazing reaction. She beamed at him, and strangely enough, she felt pretty and wanted and desirable. He was gazing at her as if he'd never seen her before, and all of that because of a sweater. How odd. "Shall we go?"

He crooked his arm in her direction, and she put her hand in his elbow, and off they went.

Painted Barrel didn't have a ton of reception halls or places to hold a party. Actually, there was really just one, the local "saloon" run by Wade. It was the town's only restaurant and doubled as a meeting place for all kinds of things. Sometimes they had town hall meetings here, sometimes Bible studies or the occasional book club meeting. Tonight it was closed for a private party—Greg and Becca's rehearsal dinner. The interior of the place was done up beyond its normal country pub look. Tonight, it was festooned in white flowers and garlands, and the tablecloths were red with white napkins, plates, and floral arrangements. A big CONGRATULATIONS banner hung down the length of the bar, and behind it, Wade was pouring drinks. People were already crowding inside to get out of the snow, and as they entered, she saw Greg's older brother was taking coats while Greg and Becca greeted everyone at the front.

"Here," Jason said, and helped her remove her coat.

The moment she was free of it, static made strands of hair float around her head and her slinky sweater stuck to her skin. Lovely. She fussed at her clothing as Jason deposited their coats, and when he came back to her side, he put his arm around her waist. "Stop fidgeting. You look fantastic."

She did? Sage stared at him in surprised pleasure. He gave her waist a squeeze, and she remembered that this was all a game. Right. He was repaying her for some of the lessons. It wasn't a real date.

Not that she'd know what one of those felt like, either.

There was Greg, standing next to Becca in a gray suit. He was wearing a red tie that matched Becca's festive red dress and smiled at guests as they approached. Becca was clearly more in her element, chattering and beaming at everyone. Greg looked at Sage in surprise as they moved forward. "You made it."

"Of course. I wouldn't miss your rehearsal dinner." She beamed at Becca, who gave her a giddy smile.

"Who's your boyfriend?" Becca asked, gazing up at Jason.

Sage turned to him, and as she did, she realized how tall he was in comparison to everyone else. He towered over Greg and Becca both, and even Sage felt dainty next to him, and she wasn't all that dainty a girl.

"I'm Jason," he told them, sticking his hand out in greeting. She noticed he didn't correct them and say that he wasn't her boyfriend, and she could feel her face growing redder by the moment.

"How long have you and Sage been dating?" Becca's eyes were wide, and she kept glancing over at Sage as if full of disbelief. "She hasn't said a thing."

"She's good at keeping secrets," Jason told them, and

looped his arm over her shoulders as if it were the most casual thing in the world. He smiled at them. "We kinda wanted to keep it just us for a while. You know how it is."

"That's so sweet," Becca gushed, clinging to Greg's arm. "Isn't it, baby?"

"Sure is." Greg gave Sage an almost hurt look, as if he felt betrayed that she'd never shared such a secret with him. He didn't look happy to meet Jason.

"We're just having fun," Sage managed to choke out. Isn't that what people said when they were dating casually? It was just for fun? She couldn't imagine. No one ever dated her, much less just for fun. But it sounded good enough.

Jason chuckled. "Yup." He leaned in close to Sage and touched one of her earrings. "You've got a strand of hair stuck here, sweetheart. Let me get that for you."

She remained perfectly still as his fingers moved over her earring, and a shiver went down her spine as he grazed the shell of her ear. "Thank you."

"Come on, let's go get a seat." Jason nodded at Becca. "It was nice to meet you both."

"You too!" Becca gave Sage a look that promised a grilling later on. Not that she'd ever been that close to Becca, but they still talked. Sage suspected she was going to get a visit at the office this week just to hang out and fish for gossip. But hadn't she expected that? She knew that coming to the party with a date meant that people were going to talk, and she was ready.

As Jason steered her toward a table, he pulled her close in a half hug, his lips going to her ear. "You need to stop blushing so much, sweetheart."

Oh gosh, like she could stop now? Just hearing his sexy whisper and feeling his breath tease her ear was making her face turn bright red. Other parts of her were thrumming with heat, too, which just added to her shyness. "I'll try."

"I mean, I think it's utterly adorable, but people are going to wonder how long we've really been dating if you keep blushing like that every time I reach for you." His voice had a sexy growl to it, pitched low so only she could hear it, and it was making her feel all kinds of things. He thought she was adorable? He'd pulled her so close that his face was practically in her hair, her body pressed against his. Sure, it was just to hide his whisper, but it felt so darn good, so right.

Her hand moved to his waist, and for a moment, she wished they could stay like this forever. "People are going to wonder, anyhow. They're going to be bugging me all week, laughing that Sage finally got herself a boyfriend at the old age of twenty-nine." Funny how that didn't bother her as much as she thought it would. She'd initially thought that the questions would be a terrible price to pay for not looking like a loser, but right now? It didn't seem so terrible. At all.

He pulled away from her ever so slightly and looked down. "You've never had a boyfriend?" The look on his face was full of disbelief.

Well, now she felt like a huge loser. How could she explain to him that this town was so small that the dating pool wasn't that big to begin with, and she'd always been painfully awkward? To add to that, her father was the mayor, so he'd dragged her along with him on all kinds of projects and jobs that kept her busy enough that she didn't hang out with the others after school. They'd had a very small class size—twelve people her age—and the girls had always outnumbered the boys. Now that they were older, it was even harder to find someone to date. It was just one of those things that she kept waiting for but never happened. She knew it made her a big dork, but hearing the surprise in his voice just made things worse.

"Long story," she managed to choke out and then pointed at a table nearby. "I think I see our place cards."

Jason gave her a skeptical look but said nothing else, leading her toward the seating and pulling her chair out for her.

Relieved, she sat down and smiled at the couple across the table from them. Becca's cousin and her husband. Sage had met them a few times before, and they wouldn't give her weird looks for having a date, which was a relief. Jason sat down next to her in his chair, stared down at the place setting, and then leaned over. "Don't look now, but there's mistletoe on the plates."

What?

Sage stared down at the place setting. Sure enough, the dainty white plates and bowls set at each seat had a cluster of leaves in the middle of the bowl. She'd thought with a quick glance that it was holly, but now she could see that it was mistletoe. It was cute for a wedding . . . except that she'd brought a fake date. Oh no.

"Well?" Becca's cousin Simone prompted, laughing at them. "You're just going to ignore it?"

"Never," Jason said, and pulled Sage's chair a little closer to his. He touched a fingertip to her chin, turning her toward him, and before she could say anything, his lips brushed over hers in the barest of kisses.

Oh.

Oh my.

He'd just kissed her as if it were nothing, but it was everything to her. Sage's mouth felt as if it were throbbing with sensation, and she wanted to touch her lips and savor the kiss, but Simone was watching. Even as the tables filled up and Jason talked with Simone and her husband, Sage was quiet. She couldn't stop thinking about that kiss. The feel of his mouth against hers. It had been the briefest of caresses, but what would it have felt like if it were more?

What would it have felt like if they weren't pretending?

Jason cleared the mistletoe off her plate and gave her a look that took her breath away.

Sage didn't say much as people got to their seats and the dinner was served. She was barely aware of her surroundings, keeping her answers to Simone's questions brief but pleasant. She knew she wasn't being great company, but her mind was still focused on that kiss. And when she'd looked over at Jason after their kiss?

It was like he was thinking of it, too.

After they were done eating, Jason pulled her chair closer to his and put his arm around the back of it, as if hugging her close. Gosh, he really was good at this pretending. He was making her feel cherished and cosseted, and it wasn't even her wedding. He'd lean in to whisper a comment into her ear, and just knowing that made her blush all the more.

She saw Dustin and Annie across the room, waved at them, and hoped Jason hadn't noticed they were here. She hoped that their presence wouldn't make him nervous.

At some point, he leaned in again. "Look at Greg's face." His lips brushed against her ear, and it took her distracted mind a moment to figure out what he was saying.

She forced herself to quit staring at him and turned to look at Greg. Sure enough, he was sitting across the room, next to Becca, who was beaming at the people at her table. Greg was looking directly at Sage, and the look on his face was confusing. He didn't look happy for her. As she watched him, Jason leaned over again, and Greg's eyes narrowed.

"He looks like he's ready to spit nails," Jason murmured.

"I just . . . Maybe he's stressed?" There couldn't be any other reason Greg would look so unhappy that she had a date.

"Or maybe he's realizing you're not going to wait around for him forever?"

But that was ridiculous. Greg wasn't interested in her. He just liked to talk to her and wanted her to make cookies for him and run errands for him. There had never been anything romantic there, and Greg had always teased her about her crush—everyone had. It wasn't a secret that Sage Cooper had been madly in love with Greg Wallace. In this town, everyone knew everyone else's secrets. But now Greg didn't look happy for her, and it was confusing. He didn't look happy for himself, either. He was getting married in a matter of days. Why did he care if she dated?

"I don't understand," she whispered back at him.

"Me either, but who knows what he's thinking." Jason gave her a thoughtful look and then reached out and tucked her hair behind her ear. "All I know is that he glares at me whenever I touch you."

It was on the tip of her tongue to shamelessly suggest he keep touching her, but someone tapped the microphone, indicating that speeches were about to begin now that the dining was done.

Somewhere in the kitchen, a stack of plates was dropped in a loud crash.

Sage jumped in her seat. Everyone did, and then a wave of nervous titters filled the room. Jason jolted to his feet, moving in front of her, and Sage noticed he'd gone deathly pale.

Oh no. The crash of dishes had triggered him.

She carefully got to her feet even though everyone was staring at them. Even Greg and Becca were frowning in their direction as Greg's father held the microphone and looked at Jason and Sage.

Jason wasn't moving. He was breathing fast, and his pupils were dilated, making his eyes seem incredibly dark.

"Jason," she murmured, touching his arm gently. "Look at me."

He whipped around, giving her a wild-eyed stare, and for a moment, she thought he was going to bolt.

She wrapped her hands around his arm like a clingy girlfriend. "Let's get out of here, all right?"

A few quick breaths panted out of him, and then he grabbed her hand and hauled her out of the party. She knew he wasn't trying to drag her like a sack of potatoes—he just had a desperate need to get out of there, to compose himself. So she let him pull her with him, rushing out of the crowded pub and into the snowy street outside.

There were dozens of cars lined up and down the street thanks to the party, but the street itself was empty, most of the town was at the celebration or gone home for the day. Fat snowflakes drifted down, and somewhere distant, Christmas music was playing.

Jason's clammy hand squeezed hers, and he panted heavily, as if trying to compose himself. His gaze darted back and forth, and she recognized that almost hunted look in his eyes. She could help with this, she decided, and took his arm, holding on to him. "Let's walk the street so you can check everything out. Come on."

So they walked. She let him set the pace, let him pause in front of as many buildings as needed, or check the narrow alleys between shops. It was brisk out, but the wind had died, so it wasn't so bad, even without a coat. She was a Wyoming girl, and she'd been through worse. She wouldn't die from a little time outside in only a sweater, and Jason needed her more than she needed her coat.

Eventually, his breathing slowed and the wild-eyed look on his face went away. She still held on to his arm, and she was surprised when he gently touched her clasped hands and looked over at her. "I'm sorry, Sage."

She frowned up at him. "What are you sorry about? There's no need for an apology."

"I ruined your evening."

"You absolutely did not." She squeezed his hand. "I'm the one that's sorry. I put you in a situation that made you uncomfortable."

"You didn't know that someone was going to drop some dishes and make me flash back." He raked a hand through his short hair, and it stuck straight up, which told her he was sweating. "You should return and try to enjoy the party. I should get home."

She wanted to tell him that he was the only enjoyable part of it, but that might have seemed too bold. He still looked scattered and distracted, and they'd ridden in one car tonight—hers. Either way, they'd both have to go back to her house for his vehicle. "Let's finish our walk. Why don't you come stay at my house tonight?"

Jason looked down at her in surprise. "Stay with you?"

Selfishly, she wanted him to stay just because she loved his company. Because she was crushing on him. Because she cared for him and wanted him close by where she could watch over him and help him if he struggled through the night. "Why not? Your truck's already at my place and it's snowing." She put a hand in the air as if to catch a handful of the fat flakes drifting down. "You look like you need to get away for a bit, so come stay with me. Text Dustin or Eli and let them know you'll be there in the morning, but I'm weeping over the loss of Greg and you're doing your best to comfort me." She gave him an impish smile. "It's a totally believable lie."

But he frowned down at her. "Sage, I don't want to make you sound like an idiot just to cover for me. That's not fair to you."

She shook her head. "Jason, I don't care what I sound like to the others. I don't care what they think. I'm leaving them all behind as soon as it's spring, remember?"

"That doesn't mean I like it." He cupped her face with cold hands. "I shouldn't have to sabotage you just to try and make me look like less of a coward."

He thought he was a coward? That was insane. Sage shook her head and put her hands over his, as if she could let him see how she viewed him with that small touch. "You're anything but a coward. You're one of the strongest, most determined people I've ever met. Don't you ever think otherwise."

Jason smiled down at her, and his thumb brushed over her cheek. For a moment, she held her breath, hoping against hope that he'd kiss her again—really kiss her, not just brush his lips over hers. She wanted tongue and lips, his breath mingling with hers, and sexy nibbling. She wanted it all.

But he just smiled. "You really are the nicest person."

And for a long, despairing moment, she worried that she was turning invisible all over again. That no matter what she did, no one would ever look at her as if she were girl-friend material. She would always be Sage Cooper, depend-able and forgettable.

Of course, that was selfish of her. He was struggling

with post-traumatic stress and here she was mentally pouting that he didn't kiss her? She shook herself out of it and patted his hand. "Come on. Back to my house where we can hide away from the world for a while."

"If you're sure . . ."

She was more than sure.

CHAPTER TEN

They drove back to Sage's house, and as if the weather was in cahoots, the snow started pouring from the skies, thick and heavy. Good. All the more reason for him to stay with her overnight, since it would be dangerous to drive in this after dark. He texted Dustin to let him know where he was, and while he checked the perimeter of her house, she went into the kitchen to make hot cocoa and texted Cass to let her know that he was staying with her tonight and he'd be back after sunrise in the morning.

It made her feel guilty to go behind his back like that, but she also didn't want him to lose his job, either. Cass texted back in agreement, and then Sage turned her phone off so it wouldn't ping while Jason was with her.

He came inside, covered in snow and hollow eyed, but she handed him a hot cocoa, said nothing, and led him to the couch. She'd gotten out blankets and pillows and made a comfy nest, and she turned on one of her favorite Christmas movies, *Die Hard*, and they watched it in silence, curled up on the couch together. At some point, long after she'd finished her cocoa, she nodded off in the movie and woke up to find that Jason's arm was around her and her head was tucked against his neck.

"Oh," she murmured, wiping at the corners of her mouth in case she'd drooled. "I fell asleep on you. I'm sorry."

"Don't be. You want me to help you up to your room?"

"Actually, I thought we'd both sleep down here. There's plenty of room on the couches, and you seem like you need the company tonight." She gave him a sleepy smile.

"You don't have to do this, Sage."

"I know. But I don't mind it. I like your company."

He smiled at her and squeezed her hand. She realized belatedly that his arm was around her waist, and it felt good to curl up against him and relax. "You can lean against me and nod off again if you want," he offered.

Sage took him up on it. She leaned against him, cheek on his shoulder, and watched the movie for a time before her eyes started to close again. At some point, she was aware of the movie turning off and the room going quiet, but Jason's arms were around her and he was stroking her back, and she felt too good to move.

So she went back to sleep.

Jason didn't deserve someone like Sage Cooper as his friend. He woke up the next morning feeling curiously refreshed despite the crick in his neck. He blinked at his surroundings and then glanced down at the beautiful woman curled up against his side. They were both wedged onto one of her large sofas, Sage's body tucked along his and her breasts pushing against his chest. Her hair was everywhere, and she slept with her mouth slightly open in a way that was completely adorable and somehow sexy at the same time. Her hand was curled against his chest, her leg between his, and he had a raging case of morning wood.

God, he wanted to touch her right now.

He closed his eyes and willed his body to behave. Sage deserved better than him. He was a mess, and she was just being friendly and kind. She was hung up on that dumbass Greg, so it didn't matter that her body fit against his perfectly or that her hair was silky soft and tickled his skin. It didn't matter that he loved the sight of her dimples and how he'd stared at her in that slinky, figure-hugging sweater last night.

It sure didn't matter that he'd kissed her and she'd flushed and given him a soft look that normally told a man to kiss a woman again.

She'd just wanted a pretend date, he reminded himself. She'd never indicated to Jason that she wanted more than friendship, so lusting after her was a bad idea. Very bad, even if she was incredibly soft and sweet in his arms. She was snuggled against his side, and when he shifted his weight, she moved even closer to him, her hand sliding to his waist.

And then he had a really hard time thinking innocent thoughts. That hand was edging into dangerous territory. He wouldn't let it go any farther, but he'd leave it there and just . . . daydream about it for a bit. He thought about peeling that clingy sweater off of her and revealing her pale skin and seeing if she flushed everywhere. He wanted to graze his knuckles over the tip of one breast and watch it harden in response. He wanted to hear her moan with passion.

He wanted a lot of things from Sage, and none of them were friend-zone type things. That was a problem. The more time he spent with her, the less he wanted to just be her friend and the more he wanted to kiss her. That quick peck he'd given her last night had been too easy and over far too fast. He should have knotted his hands in her silky fall of hair and held her to him while he kissed the day-lights out of her.

But . . . then he probably would have lost her as a friend. And right now? Sage was the only thing keeping him balanced. He was pretty sure that without her, he'd have been fired from the Price Ranch and sent packing.

The Price Ranch. Damn. He had to return. He glanced out one of the big windows, and the sun was creeping over the horizon. That meant it was time to go. They'd be expecting him, no matter how badly he wanted to stay curled up with Sage.

Last night, she'd been so kind and understanding when he'd acted like a fool. She hadn't judged him or made him feel stupid for his knee-jerk response. She'd taken action, ushering him out of there, and then let him go up and down Main Street patrolling until the edge wore off. She'd never complained . . . and she hadn't left him alone. Having her support was the difference last night, and he needed to find a way to thank her for her generous, kind heart.

It'd have to wait, though, if he planned on remaining employed.

Easing his body off of the couch, he watched Sage to see if she woke up. She just mumbled and turned over, burying her face into the pillows, and that was kinda cute. Clearly, she was a heavy sleeper.

He made it out of the house without waking her, then stopped to feed her cattle and give them water. It was rather cold outside, the temperature having plummeted overnight, so he didn't let them out into the pasture. Instead, he gave them extra cake pellets like she'd shown him, and he thought of her and her lessons while he did so.

By the time he drove out to the Price Ranch, the sun was up and glaring on the new snow, but he was . . . in a good mood. He couldn't wait for Sage to text him. He was curious what she'd have to say about how she slept, or if she'd noticed that he'd taken care of her cows . . . or heck, he just wanted to talk to her.

When he parked his truck, he headed inside the house. He could hear the dishes clanking in the kitchen, and the place smelled of bacon. Christmas music played in the living area, and the dogs were gone from their beds by the fireplace, which meant that Eli and Dustin were already out and hard at work.

He should probably poke his head in and let Cass know that he was back so he didn't startle her. When he got into the kitchen, though, he was surprised to see Eli was there, waiting for him. He was talking to Cass in a low voice while she stirred something on the stove, and both of them looked up when he came in.

"Sorry I'm late," Jason said. "Sage insisted I stay overnight at her house."

"No problem!" Cass said, her voice utterly cheery. "You need breakfast?"

"I'm good. I'll just change clothes and then head out to the barn and get started."

By the time he got out to the barn, though, Eli was there, waiting for him once more. The big cowboy offered him a hat, a deep-brown cowboy hat with a pale band. "This'll be better for keeping the sun out of your eyes than that baseball cap," Eli said and held it out to him.

"Thanks." He wasn't entirely sure if it was a gift or if Eli was giving it to him because he thought Jason was lacking some sort of vital gear. Either way, it'd be a better hat than the one he had on, and he switched them out.

As he took it, he went to step past Eli, but he put a hand on Jason's chest, stopping him. "We need to talk."

Jason immediately tensed. "About what?"

Eli frowned in his direction, and his entire stance was that of disapproval. "What are your intentions toward Sage?"

Intentions? "We're friends."

Eli gave him a suspicious look. "You stayed over at her place last night. I know she's an adult, but she's also alone and needs someone to look out for her. She's a good girl, and you don't go breaking her heart."

He . . . couldn't even be offended at that. Instead, he was touched that Sage was thought of so highly that Eli would take him aside to lecture him. "I know she is," he said. "And I'll be careful."

Eli nodded, then picked up a pitchfork that was leaning against the wall. "There's some cow shit calling your name."

There always was.

CHAPTER ELEVEN

SAGE: I must have overslept. Thank you for feeding Lucy and Ethel!

JASON: My pleasure. Thanks for letting me stay overnight.

SAGE: Of course! What are friends for?

JASON: Speaking of friends, Eli had a chat with me this morning. Told me not to break your heart.

SAGE: Oh boy, this is embarrassing.

JASON: I told him we were just friends but not sure he believed me.

SAGE: I'm sorry. That has to be awkward for you.

JASON: Nah, it's all good.

A ll good? What the heck did that mean? Sage touched her mouth, thinking of that brief kiss from last night, and leaned against the counter at the office. She couldn't figure out what he meant. Was he annoyed with Eli for trying to protect her? Gosh, she was embarrassed that his favor to her was going to end up with further-reaching ramifications than she'd thought. She'd foolishly assumed that they'd "date" for the one night and the wedding, and then it would just quietly go away. She'd forgotten that this was a small town and everyone gossiped and got into everyone else's business.

This was going to follow her until she moved.

It was going to follow him for as long as he was here.

That was . . . a problem. She made a mental note to talk to him about it. Maybe when they "broke up" they could do so in a way that would make him look awesome and her like the fool. That wouldn't be too hard to do, really, given that everyone in town already couldn't figure out why he was supposedly dating her. Should she text him back? Offer an apology? Should they meet up to discuss a game plan?

Or was she just using that as an excuse to see him again?

The door to the office opened, and she immediately hid her phone, her cheeks flushing. It was Greg, wearing a bright red sweater that made his color look washed-out and his blond hair a little too pale. Of course, he didn't compare to Jason in the looks department, but who did? Man, she had it bad. "Hey, stranger," she said cheerfully, turning to the mail tub and flipping through for his mail. "Just catalogs today, I'm afraid—"

When she turned around, Greg was at the counter, his hands planted, a somber look on his face. "We need to talk, Sage."

Uh-oh. She blinked at him. "Is everything okay?"

He took a deep, dramatic breath and then fixed his gaze on her again. "I need to know if you have feelings for me."

Oh dear.

This was awkward.

She tried not to show her shock, but she suspected she failed on that front. "Greg . . . you're getting married next weekend. Why does that even matter?"

He clenched his jaw and drummed his fingers on the countertop. "Maybe I shouldn't."

Oh no. This was a nightmare. "What do you mean?" If he broke up with Becca because he thought Sage still had feelings for him . . . this was worse than a nightmare. "We're just friends, Greg. You know anything that I ever felt for you was just a girlish high school crush. I'm sincerely and truly happy for you and Becca both."

He gave her a woebegone look. "You don't love me?"

"Ah . . . we're friends, Greg. What do you want me to say?" She reached out and patted his hand awkwardly. "I think you're just getting cold feet. That's normal before a wedding." And she tried to smile. "It's going to be okay, really it is."

"I don't know if it is, Sage." Greg shook his head and snagged her hand, clasping it in his. "Becca doesn't look at me the way you look at that guy."

"Jason?" She blushed. "Uh, how was I looking at him?"

"Like he was the entire world. You used to look at me like that, Sage. I remember that now. And I think I want it back."

With a yelp, she pulled her hand from his. "No, you don't," she told him quickly, and did her best not to wipe her hand on her jeans. There was something weird about Greg's touch. She'd never held his hand before, but it was . . . soft. His nails were manicured, too, likely because of Becca. After touching Jason's calloused hands, it didn't feel the same.

She didn't like it.

"You're just worrying," she told him again. "You know as well as I do that there's never been anything between us."

"But there could have been," he said desperately. "And I'm wondering if I was too stubborn to see what's been under my nose this whole time."

Was he serious? Sage stared at him. She'd crushed on him for years. She'd made it obvious—because she couldn't hide her feelings—that she'd adored him, and he knew it. How many times had she made cookies for him? Cooked for him? Done special little favors for him because he'd asked? He could have had her any of those times, and she would have jumped for joy to get even a sliver of his attention.

But now? Now it irritated her.

"You have cold feet," she repeated again, her voice firm. "I won't tell Becca about this."

"I thought you left the party last night because you still had feelings for me," he told her. "That you couldn't stand to see me marry someone else." His gaze searched her face, looking for confirmation.

"That is not it. There was a ranch emergency and Jason had to go."

"Jason, huh? He's too tall for you. A skinny beanpole with mean eyes."

Mean eyes? Skinny beanpole? Were they talking about the same person? "I think he's wonderful," she said dreamily, picturing Jason and the way his eyes crinkled at the edges when he grinned. His eyes weren't mean at all. They were . . . delicious.

Just like the rest of Jason.

"I heard you were spending every moment with that guy. I just don't want someone taking advantage of you, Sage."

Greg was the second person this morning to act like she was a pea-brained idiot that didn't know a good guy when she saw one. First Eli, and now Greg. "That's sweet of you to think of me, but I'm an adult, Greg. I can make my own decisions, and Jason is great. We're just having fun together."

"We have fun together—"

"Cold feet," she repeated. "It's just cold feet."

He sighed heavily and put his head in his hands. "I just don't want to make a mistake, Sage. I love Becca, I do . . . but she's so controlling."

Sage didn't know if that was a bad thing. Greg always seemed really happy with Becca's pushiness until now. He wasn't the most motivated of men, and now that she had some distance, she could see that. She kept her voice polite, though. "Oh?"

"She told me that after the wedding, I needed to step up my real estate game. That I wasn't selling enough houses to make a living and I needed to think long term. I needed to think of her and the children we were going to have. Children, Sage. She's already planning children!"

"You guys haven't talked about children before now?"

"Well, we have. It just always seemed like it was in the distant future. But now I'm starting to realize that I'm about to marry her, and then the future is now."

He was babbling, she decided. All of this was definitely nerves. Poor Greg. "I'm sure you guys will figure it out. Just think how stressed she is right now, too. She's got a lot on her plate, and I'm sure some of it is spilling over to you."

Greg propped up his chin on his hand and looked up at

her. "Speaking of real estate, you're going to let me list your ranch, right? In the spring? Since we're friends?"

Sage couldn't help but feel a little manipulated. Is that why he'd come over and been so dramatic? She never knew what to think with Greg. "We'll figure something out," she said and hoped it was vague enough to pacify him. Other than the whole nebulous "spring" date, she hadn't given much thought to selling her home. It would be hard to leave everything behind, but harder still to stay and grow old alone.

She had to leave this town.

Greg forced a smile to his face, thumped the counter, and then headed for the exit. "Thanks for the pep talk, Sage. I can always count on you."

He could, couldn't he? She was starting to feel like a babysitter for a man-size baby. "Bye."

The moment he was out the door, she sat down on her stool and texted Jason.

SAGE: I just had the weirdest visit from Greg.

JASON: Let me guess, he's jealous.

SAGE: I . . . suppose? He came here to talk, and it started out with him saying he wanted to cancel the wedding and ended with him trying to strong-arm me into using him as a Realtor.

JASON: I saw the way he looked at you last night.

JASON: He's flattered by your attention. He likes having you do stuff for him. And now that he thinks you're moving on, his ego doesn't know how to handle it. It bothers him that you're no longer pining with love for him.

SAGE: Yeah, well, it bothers me that he thinks of me like that. Like I'm going to sit in the wings and wait for him to notice me. I'm not a doll.

JASON: We'll keep shoving our relationship under his nose, then. :)

JASON: When's your next outing that he's sure to be at?

Jason wanted to go out with her again? Other than the wedding? Was this just to rub Greg's nose in it? Jason didn't seem like the petty type, but he was rather protective of her, and she could tell he didn't like Greg.

SAGE: The town Christmas festival is tomorrow night. I'm sure he'll be there. Everyone shows up for it. It's a very sweet event for the kids, and everyone else socializes. I usually run the thing.

JASON: Can I be your date?

SAGE: You absolutely don't have to. I'm going to be dressed as an elf and handing out presents. That's not exactly date material.

JASON: Nonsense. You're there. I'll be there. Greg will be there. We can look lovey-dovey and make him crazy. It'll be fun.

JASON: I'm not dressing like an elf, though. Bad enough I have to wear this cowboy hat Eli gave me.

He sent her a picture, and her heart thumped. Even if he had to wear the cowboy hat, he looked utterly gorgeous in it.

SAGE: If you're sure . . . You really don't have to, Jason, I promise. I can tell everyone my boyfriend is busy.

JASON: Nonsense. Just tell your boyfriend what time to be there.

SAGE: I'm going to start putting up decorations at five.

JASON: I'll tell Eli I need to come help you, then. He won't mind. He likes you. It's me he hates. :)

SAGE: He doesn't hate you!

JASON: Ask me how many stalls I've mucked out since I started here.

SAGE: What did you think ranching was? Riding a horse and yelling yee-haw? There's a lot of poo involved, my friend, a lot of poo.

JASON: No one ever tells you about the poo.

SAGE: Just you wait until spring and you have your hands in a cow's uterus all day long.

> JASON: I'm trying really hard not to think about that, thanks.

And she couldn't stop giggling.

Once her laughter died down, she stared at her phone thoughtfully. She knew that Jason put on a brave face in their texts, but it was clear after last night he was still struggling, and would continue to struggle no matter what. She thought about what he'd said about his service dog, how he'd tried to get another and been wait-listed for over a year, and even then it would be tens of thousands out of pocket. She wanted to help him, but how?

After searching on her phone for a good hour, she had an idea. She texted Cass, asked for Annie's number, and then called her.

"Hi, Sage," Annie said, her voice a whisper. "I'm talking soft because the baby's finally asleep. What's up?"

"I was wondering if you could tell me the difference between a service dog and an emotional support dog."

"Oh. Gosh, let me think. I've trained dogs with basic commands to be emotional support dogs, but a service dog has specific training and tasks it can do. You can take a service dog everywhere with you, no questions asked."

"And an emotional support animal?"

"It's a slightly different beast—no pun intended. Basically, they can accompany you in order to provide emotional stability and a calming presence. They can be trained to do certain things, of course, but there's not specific criteria, and because of that you can't take them a lot of places." She paused. "Why do you ask? I think I can guess, but I'm curious."

Sage hesitated, but she was already this far in, so she might as well go the full distance. "I'm sure Cass told you about Jason?"

"I'm not sure if I'm supposed to know, but yeah. I had concerns, so she told me. We won't let him know that we know, though."

"It turns out that he used to have a service dog and he did a lot better with handling his PTSD, but it died last year and he's been struggling. I wanted to see about replacing it for him. I don't know anything about service dogs, but then I started reading about emotional support animals and . . ."

"And you wanted to know if I could train one for him?" Annie guessed.

"Well, you are a dog trainer." Sage could feel herself blushing. "I know it's an imposition—"

"Not at all, and we're both on the same track. I actually talked to Dustin about this a day and a half ago, when I first heard he had PTSD. Of course, I'm not supposed to know about that, so we've been figuring out the best way to introduce a dog to him without him getting suspicious."

"Any ideas?"

"Yes, actually. I've got a few things in motion and I need another day to implement it . . ."

CHAPTER TWELVE

The next day, Sage lined up the rows of felt stockings she'd spread out on the table at the office. Most of them were stuffed, and she'd do the rest tonight before getting ready for the celebration. She'd managed to move most of the furniture to one of the back rooms while Bill, the current mayor, had taken on the street decorations. The sidewalks were lined with hay bales and festooned with garlands, wreaths hung from every window, and a big banner in front of the municipal office read SANTA'S WORKSHOP. Here, a big chair was set up for Santa, the raffle presents were carefully stored, and there were souvenir stockings for every child who came to the celebration. Across the street, a cotton candy machine was going, and Sage could see more food service tables being prepared. There were all kinds of treats for the young (and young at heart) and hot sandwiches and cups of soup for everyone else. The scent of hot cocoa filled the air, and she knew that if she went down the street, there was a "snowman building area," a reindeer petting zoo, face painting, and other fun games. There was even a donation area for winter clothing and extra food, and anyone that donated got free tickets for the raffles and games, and they always had a good showing. It was one of Sage's favorite things, just seeing the community come together to help one another out.

Now she just needed Old Clyde and Hannah to show up in their Santa and Mrs. Claus costumes. Sage was already wearing her elf outfit, her dress a short green baby doll with bright red dags at the collar and hem, and she wore red fishnets and big, fuzzy, green boots. She wore a bright red Santa hat, her hair was pulled into pigtails, and two cheery, glittery spots were painted on her cheeks. She knew she looked ridiculous, but did it matter? This was about fun, not fashion.

The door to the office opened, and Sage turned, ready to point out that the celebration wasn't going to begin for another hour, when she realized it wasn't partygoers, or Hannah and Clyde, but Jason. He stared up at the ceiling in surprise, pushing aside the glittery paper snowflakes that she'd spent all afternoon hanging. She'd done a good job with the office, she thought. Puffs of thick craft cotton made the tile look like clouds, and she'd hung the snowflakes. With large sheets of bulletin board paper, she'd managed to wrangle together a paper mural of Santa's workshop, and the furniture she hadn't been able to move to the back office was wrapped to look like giant presents.

"This place looks different," Jason commented as she rushed out to meet him.

"Does it look okay? Festive enough?"

His gaze moved to her and then stopped. Jason stared at her pigtails and glittered cheeks, then began to smile and kept eyeing her even as his gaze traveled downward. "It looks great. Nice costume."

"It's a little loud."

"It makes your legs look like they go on for miles. Greg's gonna have a heart attack." He grinned at her, but she noticed he was sneaking extra looks at her legs himself, and she could feel her cheeks heating in response. Okay, that was flattering.

"Thanks for coming, but you really didn't have to do this, Jason. I'm afraid you're going to be bored."

"Me? Not at all." He moved to her side as she bustled to the back table, stuffing the last of the stockings. "I like spending time with you."

"Well, the most exciting thing that will happen tonight is when I inevitably take Mayor Bill's keys away from him because he's hitting the eggnog too hard." She smiled at Jason over her shoulder. "The rest is just good, clean family fun but nothing exciting."

"I'm fine with boring and not exciting." He smiled and glanced at the table and the spread of half-stuffed stockings she had laid out. "Show me what I can do to help."

"You don't have to—"

"I know I don't, but I'm happy to. Now, let me help you, Sage, or I'm gonna find some mistletoe and drag you under it just to distract you."

She blushed bright red.

As things swung into gear, Jason stayed close to Sage's side. She'd warned him that this would be a very busy night, but he'd had no idea. Every time he'd been in Painted Barrel, the sleepy little town seemed practically deserted except for the few sparsely populated businesses. Tonight, though, everyone in Wyoming seemed to have descended upon the tiny town. The streets were packed with people, men with children on their shoulders, women in Santa hats, and everyone was looking to have a good time. The food booths had lines of customers, the kiddie rides and petting zoo were a huge success, and everywhere he looked, he saw smiling faces.

This was a happy place, this town, and Sage did her best to make it that way for everyone. He knew she was the mastermind behind this big celebration. As the evening progressed, he watched as person after person went up to her for assistance. This person needed change for their booth, that person needed raffle tickets, this vendor needed a nutritional information card for a parent with allergic children. Sage handled all of it with grace and skill, as if she'd managed such things all her life. Perhaps she had—even the mayor deferred to her when she suggested something, and sure enough, she snagged the man's keys about an hour into the party.

The mayor only giggled like a schoolboy and handed them over to her with a smile.

It was clear that Sage might not think she was anything special to these people, but she was the one that made this town run. His respect for her grew by the minute. She was never ruffled by anything, not crying babies who wailed the moment they were put on Santa's lap, not fussy parents or the occasional rude partygoer, not anything. She just handled it all and managed to look adorable in her elf costume the entire time.

That elf costume . . . He'd never been so turned on at the thought of Christmas.

Jason was doing his best to be helpful. He was handling the raffle ticket turn-ins so it would be one less thing Sage had to manage by herself. As he did, he couldn't help but stare at her long legs in that too-short dress. They were taut and well muscled, and they seemed to go on for miles. Sage was on the tall side, but tonight her elf boots had heels, and they made her look staggeringly leggy. The pigtails were pretty damn sexy, too.

Really, all of it was turning his crank, but the thing he loved most of all was the sheer joy and happiness that radiated out of her.

Well, that and the short hem of her dress.

Jason couldn't stop thinking about that brief kiss at the dinner. He wanted to kiss her again, but this time for real. This time, he wanted to pause over her lips and taste her, really and truly taste her. He wanted to slick his tongue against hers and hear the soft little moans tear from her throat. He wanted to see if she'd blush when he kissed her, or if she'd fling her arms around his neck and demand more.

And all of the kisses he was thinking about? They weren't kisses between friends, or the kinds of kisses that you shared when you were in a fake relationship.

He was thinking about real, deep, sultry kisses. Kisses that would make her toes curl and his balls ache. Kisses that would leave her dazed and clinging to him. Oh yeah, he was definitely thinking about kissing her again.

She'd missed the hint he'd dropped earlier, though. He'd made a mistletoe reference just to see how she'd react, and Sage had immediately turned bright red and made herself very busy. She was hard to read. He wasn't sure if she was so shy because she wasn't used to flirting or because she wasn't interested and he was making things awkward for them.

There was only one way to find out, but Jason wasn't certain he wanted to push things to that level. If he did and she wasn't interested, he'd lose her friendship. Right now, that friendship was the only thing keeping him sane. Her little texts and funny pictures she sent throughout the day helped ground him and prevented him from getting too locked up in his own thoughts. Instead of focusing on the potential hiding places or theoretical snipers, he was focused on listening for his phone's next buzz with an incoming text, and what he'd send to her in reply. So far Eli and Dustin had him working on miscellaneous chores around the barn while they did the field work, and that meant he had a lot of time to text. And at night, on the nights that they weren't together? They both texted all night long, and they'd even FaceTimed each other when their fingers got tired of all the typing.

He liked her, a lot. She was smart, she was funny, and she was kind. She was a happy person—so happy. He loved that about her. He'd never met someone so full of joy. It didn't matter to her that she had a boring job for a small, nondescript town. She wanted to make everyone's experience the best it could possibly be and went out of her way to ensure that people, no matter how big or small, left her presence smiling.

And Jason wanted to return that favor. He wanted to make Sage smile. He wanted to see her beam with pleasure at him—no, better than that, he wanted to see that shy, sweet smile that told him she was shocked and pleased, as if she never thought she deserved whatever small kindness he bestowed on her.

Sage was a girl that deserved showy displays of affection. She should have had a boyfriend that lavished attention on her, got her flowers every time she turned around, and made her realize what a wonderful person she was, how pretty she was. How sweet.

But no one had. She thought no one ever noticed her.

Hell, Jason couldn't stop noticing her.

So when he saw someone walk past with a small bouquet of red and white flowers, he decided Sage needed some of those, too. He excused himself and let Mrs. Claus—Hannah, the town's innkeeper—run the raffle booth for a few minutes while he headed outside and went down the vendor row again. There were a few people selling crafts, others selling food, and at the very end of the line of stalls, he saw someone with Christmas plants. His eyes landed on a huge bouquet of white roses surrounding a trio of poinsettia and wrapped in sparkly silver paper.

Five minutes later, his wallet was a hundred dollars lighter, but the bouquet was his.

He headed back to the municipal office—aka Santa's Workshop—and just outside, he saw Greg and his fiancée, Becca. Becca was chatting excitedly to two other women as Greg stared into one of the frosted windows, and as he did, Jason knew his gaze was locked on Sage. And as Sage bent down to greet one of the children and revealed a lot more leg and cleavage than she probably realized, Jason cleared his throat. "Greg, right?"

Like he didn't know who the creep was.

Greg whipped around and gave Jason a skeptical look. His gaze flicked to Jason's face, then the large bouquet in his arms. The sour expression on the man's face grew even sourer. "Sage's new little friend, right?"

"Her boyfriend, yes," he corrected, and smiled widely at the bride-to-be, who deserved better than the chump at her side. "I was just getting my girl a little present. You enjoying the celebration?"

"It's so great this year," Becca gushed, clinging to Greg's arm and beaming up at Jason. "Tell Sage she did an amazing job."

"She did, and I will," Jason said proudly. He was glad that others were realizing just how much thought—and work—Sage put into other people's happiness. "You guys coming inside? I'm sure she'd love to say hi."

Greg nodded, and at the same time, Becca shook her head. "Oh no, the dancing's about to start in the square. I want to be there so Greg and I can practice for the big day." She bounced happily.

Greg looked less happy.

Dancing, huh? Jason wondered if Sage liked to dance. It would definitely be a way to stick it in Greg's face again—something that Jason had to admit he was getting far too much pleasure out of. "Maybe we'll see you over there."

Becca gave him a happy wave and then dragged her morose fiancé away. Jason couldn't help but notice that Greg managed to get in one last look at Sage, and he hoped the man choked on Sage's happiness. To think that he'd had Sage sitting right under his nose, her heart in her eyes, and he completely ignored her until someone else paid attention to her. He hoped Greg was miserable for the rest of his life . . . but at the same time, he felt bad for Becca, who seemed like a nice, if excitable, woman.

It wasn't his problem, though, he reminded himself, and he stepped back inside the crowded office. The heat hit him full blast in the face, and he shook the snowflakes out of his short hair. People were shoulder to shoulder in here, and as he looked around for Sage, he saw her in the back comforting a crying child as she hastily stuffed goodies into her hat. They'd run out of stockings a half hour ago; apparently, they hadn't purchased enough, and Sage looked like she was compensating by taking off her own hat and cramming it full of as many treats as she could.

He lurked off to the side, watching as she soothed the

crying child and the embarrassed parents and then talked to them for a few minutes. When they left with a wave— and a happy child now sucking on a Ring Pop—Jason approached.

"Merry early Christmas," he told her, holding the flowers out. "You've made this celebration a huge success for everyone, and someone should be thanking you."

Her jaw dropped and she looked at him in surprise. "Oh, Jason. You didn't have to thank me with flowers! I'm just doing my job." She beamed at him and took the bouquet slowly, the paper crinkling as she held it against her chest. "But that's awfully sweet of you."

"I didn't get them because you did a good job," he told her. Was she just willfully misunderstanding, he wondered, or was she truly that clueless about how he felt? Maybe he wasn't showing his own emotions very well. He decided to be a little bolder. "I got them for you because I thought you deserved flowers from your boyfriend."

Sage's face immediately colored as red as the glittery dots on her cheeks. She buried her face in the flowers and then gave him another shy smile. "You're too sweet," was all she said, and he could tell from the way her expression immediately eased that she thought this was just more of their pretending. He was obviously going to have to keep pressing her to make her realize that sometime in the last week, his feelings had changed.

He hoped hers had, too.

"I saw Greg outside," Jason said carefully, just to see how she reacted.

She made a face, and his heart swelled. "I knew he'd be here. I hope he's giving Becca a lot of attention."

"He was staring at you through the window. I saw him and he gave me a dirty look."

Sage just sighed. She didn't look pleased that her old crush was stewing with jealousy. "I feel so bad for Becca. He's got cold feet, but it's going to hurt her feelings if she finds that out."

"It's more than just that. He's realizing he settled for her when he could have had you."

She laughed and shook her head. Her chuckles died when she realized he wasn't laughing with her—that he was serious. "Jason, you make it sound like I'm some prize—"

"You make it sound like you're not."

The look she gave him was helpless, as if she wasn't entirely sure how to respond to that. "He could have had me at any point in the last ten years. The fact that he's even thinking about me now is nothing more than cold feet. Trust me, I know Greg."

Sage was an adult, but for all that, sometimes she was incredibly naive. Maybe that was the part that irked him— not her innocence, but that she wasn't lying. Greg really could have just snapped his fingers and Sage would have been thrilled at any ounce of attention he'd thrown her way. That ate at Jason. She deserved so much better than some douchebag's scraps. She deserved to be loved for the amazing, beautiful, sexy, kind, generous person that she was.

Jason wanted to be the man she looked to for that attention, but she was completely clueless about it. So he tried again. He nodded toward the windows. "There's dancing about to start in the square. You want to go?"

Her eyes widened and she looked around at the crowded room and then shook her head. "No, I should really stay close in case anyone needs anything. I'm the one running the event, after all."

He couldn't be mad at that; she'd told him before that

she was working the event. But he still wanted to dance with her, if nothing else because he'd be able to pull her in his arms and hold her close. "If things quiet down, maybe we can slip away."

She chuckled and batted at his arm. "Wow, you're determined to rub Greg's nose in it, aren't you?"

Yeah, that actually wasn't it at all. But he just gave her a vague smile and returned to the raffle desk.

Sure enough, a few minutes later, music started up outside, the strains of "Jingle Bell Rock" sliding through the air. It was like the office had an exodus—people cleared out, heading for the square, and then it was just him and Sage, and Mr. and Mrs. Claus.

The man playing Santa got to his feet and adjusted the pillow tucked under his belt. "You want to go dance, Mrs. Claus?"

The older woman tittered and took his hand, and then it was just Sage and Jason alone in the office.

He got to his feet, and she smiled at him, curious. "You know, Sage, we can dance here."

Her brows furrowed. "We'll look silly to anyone that peeks through the windows."

"So? I don't care. Let them see Sage Cooper dancing with her weird boyfriend."

She shook her head at him. "You're not weird."

"Weird or not . . ." He extended his hand to her and stood in the middle of the floor.

Her cheeks were pink, and for a moment, Jason thought she would decline. But she moved to his side, put her hand in his, and then "White Christmas" began to play. Perfect, a slow song. He pulled her against him, their linked hands raised in the air as his other hand went to her waist. It was a slow dance, but he held her formally a few inches away from him as they spun around the room. He could tell she was uncomfortable, as if she didn't belong in his arms.

Which was craziness.

So he closed the distance between them and changed the angle. "I don't think that's how a guy should dance with the girl he's crazy about," Jason murmured, and his other hand slid to her waist. He pulled her closer and leaned in, murmuring in her ear, "Put your arms around my neck."

Sage did, and the scent of her hair tickled his nose. She was the perfect height, and as he held her close, he swayed to the music. She was a little more relaxed now, but she wouldn't look up at him. "You feel good in my arms," he told her to try to break the ice. After all, it was just the two of them in the room. What did she have to be shy about?

She looked around and then glanced up at him, her cheeks bright red. "Jason, we don't have to keep pretending. There's no one else here right now."

He was tired of pretending, all right—tired of pretending that he didn't want to kiss her. He spotted the cluster of mistletoe hung over the door and gently steered her toward that, dancing underneath.

"What are you doing?" she asked.

"Kissing my 'fake' girlfriend," Jason told her and then touched a fingertip to her chin and lifted her mouth to his.

He could hear her gasp, but it was swallowed as his mouth covered hers. And then they were kissing. This wasn't just a brush of lips quickly over the other. It was a real kiss.

At least, it was on his part. She was still stiff against him no matter how much he tried to coax her mouth to open. After a moment, he lifted his head.

Sage looked up at him with confusion. "Jason, you don't have to—"

He kissed her again. Did she still not think he truly wanted her? He'd just have to show her, then. He cupped her neck with both hands and gently kissed her mouth again. And again. Over and over, he nibbled at her lips until she softened against him, her stiffness melting away. When her lips finally parted under his, he knew she was his. Deepening the kiss, he swept his tongue into her mouth.

Sage moaned against him, her hands curling in the front of his shirt.

Damn, but he liked that moan.

He deepened the kiss, enjoying her taste, loving the way her mouth felt against his, the way she sagged against him, the feel of her. He'd kissed women plenty of times before, though it had been a while. Something about this made it seem special, though. Perhaps it was Sage's unpracticed, shy responses when her tongue grazed against his. Perhaps it was the little sounds she made in her throat as he kissed her and kissed her, as if she couldn't handle all of the pleasure.

Perhaps it was just that it was Sage, and he was falling for her and her marvelous dimples.

In the background, something electronic pinged.

He lifted his head when her body jerked in response. "What is it?"

Sage was dazed, her dark eyes glazed with passion. She stared up at him for a moment, uncomprehending, her mouth pink and swollen from his kisses. She looked so soft and pretty that he immediately wanted to kiss her again, when the electronic ping happened a second time. That made her focus, and she gave herself a little shake and stumbled away from him. "I think it's my phone? I think."

Jason watched, secretly pleased, as she wobbled over to

where her purse was stored. He liked that he'd made her weak in the knees. He liked the languid look in her eyes and the way she'd felt against him. He was going to be kissing her a lot in the next while, he hoped. He watched her with a possessive, satisfied gaze as she picked up her phone, her cheeks bright pink. He was imagining her under him, the awestruck look on her face when he kissed her—and did so much more.

Dating Sage would be such a pleasure, he decided, and he wanted it more than he'd ever wanted anything in his life.

And then her eyes widened in surprise. "I got a hit on a dating app."

That was a bucket of cold water over his arousal. "You what?"

Sage looked up at him in confusion. "I . . . It's a notification from a dating app. I got a match. Some guy named Walter wants to chat with me."

"You're on dating apps?" His ego felt like it had just been struck by a boulder.

She tilted her head at him. "I told you I was, remember? You were going to help me figure out why I couldn't get any matches."

Right. He *had* told her that. Damn it. Somewhere in the middle of all of that was going on, he'd totally forgotten about her dating profiles. He'd forgotten that she was moving precisely because she was lonely and wanted to go somewhere where she'd have the opportunity to date more, because everyone in town acted like she didn't exist.

He'd been fine with that a few days ago, when he barely knew her. Now he knew Sage better than he knew a lot of people. He saw what a devoted, caring, kind person she was. He'd seen her sleeping and laughing and teasing, and he'd grown addicted to those dimples. Jason might have said he would help her a few days ago, but now the thought ate him up with jealousy. "I think you and I need to talk."

"We do?" she echoed, clutching her phone to her breast.

"We do," he repeated firmly, and crossed the room to her side and took her hand. She was wearing a short dress, so it was probably a bad idea to take her outside in the cold, snowy weather. Instead, he looked around and then headed for a door at the back of the office. Inside there, all of the furniture from the front of the office had been pushed together into a hodgepodge of desks. But it was empty, and private, and perfect for a heart-to-heart conversation with her where they wouldn't be interrupted. He steered her inside and then sat on the edge of one desk as she sat across from him, confusion on her face.

"I don't understand," she told him as he shut the door. "All of this . . . this isn't real, is it?"

Jason studied her face, curious to see her reaction. "What if I want it to be?"

Her mouth opened slightly. "Oh."

That was the only reaction he got? "That's all you have to say?" He didn't know if he was amused or wounded at that simple response.

She averted her eyes and nervously moved her hand to her ear, as if trying to tuck a piece of hair behind it. Her hand fluttered, and then she dropped it into her lap, and he realized she was nervous, her cheeks flushed bright red. She looked up, and the expression on her face was so vulnerable and full of yearning that it made his heart hurt. "I just . . . Why would you want to go out with me?"

"Are you crazy?" He chuckled and took her hand in his. "Sage, ever since I ran into you, you've been nothing but the best, kindest, most generous person I've ever had the chance to meet. You've never made me feel like I was a mess, or an idiot." When she frowned at his words, he continued. "You'd be surprised at how many people act like because I have PTSD, my brain is broken. And maybe it is in some ways, but I'm not a drooling moron."

"You're absolutely not," Sage injected, her expression indignant. "I'll correct anyone that ever even suggests such a thing in my presence."

And that was another aspect he loved about her—her fierce defense of anyone and anything she cared about. "You don't see yourself the same way I see you. Heck, you don't even see yourself the same way everyone in this town sees you. When I look around at this party you put on for the town, I see hundreds of happy faces, and you know every single one of them. They know you made this possible for them, and they love you for it. You're not as invisible as you think."

She ducked her head shyly. "Being friends with people is different than dating someone. I'm not exciting enough for anyone to date."

"That's bullshit and you know it."

Sage looked startled at his vehement denial. "Why?"

"Greg might never have noticed you because his head is so far up his own ass." Jason rolled his eyes. "And maybe he scared off the other guys in town from being interested in you. Or maybe they knew you had a crush on him and never bothered to pursue you on their own. But just because they're blind idiots doesn't mean that there's something wrong with you. It's their loss and my gain." She was staring at him so hard with those deep eyes that it made his heart hurt. He reached up and brushed his knuckles over one soft cheek, not caring that it got bright red glitter all over his hand. "I've been falling hard for these dimples ever since I met you, but I held off because I know I'm a mess. I still am a mess. And if that makes you uncomfortable, I understand and I'm totally fine with being your friend, but I want you to know that you're amazing and beautiful and any guy would be thrilled to date you."

She was quiet for so long that for a brief moment, he worried he'd offended her. But then she gave him another slow, shy smile. "You really mean it?"

"I do."

"Then will you kiss me again?"

Oh, he'd absolutely kiss her again. He'd kiss her until both of them were panting with exhaustion . . . and then he'd kiss her again, just to show her how much he liked her. He pulled her into his arms, gazing into her lovely eyes.

As he leaned in to kiss her again, though, she pulled back, pausing. "I'm leaving in the spring, though. Are you sure we should date?"

"It's just dating, Sage. We're not getting married." Not yet, at least. But he could suddenly see himself growing old with someone like her. "Plenty of time between now and then to just enjoy ourselves and see where this leads."

"If you're sure."

"I'm sure. Now, stop worrying and let me kiss you."

She smiled and put her arms around his neck again, leaning in.

He could feel her shyness as he pulled her close, but he wasn't going to let that deter him. Jason ran his fingers along the line of her jaw, almost petting her as she leaned in. Her nose brushed against his, and she gave the tiniest of sighs. His sweet Sage. "So does this mean you want to date me?"

"Yes," she said, and blushed.

"Good," he murmured and then nipped at her lower lip.

He loved the sultry little gasp she gave. She made it seem like it was all so new to her. He nipped at her lip with his teeth again, careful to be gentle. Her mouth was soft and slightly pouty, and when he slicked his tongue over her lips in a teasing caress, he tasted peppermint, as if she'd stolen a candy cane and been nibbling on it when he wasn't looking. When she gave another little shuddering moan, he claimed her mouth with his, his tongue possessing hers. The kiss grew deep and intense, his mouth slanting across Sage's over and over, until they were both panting and breathless.

"Oh," was all she said when he pulled away, that sexy, dazed look still on her face. "How . . . how was that?"

"Amazing," Jason told her, and meant it. "But I always knew kissing you would be."

She bit her lip, and the sight of that made him want to lean in and kiss her all over again. "Would it make you think I'm a loser if I tell you that was my first real kiss?"

He'd suspected as much with how utterly shy she was. "No. It'd just make me think even more that the men here are idiots."

And he loved the dazzlingly sweet smile she gave him in response.

CHAPTER THIRTEEN

Tonight had been something out of a fairy tale, Sage decided. Or it was a scene from a superromantic movie that she'd fallen asleep to, and she'd wake up to find out it was all a dream.

Men like Jason didn't look at women like Sage. They sure didn't kiss them.

And Jason had kissed her until her toes had curled in her boots and she was sure her face was permanently flushed. Once he'd told her how he felt about her, they'd kissed in the back room until Old Clyde and Hannah had returned, and then she'd spent the rest of the evening blushing and trying not to notice how much of the glitter on her face had transferred to Jason's face.

No one ever saw her, but she realized that all of Jason's pretending *wasn't* pretending. He wasn't good at faking it. He truly was interested in her. He wanted to kiss *her*.

Sage Cooper, man-repellent.

Goodness, now she was thinking about so much more

than just kissing. Her cheeks were aflame for the rest of the evening, and she wasn't entirely sure how she managed to handle the raffle, but she did. And if a few people were smirking at Jason's glitter-spattered grin, well, did it even matter? They all thought he was her boyfriend anyhow.

Once the festival officially wrapped up and people began to drift away, the work was only half done. With some volunteers, Sage, Bill, Jason, and a dozen others stayed behind to clean the streets up, remove hay bales, and ensure that the place was tidy for the next morning. The office was still a mess, but she could clean it up on her own tomorrow when she was "off" work.

It was late when they wrapped up, and Jason kissed her good night one more time before promising to text her in the morning. She'd almost asked him to stay over, but she didn't want to sabotage his job. So he left, and oh, it was hard to climb into her Jeep and head back to her quiet, lonely ranch alone, even if it was just for the evening.

She was tired, but as she lay in bed, she found it impossible to sleep. Her thoughts were full of Jason. Jason and the smoldering look in his eyes as he steered her under the mistletoe. Jason's mouth and how amazing he'd tasted when he'd kissed her. She'd never realized that kisses had tastes, but of course they did. And Sage loved the taste of Jason's mouth. She touched her lips, thinking about how his had felt there.

The throbbing between her thighs hadn't gone away, either. She could feel her pulse pounding seemingly at the vee of her hips. It was an ache that wouldn't go away, she suspected, until Jason kissed her again. Maybe not even then. Maybe not until he took her in his arms and stole her virginity.

Ha. Stole it. She'd freaking give it to him on a silver platter at this point.

Funny how she'd been starry-eyed over him and here

he'd thought he wasn't good enough for her because of his PTSD. That was just crazy to think about. He was funny, kind, hardworking . . . and gorgeous. It wasn't his fault he'd been in a bad situation in Afghanistan that had messed him up. She would never judge him for such a thing, ever.

She hoped he stayed in Painted Barrel until she moved. Even if they only dated for a few months, she'd take what she could get.

Spring suddenly didn't seem that far away, and that was depressing.

The next morning, Sage woke up to her phone buzzing with incoming texts. One was from Greg, which she swiped away without reading it. The other was from Jason.

JASON: Morning, dimples.

JASON: What's your schedule look like for the rest of the week?

SAGE: Morning. :) We have the wedding next Saturday, and work, of course, but I'm pretty free for the rest of the time? Why?

JASON: I was just thinking we should go on a real date. Something romantic, just you and me. We could head into the nearest city and get a bite to eat for dinner tonight? Is there Italian around here?

SAGE: There's not much of anything around here, but I'm game for some driving. Or I can make dinner.

JASON: You already make dinner all the time. This needs to be special.

SAGE: Hanging out with you is always special.

JASON: Okay, well, I want to impress my lady,
how's that? Can I pick you up when I'm done here?

SAGE: Of course! I'm going to hang around the
office after work for a while anyhow. Just pick me up
in town. We'll figure out plans then. :)

JASON: Sounds good. Hope you slept all right and
that you dreamed of me.

And she held the phone to her nightshirt and giggled
like a schoolgirl.

When Jason headed into the kitchen to grab breakfast,
he was surprised that Dustin's wife, Annie, immediately stood up to meet him . . . and she had a dog on a
leash. "Oh good," Annie said. "You're awake."

He was thrown off. The small, freckled redhead was
nice and polite to him, but they didn't talk much. Dustin
was the gregarious one of the two, and Annie was more or
less occupied with the dogs or the baby every time he saw
her. He looked around the kitchen, but Cass and Eli were
talking at the sink, and Dustin was already outside, no
doubt heading for the barn. Uneasy, Jason forced a smile to
his face. "What can I help you with?"

"You know Dustin and I are taking baby Morgan to my
mother's for the holidays," she said, smiling widely at him.

"You leave Monday, right?"

"Actually, we're leaving tomorrow. Sunday. Small change
of plans." She moved forward, and as she did, the dog at her

side moved with her. "And that leaves me with a problem. I need you to meet Achilles." And Annie gestured at the dog at her side.

He cleared his throat and tried not to look at the wagging tail and dark eyes. "I'm not sure what you need from me, Miss Annie."

"Oh. Well, Achilles here is a very good boy," she said, and immediately dropped to her knees, hugging the dog's neck. "I just pulled him from a kill shelter in Kansas, and a buddy dropped him off. I'm going to train him for one of my friends that does animal stunts back in Hollywood. Golden labs are always in demand, and I don't think he's purebred, but he's pretty enough that most won't notice." She scratched at the dog's ears, and the animal panted with delight.

"Okay," Jason said, still trying to follow what she needed. "You need me to drive him somewhere?"

"He's not going anywhere until he's trained," Annie said, getting to her feet again. She held the leash out to Jason. "But I do have a problem in that he's got attachment issues. He needs to be around someone at all times or he gets anxious and upset. That was why they were going to put him down at the shelter. He would howl and scratch at the walls if he was left alone, but around people, he's just the best boy. Aren't you, Achilles?" Her voice turned sugary sweet. "So we need someone to be his buddy while Dustin and I are gone."

Buddy? Jason took a steeling breath and forced himself to look at the dog. It—Achilles—was wagging his tail expectantly, staring up at Jason with the happy innocence only a dog could wear. He was shaggy and golden, all right, his ears slightly floppy. His eyes were dark brown, and his tail was wagging back and forth a mile a minute as he stared at Jason.

And Jason thought of Truck, and his heart hurt. "Miss Annie . . ."

"I know," she said softly. "You don't like dogs. It's evident when you look at them. But I really need a favor."

His mouth was dry. He rubbed a hand over his lips, feeling dread creep over him. "It's not that I hate them. I don't. It's just hard to be around them sometimes."

"I know, but you're the only person I can ask. Dustin's going with me, Cass has the baby and the other dogs to look after, and Eli's got enough on his plate with us going out of town. I already talked to Eli, and you can bring Achilles with you wherever you go when you're working. He's not a runner, and he's very comfortable in a harness, so you shouldn't have any problems. Just consider it another aspect of your job." And she beamed at him, an apology in her eyes. "Please. I'd hate to send him back to the shelter."

He stared down at the dog.

Achilles just kept wagging his tail. He did an excited little shimmy in place, as if he couldn't wait to say hello to Jason. He did look like a handsome dog. Happy, too. He thought about Sage, oddly enough. She'd want him to help Annie out, because that's what she would do. And she would look at him with such pride if he did, knowing how hard it was for him to be around another dog. "How long is this for?"

"He's going to need to stay with you twenty-four seven until we get back," she told him with a grimace. "The anxiety and attachment issues he has are really bad. That means he goes with you today around the ranch, and he stays with you in your room at night. Once his environment's been stabilized, we can try to move things around a little, but he needs a constant person at his side before we can get that far."

And that constant person was supposed to be him? Hell. "I was going to take Sage out on a date tonight," he said as a last-ditch excuse.

Annie just smiled. "Sage loves dogs."

And she held out the leash again.

What the hell else could he do but give in?

Eli and Dustin were out on two of the horses, running down one of the cattle that had gone missing. That meant Jason was—as usual—waiting at the barn and cleaning up after the sick cows that had been pulled from the herd temporarily. He gave them fresh water and added straw to their stalls, and made notes on the wellness chart for each animal to see if symptoms were better or worse. If they were better, and the animal responded to antibiotics, it could rejoin the herd soon. If not, they'd probably have to call the vet. So he judged the amount of snot running from cow noses and made notes and tried not to look at the dog at his side. It was a calm dog, at least. Other than the tail that wagged a mile a minute, he was quiet. He didn't bark, didn't chase the horses or the sick cattle. He just stayed at Jason's side as if he was happiest right there.

In a way, it reminded him of Truck's constant presence and made his heart ache. He finished mucking one stall, washed his hands, and then sat down on a bale of hay to try and compose his thoughts.

Achilles immediately put his head on Jason's knee and gazed up at him with sad eyes.

"Stop it," he told the dog. "We're not going to be friends, you and me. This is just temporary."

The tail wagged harder, but his chin didn't move from Jason's knee. He looked as if he was dying for a head scratch, and with a sigh, Jason complied. He scratched behind the ears and along the muzzle, and Achilles closed his eyes and groaned as if in pleasure. "Don't get too comfortable," he muttered.

He smiled when he lifted his hand and the dog immediately put a paw on Jason's arm, demanding more pets. With one hand rubbing the dog's thick fur, he scratched at his new "friend" and texted Sage with his other hand.

JASON: Guess what?

SAGE: You changed your mind about us?

JASON: God no. Don't even think that.

SAGE: Then what?

JASON: I got stuck with a dog.

SAGE: You what?

He took a picture of Achilles—who was rather photogenic for a mutt, really—and sent it to Sage.

JASON: He has attachment issues. Annie needs me to watch over him night and day until she gets back from LA. She already cleared it with Eli, and I don't get much of a say in the matter.

SAGE: Oh. I mean, he's cute? Is he a good dog?

JASON: He's pretty chill from what I can tell. Happy, too.

JASON: Hope you don't mind a third wheel at our sexy dinner tonight.

SAGE: You know I don't mind. :)

He looked down at the dog as he scratched his ears. "You're going to be a real pain in my ass for the next while," he told Achilles. "But you get to come with us tonight as long as you follow my rules. Understand?"

Achilles's tail wagged.

"Just remember she's my girl. No sad eyes at her. She's got too soft a heart as it is." He paused for a moment and leaned in. "The sad eyes are *my* move."

Achilles just squirmed with delight, and Jason found himself chuckling.

CHAPTER FOURTEEN

For some reason, the day raced past despite the complication of having a new friend at his side. He learned that while Achilles didn't give a damn about horses or cattle, the chickens made him lose his mind. The dog went on high alert the moment he heard birds, and he raced over to the cage to stare at them with death in his eyes, as if he were somehow protecting Jason from the feathered menaces. Jason wasn't much of a chicken man himself (unless it was on his plate), but it was rather funny to see how Achilles acted. That was a habit he'd have to break him of, though, and with a few stern "no" commands and a tug on the harness, the dog obeyed. He even stayed at Jason's side without complaint as Jason saddled up onto Buster and rode out to meet Dustin and Eli at one of the south pastures, where the fencing had been torn down by leaning cattle.

By the time the cows were settled for the night and the horses curried and hooves cleaned, it was completely dark out. He grimaced at the sight and hoped Sage wasn't too impatient waiting on him. He washed up inside the house, told the others he was going to dinner with Sage, and headed out with Achilles at his side. He'd had a moment where he'd considered leaving the dog with Annie tonight, but the babies were crying and Dustin was packing their car and everyone seemed frazzled. Achilles needed stability, she'd told him, and tonight at the Price Ranch, the living room was crowded and noisy. So he took the dog with him without complaint.

Achilles seemed to love a car ride, too. He hopped up on the towel Jason spread on the seat as if he'd done that a hundred times before, didn't squirm when his harness was buckled to the seat belt, and pushed his nose against the glass as Jason drove into town.

If he had to have a dog with him, he supposed Achilles was a pretty good dog.

He hoped having the dog with him wouldn't ruin their evening together. He'd wanted to take Sage to a nice dinner, something memorable for their first official date, but now he didn't know if that was possible with a dog in tow. He'd talk to her and see what she wanted to do. He didn't much care what they did as long as he got to spend time with her.

Jason pulled up to the post office, then took Achilles for a walk so he could do his business. They circled around the buildings like he always did, but his thoughts were less wild tonight. His focus was on Sage and the dog-slash-problem at his side. By the time they went back to the front of the office, Sage was there, smiling at him from the doorway. "How's your new friend?"

"Bit of a pain in the ass, but we're getting to know each other." He looked down at the dog and then at her. "His name's Achilles, and it seems that Annie rescued him just in time to leave town."

"Oh?"

"I'll tell you all about it on the way to dinner." He studied her, noticing that her usual "ugly" sweater was gone.
She wore jeans and a plain cream turtleneck sweater with
an oversize collar that draped over her shoulder and made
her look touchable. Her hair was pulled into a sleek ponytail and emphasized the soft, pale skin of her neck, and for
a moment, he desperately wanted to go back inside the office and kiss the hell out of that neck, forget dinner.

But that was him thinking with his dick, and he knew it.

"You look beautiful, by the way," he told her. "I should
have said that right away."

She gave him a shy smile. "The fact that you said it at all
makes me happy." She didn't look happy, though. Those
dimples weren't showing. In fact, she was almost as pale as
her sweater and looked as if she were about to vomit.

"I mean it. You're gorgeous." He reached for her, and
when she put her hand in his, he squeezed it. "Don't look so
nervous, all right? It's just me."

Sage didn't smile back at him. "Yes, but everything is
different now. I don't want to mess anything up. More than
that, I don't want to disappoint you."

What could possibly disappoint him? It was on the tip of
his tongue to say she was being silly, but he knew she was
deadly serious. She truly was worried she'd somehow
"mess up" their relationship. "You want to get it out of the
way first, then?"

Her brows furrowed. "Get what out of the way?"

"The good night kiss. That's the part you think you'll
mess up, right? Because you and I talk all the time, so you
can't be nervous about that." When her cheeks colored pret-
tily, he knew he was right. "So let's get it out of the way.
We'll kiss first, and then you can relax for the rest of the

evening." He tugged her closer to him, leading her hand to his neck.

The look she gave him was skeptical. "I'm trying to decide if this is just a ploy to get me to kiss you."

"Possibly." Jason grinned. "Does it matter if it works, though?"

"I guess not." She put her hands to his neck and took a deep breath. "Let me know if I'm not very good, and I'll try to do better."

Is that what this was? She was shy about kissing him because she was afraid she wouldn't be very good at it? "I kissed you before and thought you kissed just fine, Sage. Even if it was a terrible kiss, I wouldn't care. In fact, it might almost be better."

"Better? Why?"

"Because then we could practice a lot." And he leaned in and gently brushed his lips over hers. She gave a nervous chuckle that died when his tongue flicked at the entrance to her mouth, and then her arms tightened around his shoulders. Her lips parted sweetly, inviting him in, and then they were kissing just as deeply as they did last night, and he had no idea why she worried. Every time he touched her, it made him hungry for more. It didn't matter that her responses weren't polished or expert. She kissed with enthusiasm, and she made little noises of pleasure constantly, as if she couldn't quite believe how much she liked the kiss. He swept his tongue over hers, his hands sliding to her waist. He wanted to grab her ass and haul her against him, to pull her so close that she would feel just how much he liked kissing her, but he knew he needed to take things slow. So he kissed and licked and nibbled at her sweet mouth until she broke the connection, panting.

Her eyes were heavy with arousal as she looked up at him. "How did I do?"

"Amazing," he murmured. "But we can do it again if you're not sure."

She immediately pulled him down to her again. Minutes passed before either one of them broke the embrace this time, and when she pulled back, her face was flushed, but her dimpled smile had returned. The sight of those dimples made his already aching cock even harder. "That was a good kiss, I think," she declared.

"It was." They were all good in his eyes.

She smiled at him, and then her gaze moved down to Achilles. The dog's tail immediately began to thump, slapping against Jason's leg. "Well, hello there," Sage cooed at him. "What a handsome fella."

"You sure you don't mind if we have a third wheel for our date?" he told her, rubbing his thumb against her waist. Her sweater was bunched up under his grasp, and he wanted to haul it up and reveal the soft skin underneath. Damn, but he was getting impatient with taking things slow, and here they were only on the first date. It was going to kill him to move any slower.

"Oh, I don't mind at all." She dropped to her knees and petted Achilles, who took the loving with happy thumps of his tail and endless licking of Sage's face. She laughed, and the sound filled him with joy. "You know, we don't have to go anywhere special," she told Jason, glancing up at him even as she rubbed Achilles's ears. "I don't know which restaurants in Casper take pets, but the bar here in town has pretty good nachos, and I know Wade doesn't mind the occasional dog."

"I wanted to take you someplace special so that you'd

realize how much I appreciate you. So that our first date would be important."

Her smile grew wider. "Jason Clements, you don't think this would be important to me unless you took me somewhere fancy? What's important is just being with you. I don't care where we go. We can stay here for all I care."

Jason smiled back at her, but he did want to take her somewhere. If nothing else, she could prove to others that yes, they were indeed dating. "If you want to go into town, we can go into town. But I'm buying."

She laughed. "Fine, then. Next one's on me."

"We'll see about that."

Rather than drive the hour out to Casper and restaurant hunt, they opted to go into town after all. In a way, that made Sage more nervous than a normal date would have. If they'd gone to Casper, she'd have been surrounded by strangers who didn't realize how momentous a date was for Sage Cooper. Here in Painted Barrel, everyone would know. Everyone would stare. Everyone would smirk behind their hands and gossip about it the next day if she was the least bit awkward or strange.

And she was bound to be awkward and strange. She was twenty-nine years old, and all of her dates could be counted on a single finger.

They drove into town in Jason's truck, Achilles sitting between them, and she tried to ignore the dog as best she could, even though she knew the truth of why he was there. She knew exactly why Annie had "suddenly" rescued a well-trained dog and bailed out on him. The truth of the matter was that Annie had been searching shelter databases in the surrounding states, looking for a dog that might work as an emotional service dog for Jason with minimal training. She knew Annie had come up with an excuse to force the dog into Jason's proximity for a while, and she hated that she was in on a lie.

But . . . she couldn't help but notice that he was calm tonight. That he hadn't texted her with worry, and when he'd arrived on her doorstep, he seemed . . . happy. Content.

And if the dog had a hand in that, she'd just have to live with the lie.

"You sure you don't mind this?" Jason asked her as he pulled up in front of the pub. The parking lot was full, since it was past dinnertime and people were heading out for drinks to the only place for miles around that served them.

"I don't mind at all," she answered honestly. "I'm just happy to be with you."

The smile he sent her way was dazzling, and for a moment, Sage felt like the luckiest woman alive. How did a man so effortlessly sexy find her interesting? Of all the Beccas in the world, he wanted Sage? It made no sense to her. She hadn't dressed sexy or tried to get his attention like she had off and on for so many years with Greg (who'd promptly ignored everything she did). She'd just been herself . . . and Jason couldn't stop kissing her.

She touched her lips even as he hopped out of the truck and opened her door for her.

"Stop that," he murmured as he helped her down.

"Stop what?"

"Looking like you're thinking about kissing, because if you touch your mouth one more time and get that soft look in your eyes, I'm going to grab you and kiss you until you're breathless, right in front of this bar."

Sage blinked up at him, already breathless. "Is that

supposed to be a threat? Because it doesn't sound scary. It sounds fun."

He groaned and leaned in, and she thought he was going to kiss her. Instead, he pressed his forehead to hers. "No, we're doing this right, damn it. I'm not dragging you to the back of this truck and having my way with you."

"You're not?"

"Damn it, Sage, quit looking so disappointed." He cupped her cheek and gave her a quick kiss, and she had to settle for that.

He got Achilles out of the truck, took his leash, and then offered Sage his other arm, as if he were a courtly gentleman and her a lady . . . and as if they hadn't been here just days ago for Greg and Becca's rehearsal dinner. She took it anyhow, though, because if she was being honest with herself, she liked that he was fussing over her. He was doing his best to make her feel special, and it was working.

Inside the bar, most of the patrons were seated near the bar itself, which had a mounted TV showing a sports game that drew all eyes. When Jason looked to her, she pointed at a table in the back, and they sat down. She couldn't help but notice that Jason sat right next to her instead of across from her, and even though Achilles wedged himself between them on the floor, it still felt cozy. And when he reached for her hand as they pored over the brief menu? Sage felt like she was floating in a cloud of happiness.

They ordered simple food—nachos for her, a burger for him—and Wade brought out a round, meaty bone to keep Achilles occupied. It was nice to just sit and talk about their day. Jason asked about her day and stole a chip off her plate. She snuck a few of his fries as he told her about his day at the ranch and how he was getting better at spotting when the horses were in a bitey mood. They stayed long enough to have a coffee and split a piece of cake, and she could have stayed out with him forever, just basking in his easy smile and presence.

Of course, her phone had to ring to spoil that. She glanced at the screen and grimaced when she saw who it was. "Greg."

"What does he want?"

"Attention?" she joked lightly.

Jason didn't laugh. "He's probably annoyed you're not at his beck and call."

"Oh stop. He's getting married." When Jason only shot her a look, she realized he didn't think it was funny. "He's just nervous before his wedding, Jason. It's nothing. I'm not interested in him."

"It's not you I'm worried about. You're smart, Sage, but you're also entirely too giving, and he knows that. I'm waiting for him to come up with some ridiculous story about how he needs a wedding cake at the last minute and you'll somehow need to do it for him. Or he needs the reception catered. Or any number of things where he can take advantage of you because he thinks you're his even though he's got a fiancée."

She was astonished to hear that. "He doesn't think I'm his."

"Please. He treats you like some guys treat their wives . . . or mothers."

"No!"

Jason shook his head. "Sage, baby, you can't see it because you're too close."

Baby? She was his baby? A warm, delicious flush moved through her. "But—"

"Think about it. He has you baking for him. You run errands for him. Has he ever had you water his plants? Help him clean his house? Asked you to help him with laundry?"

Sage stared at Jason, stricken. "He has asked to me pick up his dry cleaning regularly."

"Do you bring him lunch at work?"

Oh god, she did. Her hand flew to her mouth. Was she that much of an idiot that she'd never seen it? When everything was put together like that, it all sounded like things a wife or significant other did. She'd always just done little things for him that she thought other female friends would do for guy friends.

Jason gestured as if to say, *See?* "He probably comes to you and complains about things Becca does because he knows you'll support him."

He did. Oh god, he did all the time. She gave Jason a horrified look. "I can't believe I'm such an idiot."

Jason shook his head and squeezed her hand again. "You're not. You're just trusting, Sage. And that part about you never dating anyone? It didn't make sense to me . . . until I met Greg. I totally wouldn't put it past that guy to make it clear that he'd staked a claim on you, even if he never went after it."

What a horrible thing. And she'd been so lonely and miserable and . . . Greg was using that to his advantage. "Can we go?" she whispered, her stomach lurching. "I feel sick."

"I shouldn't have said anything." Jason's mouth thinned.

"No, I'm glad you did. I'm glad someone finally did." Wasn't it a big joke around town that everyone called her Greg's "keeper"? Heck, she'd even paid his water bill for him when he forgot, just so he wouldn't have late fees.

And now that she had a boyfriend, he was suddenly texting or calling her constantly. He was showing up to her office "just to talk" more and more often, and most of those talks had to do with how he wasn't sure if he should marry

Becca. Was he . . . using her? For emotional support and cookies?

That ass.

Gritting her teeth, she picked up her phone and put him on ignore. "Greg can wait." She'd go to his wedding, cling to Jason's arm, and then do her best to distance herself from Greg. If he wanted emotional support, he needed to go to his fiancée for that sort of thing, not her.

And Becca sure as hell could make him cookies.

And pay his water bill.

And pick up his dry cleaning.

"I really am an idiot," she blurted, burying her face in her hands.

"No, you're wonderful. It's not your fault he's using you." He paused. "Well, it's a little your fault." And then he grinned to take the sting out of his words. "But now you're aware of what he's doing. And you're with me. He had his chance." He pulled out his wallet and threw a stack of bills on the table. "Come on. It's getting late and I need to get you home."

"Oh." Was he ending their date because he was disgusted with how Greg used her? "All right."

They got to their feet, and when he held his hand out for her, she hesitated. But she could feel the eyes of others in the bar watching them, so she slipped her hand in his anyhow.

He immediately pulled her against him and leaned in close. "I can tell what you're thinking with that look, Sage."

"What?" She tried to smile.

"You think I'm trying to get rid of you." He shook his head slowly, grinning. "I'm a selfish man, because I want to get out of here and have some private time with you. That's all. Dinner's over, but our date isn't."

Oh.

Oh. She couldn't stop the smile that beamed across her face. And when he smiled back, it felt like her whole world was right.

She hugged Achilles against her on the drive home, and when they pulled into her driveway and he parked the car and then just gave her a long, steady look, she melted.

"If this dog wasn't in the car with us, you'd be in my lap right now," he told her, reaching over and toying with a strand of her ponytail.

Sage had never wanted to fling a poor dog out of a truck before, but she wanted to now. "We can go inside and hang out on the sofa," she told him, breathless. "Maybe have a cup of coffee and watch some Netflix."

He arched a brow at her in the darkness. "You asking me to Netflix and chill?"

Lord, she was, wasn't she? "You don't want to?"

"Oh, I want to." He reached over and ruffled Achilles's ears. "Just wondering if you've got something to keep this guy busy while we get comfy on the sofa. I'm not sure I want him thinking I'm eating your face."

She giggled at the mental image. "We can always smear some peanut butter inside a jar. That used to keep my dad's dogs busy for hours."

"Sold. Why don't I take care of your cattle while you put on some coffee?"

"All right." She knew that was probably code for him wanting to check the perimeter to make himself comfortable, and that was okay. If that was what he needed to relax, she didn't mind waiting. Heck, she'd wait all night for him if she had to. "Do you need to be back at the ranch soon?" She glanced at the clock on her phone—it was past ten, and she knew he got up early.

"I do. Doesn't mean I don't plan on kissing you until your panties are wet first." He gave her a heated look and then got out of the truck.

Oh lord, just hearing him say that made them wet. She squeezed her thighs together tightly until he came around to her side of the truck and opened the door for her. Sage didn't know how she managed to walk to the house without turning into a puddle, but she succeeded somehow. In a daze, she moved around her kitchen, putting on coffee, setting out fresh cookies for Jason (because he'd once mentioned that oatmeal raisin was his favorite, so she'd made a whole batch of them), and slathered the inside of an empty mason jar with peanut butter for Achilles. She peeked out the window, expecting to see Jason doing his perimeter checks, but to her surprise, he was coming back from the barn already. No perimeter check? And he'd been so calm tonight. Achilles's presence was helping. She was so thankful that she added another spoonful of peanut butter to the jar for that good boy.

Jason came inside the house, and she jumped a little to hear the door shut, her nerves getting the better of her. She smoothed a hand over her ponytail, hating that she'd spent the last few minutes getting out cookies and making coffee when she should have been checking her hair for strays or freshening her makeup. What if she was messy looking? Oh no—what if she had a stray jalapeño in her teeth? She ran her tongue over them nervously. He would tell her, right?

"You know we already kissed," Jason told her as he came inside. "At the beginning of the date. If it makes you this nervous, we don't have to kiss again. We can just watch something on TV, like you said."

"Oh no, I'm fine," she told him, hating the anxious wobble in her throat. This was her first make-out date and she was highly aware of the fact that twenty-nine was rather old to be as inexperienced as she was. She held the peanut butter jar out to him mutely. "I just get wound up. Don't mind me."

"So you do want to kiss?"

Gosh, her cheeks were hot. She tried to say something simple, and it just came out as a squeak.

"Beg pardon?"

Cruel man. "If you're going to make me say it out loud, yes."

He grinned wide at her, his eyes crinkling in the corners and causing her pulse to start between her thighs again. "Just wanted to hear you say it out loud." He bent down and touched Achilles's head, fondling the soft ears before offering him the peanut butter jar. Her heart ached when the dog gave him the saddest look and then gently licked the jar before looking at Jason again, as if for approval. Poor thing. She kept forgetting that he truly was a rescue, and he'd probably been abandoned himself. Maybe he needed Jason as much as Jason needed him.

"Let's bring that into the living room," she told him. "So the jar doesn't roll all over the tile floor and make a ton of noise." Plus, it felt wrong to push Achilles into another room just because she wanted to kiss Jason. After all, she was planning on doing a lot of kissing him in the future, and the dog would just have to get used to it, right?

They headed into the living room with two cups of coffee and a tray of cookies, and she turned on Netflix and looked for something appropriately boring. When *Miracle on 34th Street* popped up, she clicked it on and sat delicately in the middle of the couch, uncertain. Why was she so on edge? She'd held Jason's hand and slept curled against him the other night. He'd spent lots of time alone with her before.

Except now it was a date.

And that made everything different. Before they were just friends. Now she was his.

She held her coffee cup in her hands but couldn't drink it. Her throat felt tight, and she was nervous, watching Jason instead of the television as he looked over at Achilles when the dog started to lick the jar. For a man that didn't want a dog and resisted the idea every time someone suggested it to him, he sure was an attentive owner. She hoped that the bond between him and Achilles continued and that in a few weeks, maybe he'd approach Annie about keeping the dog. And wouldn't that just settle everything neatly into place?

But then Jason sat down next to her and pulled her against him, tucking her against his side, and she had to bite back the little sigh of pleasure that threatened to erupt. How many times had she wanted so desperately to be with someone like this? To curl up on a sofa together and just be in each other's presence? To lean on each other? She'd been alone through so much that now she was a little terrified of wanting too much. That maybe if Jason realized how desperate she was, how pathetic, he'd run away and she'd be left alone all over again. Except this time it would be worse, because she now knew what it was like to share deep, hot, wet kisses with a gorgeous man, to have him fill her with longing and need and leave her wanting more.

Sage shifted uncomfortably on the couch, aware of her body's responses to his nearness.

His hand was on her shoulder, his thumb rubbing at her collarbone through her sweater. Just that small touch was making her antsy, because it was a promise of so much more . . . so much more that she wasn't getting. Man, just a few kisses and she'd suddenly turned into the world's most impatient woman. It was like, now that she had the potential of caresses and kisses and hour-long make outs, she didn't want to waste any more time. So she slid a little closer to him, hoping it wasn't too obvious.

"I had a nice time tonight," Jason said in a low voice, watching the dog frantically work at the peanut butter–covered jar. He idly rubbed Sage's shoulder again and then stroked her arm. "Even if we didn't go anywhere special."

"I had a wonderful time, and it was special to me."

He turned to look at her and smiled. Oh, she loved that smile. It seemed like he smiled more and more with every day that passed, and that made her so happy. "You're easy to please."

"Or I just like being with you."

Jason took her hand in his, and her heart gave a tiny little flip. Were they going to kiss again now? But he only rubbed her knuckles, and the small touches were making her crazy. She wanted to fling her arms around his neck and plant her mouth on his, but she wasn't brave enough to do that yet, so all she did was nudge a little closer. "So when do I get to see you again?" he asked, his gaze flicking to her mouth.

Kiss me, she silently implored. They were snuggled up on the couch, after all, and he had one arm on her shoulders and the other in his lap, and it seemed like the easiest thing in the world for him to just lean in and press his mouth to hers . . . but it wasn't happening.

Then again, they'd kissed earlier tonight to get it out of the way, so maybe that was all she got? A pang of disappointment struck her. She'd just have to wait for more make-out time, then . . . Sage didn't want to seem too greedy or desperate, so she'd let him lead. "Well, the wedding is next Saturday. So I guess . . . then? I'm sure Greg and Becca won't mind if you bring Achilles, by the way. I'll make a cute bow tie for him, and they'll love it."

Jason leaned back, studying her with those intense eyes. "You don't want to get together, say, tomorrow night?"

Oh, she did. More than anything. Heck, she was of half a mind to tell him to stay over tonight, just because she didn't want him to go. She also didn't want to seem too clingy, though, and had no experience in how to handle these things. "Of course I do. I just didn't want to take up your time. I'm sure it gets boring being around me constantly—"

"Don't be so sure of that. I like spending time with you." And his fingers moved over her knuckles again. Goose bumps prickled up her spine, and her nipples hardened against her sweater. Oh mercy, in a minute she was going to start panting. "I don't care what we do. I just like being around you."

Sage melted against him. It was getting hard to think with his fingers tracing little patterns on her skin, but she tried to focus. "Um, I was going to go shopping tomorrow night . . . pick up a few last-minute presents for some co-workers. Did . . . did you want to come?" He'd turned her hand over and was teasing the palm, and god, had she been turned on before? She was about to come undone now.

Why wouldn't he just freaking kiss her already?

"Absolutely. Okay if I bring Achilles? He needs to be my shadow until Annie gets back."

"Of course," she said, breathless and distracted. They'd figure something out.

"Can I ask you something?" When she absently nodded, he continued. "Are you trembling because you're nervous?"

Was she trembling? Sage looked down at her hand, resting palm up atop his thigh. She was twitching all right, but it wasn't from nerves. It was from sheer arousal. She was practically humming with need. "I'm not nervous," she admitted, then slowly met his gaze. "It's just all very . . . intense."

"Does that mean I can kiss you again?" He glanced at her mouth. "Tell me no if you don't want that."

"I want that," she said quickly. Oh, she wanted that. "Please."

"Good. That makes two of us, then." He leaned forward and touched her cheek, tipping her face gently as he moved in to kiss her.

Sage bit back a moan the moment his lips touched hers. She'd been daydreaming all through dinner about more kisses, and this was the fulfillment of so many dang fantasies that she nearly cried with the pleasure of it. A whimper escaped her, and Jason only chuckled against her mouth. That was okay. She didn't care as long as he kept kissing her. She loved the feel of his lips on hers, how he managed to make every brush of his mouth on hers feel new and exciting. His tongue flicked against her mouth, and she leaned back against him, sinking into the kiss as their tongues mated and played against each other.

She didn't know how long they kissed. The world outside seemed to drift away until her world consisted purely of Jason's lips, Jason's mouth, and the feel of Jason's body pressing against her side. He took her hand from his thigh and put it to his neck, and she clung to him, biting back another moan as his tongue swept deep into her mouth. It was like he was licking her.

And she felt every lick right down to her core.

This time, she couldn't stop the moan that built in her throat. She shifted against him, restless, as his mouth devoured hers, the faint stubble on his cheeks rasping against her skin in the most delicious way. Heat throbbed all through her body, and if he put his hand on one of her aching breasts right about now, she'd fling her sweater off so he could do with her as he liked.

Jason lifted his mouth and then pressed his forehead against hers. "I should get going soon."

Hot disappointment rushed through her. "Oh? Oh, okay." He didn't want to stay and kiss her some more? Because she felt like she could kiss him forever.

He nipped at her lower lip, making her whimper with need again. "You keep making those sexy little sounds and it's driving me crazy, Sage." He pressed another light kiss to her mouth, then continued. "If I stay any longer, I'm going to have a hell of a time controlling myself."

"And . . . that's a bad thing?" she asked, breathless. She was okay with him losing control. Heck, she was more than okay with it . . . she craved it.

He chuckled, and she felt liquid heat ripple through her at the sound of his sultry laughter. "It is a bad thing, because I don't want to rush things with you."

"I want to go on the record and say that I'm one hundred percent fine with rushing things," she whispered, reaching up and tracing her finger along that delicious, stubbly jaw. Was it strange that she wanted to lick it? Because now that the thought was in her head, she couldn't get it out of there. He looked positively lickable, she decided.

He took her hand and kissed the palm, grinning at her. "Just trust me, all right?"

"One more kiss before you go, then?"

Jason arched an eyebrow at her and then groaned and pulled her back against him again. The second "kiss" turned into a fiery storm of multiple kisses, and by the time he finally let her up for air, they were both panting. "Damn it," he murmured. "Leaving you is the hardest thing I've ever done."

"Then don't leave."

"I'm determined to do things right," he told her, and kissed her one more time, just because. When he eventually got to his feet, she noticed that the front of his pants strained with his erection, and she felt a curious sense of pride. She'd done that. She'd made him that hard.

And giddy, she couldn't wait to do more.

CHAPTER FIFTEEN

It was hard to pay attention the next week at work. Sage had a routine, but that routine had never contended with her being distracted by late-night make-out sessions, which she'd been almost every night this week. She smiled to herself every time she yawned, knowing that the reason she'd stayed up late was because of Jason. They'd kissed while he'd put his leash on Achilles, they'd kissed good night at the door, and then she'd walked him out to his truck and they'd kissed again just because. She'd dreamed of him and his amazing mouth, and had woken up each morning with her body aching and needy, and her thoughts flitting with distraction. The distraction continued at work, when she realized she'd sorted all of the mail into the wrong folders and had to go back and redo everything, and she'd been working on a billing spreadsheet for the water department for hours. She hadn't even cared that some of the town teenagers came in and monopolized the library computer, because her thoughts were too focused on Jason to fuss over what a few kids might be looking at on YouTube—or worse.

Just thinking about Jason made everything better.

She was always determined not to be the first one to text, though. Wasn't that one of the rules of not being too desperate? That you had to wait for the man to make the first move? She watched her phone impatiently for hours, checking the screen over and over until it finally pinged and she snatched it up with shaking hands.

JASON: Did you oversleep?

JASON: I normally hear from you by now.

SAGE: No, I'm here! It's just been a busy morning.

Yeah, she was going to hell for that whopper.

JASON: Same here. A few of the cattle are sick, so we've been separating them from the herd and then taking them to the barn for medicating. It's just me and Eli, so it's been a hell of a lot of work.

JASON: The man never stops, either.

JASON: BRB—more Eli.

Oooh. Sage winced at her phone, hoping that Cass's hard-edged husband wasn't going to make Jason too miserable. It was a good sign that they'd kept him on, though, wasn't it? Cass hadn't said anything else to her, and Dustin and Annie had gone on to Los Angeles for their Christmas vacation, and they wouldn't have if Jason was going to be a problem. She knew that helping him with some of the ranch basics had probably been the difference between him staying employed and getting fired. Jason knew how to handle himself around cattle and how not to panic them, and everything else could be taught, really.

Which meant he'd be sticking around, hopefully, until spring.

Sage let out a dreamy sigh, imagining an entire winter of cuddling with Jason by the fire, Achilles at his feet. Holding hands and watching the snow fall outside. Sharing hot mugs of cocoa or coffee and curling up to watch a movie . . . or make out. Just the thought made her happy on a soul-deep level. His job would keep him busy, but they'd find ways to get together. She wasn't nearly as busy as him, and she could always go over and hang out. She could bring him lunch . . .

And then she realized that what he was saying about Greg was true. She had been waiting on him like a girlfriend—or a wife—and never realized it. No wonder he was so pissy about her dating Jason. He was losing out on an unpaid maid, assistant, and emotional support. Well, no longer. Becca could have him.

She set her phone down on the counter, humming to herself as she went through another bundle of mail, checking the screen every so often to see if Jason had sent another text. They had long pauses throughout the day in which she wouldn't hear anything, no doubt because he was busy with the cattle or some backbreaking chore that Eli had given him, but he'd text her soon enough.

The door to the municipal office opened, and Sage looked up to see Hannah from across the street. Her eyes were sparkling as she approached Sage's desk, her gray hair layered into an immaculate beehive of curls. "Did you see?"

"See what?" Sage put down the stack of catalogs and tried not to frown. Hannah was sweet, but she was also responsible for about 90 percent of the town's gossip, and Sage had learned to be careful of what she said around her.

Hannah leaned in, a knowledgeable look in her eye. "Becca's salon is closed today."

Sage glanced down the street, trying to see the tiny floral sign of Becca's Beauty, but the snow and the Christmas decorations in the window blocked everything. "I hadn't noticed. Maybe she's taking an extra day off to prepare for the wedding tomorrow?"

Hannah shook her head, her lips pursed. "I had an appointment for my weekly today." She touched her silver curls. "Normally, if Becca's not feeling well, she texts me to let me know we need to reschedule. I haven't heard anything from her, and neither has anyone else. It's been completely quiet, and she never bothered to show up for work."

A funny feeling started in the pit of Sage's stomach. "Maybe she's just getting nervous about the wedding? Or maybe she overslept. I don't know that there's anything to worry about." She hoped for Becca's sake that everything was normal, but she couldn't get out of her head how weird Greg had been acting lately. How he'd complained about Becca.

And the wedding was tomorrow.

Hannah gave Sage a disbelieving look. "I called the church to check on things, and they said there was a cancellation, but they wouldn't say who." She tapped the counter as if to emphasize the news. "How many other people are getting married tomorrow? This just all doesn't seem to add up."

"I hope it's nothing," Sage said, only half listening as

Hannah continued to gossip. She managed to nod and make the appropriate noises as Hannah kept up the one-sided conversation, but Sage's mind was on her phone.

Greg had texted her, and she'd blocked him. Why did she feel guilty over that? It wasn't like she could force them to marry, but she still somehow felt responsible, like she hadn't convinced Greg that he loved Becca enough to go through with things. Poor, sweet Becca would be devastated if Greg really had broken it off with her.

Everyone in town would think Sage was the problem, too—especially if Greg kept trying to hang around her. Her stomach clenched again. She was utterly relieved when Hannah took her mail and left. Sage immediately snatched her silent phone off the counter and scrolled through her contacts. She unblocked Greg, waiting to see if he'd sent her any more messages. Nothing came through—nothing would while she had him blocked. Crap. Should she text him to see what was going on?

How could she not?

Sage glanced up from her silent phone and noticed Hannah going over to the souvenir shop instead of back to her hotel, likely so she could gossip with even more people. Ugh. It would soon be all over town that the wedding was canceled, so if it wasn't true, Greg needed to step in. If Sage was truly his friend, she needed to help, didn't she? And while she was frustrated with Greg for a variety of reasons, she couldn't just sit back and let the gossip mill go nuts. After a moment's hesitation, she texted him.

SAGE: Hey, is everything okay?

The answering reply was swift.

GREG: I see you finally decided to answer.

SAGE: Let's not get into that right now, okay? Friend
to friend, I'm checking in on you.

GREG: I've needed a friend for days, and you've
been ignoring me.

SAGE: Fair point, but I'm here now. Asking again,
are you okay?

She was not going to let his guilt trip bother her. She just
wasn't.

GREG: And I appreciate it. :) :) :)

GREG: Can we meet for lunch? I really want to talk
to you. I NEED to talk to you.

SAGE: Oh, I can't. It's super busy today.

Sage looked around the empty mail room, hoping he
didn't show up to prove her a liar. But meeting for lunch?
When everyone was speculating that he'd just broken up
with his fiancée? Terrible idea. Terrible, terrible idea.

GREG: I really need to talk, though. What if I come
up there?

SAGE: Greg, everyone's gossiping about the
wedding. Becca never went to her salon today.

GREG: Dinner tonight, then?

For a moment, Sage wanted to throw her phone through the window. What about this was he having a hard time freaking understanding?

SAGE: Greg, did you break up with Becca? Is the wedding still on?

SAGE: I hate to ask so bluntly, but people are talking around here and I'm concerned.

GREG: It's over.

GREG: I should have never asked her.

GREG: And that's why I need to see you. So I can get this all off my chest. Please help me out, Sage.

GREG: You've always been there for me in the past. I need a friend right now more than ever.

GREG: So . . . dinner?

She pressed a hand to her mouth, horrified. The wedding was off? And he was insisting on seeing her? Oh no, this was very, very bad. Funny how a year ago this would have been her dream scenario—Greg tossing over his fiancée because he finally realized how wonderful Sage was . . . but now that it was playing out, it was just a nightmare. Her stomach clenched and she felt sick, not only for herself but for poor Becca, who never hurt anyone and always had a smile on her face.

SAGE: Greg, I'm sorry. I have plans.

SAGE: I really think you should talk to Becca.
Not me.

SAGE: And if the wedding is really off, you need to
tell all your guests.

GREG: Can you help me with that? If I show up
there tonight?

GREG: PLEASE, Sage. I'm begging you.

SAGE: I can't switch my plans. I'm sorry, I really am.
Maybe talk to your brother Robert?

When her suggestion to talk to the best man didn't elicit
a response, she set her phone down. Of course he didn't
want to talk to Robert. Robert would tell him he was being
silly. He wanted to talk to Sage because she'd support him
and reassure him that he was amazing no matter what . . .
wouldn't she? Somehow, she didn't know if she would anymore. She felt like that Sage had disappeared. The new
Sage wasn't quite so thirsty for approval and Greg's scraps.

Not when she had someone like Jason to tell her she was
amazing. With a warm flush, she picked up her phone
again, pulled up Jason's screen, and sent him a picture.

SAGE: Like my sweater?

JASON: It's hideous. Can I pull it off you later?

And she shivered with anticipation.

CHAPTER SIXTEEN

Jason was whistling to himself as they headed into the house for the day. It hadn't been his favorite working day—the cattle had gotten into some boggy mud and a few heifers got stuck, which meant he'd had to get in there and tug them free from the half-frozen muck. Between that and spending half the day on horseback, Jason was cold, wet, and tired, and he was pretty sure he had mud squishing between his toes. But the day was over, and he'd see Sage soon. He'd get to kiss her and hear her sweet voice and see those glorious dimples, and that made everything worth it. Achilles pressed his head under Jason's hand, eager for petting as they walked back to the house, and that was growing on him, too. The dog was ever present, but not annoying.

At his side, Eli shook his head at Jason. "You're in a good mood."

"I have a date with Sage tonight."

Eli grunted, but Jason was learning that that didn't mean disapproval; it was just Eli's way of acknowledging that he'd heard him. "Hope you don't fall asleep on her. Been a long damn day." He looked at his own mud-splattered white dog, Frannie, and shook his head. "Cass's gonna kill me when Frannie gets into the house. She's gonna get mud under the tree. You watch."

"Guess I'm lucky. Achilles didn't chase the cows like she did." The dog had stayed glued to Jason's side, which made cleaning up muddy paws a whole heck of a lot easier.

Eli just grunted again. "Damn dogs." But Jason noticed he bent down, gave Frannie's head a loving rub, and then petted the heads of all the other ranch dogs that clustered in. Dustin and Annie had taken their dogs—Moose and Spidey—with them, but that still left several of the dogs at the ranch with Eli and Jason, and Jason was getting more used to their presence as the days passed. He didn't ignore them anymore, and when they helped with rounding up the cattle, he made sure to praise their hard work and lavish attention on them. Seeing the liquid eyes and wagging tails didn't make his heart ache for Truck anymore. He still missed his dog—probably always would—but the pain of that was fading, and he had to admit that being around the other rambunctious dogs probably helped.

Achilles helped a lot, too. He was getting fond of that big yellow critter. Achilles was clingy, just like Annie had warned him, but he was also calm and well-behaved. Occasionally, he'd show a bit of puppyish behavior, like chasing a stick, that made Jason wonder what Achilles would be like when he was truly comfortable and all the fear went away. He hoped he got to see that.

He really hoped Achilles's new owner would love on him and tell him what a good boy he was constantly, because he deserved it. He'd have to talk to Annie when she got back, make sure that the new owner would treat his buddy right.

Until then, though, he and Achilles had a date with Sage.

They went inside, Cass squealing in outrage at the muddy dogs and boots that tracked into the kitchen. The baby in her arms giggled, and then Eli laughed, and suddenly the small kitchen felt full of happiness and laughter. Jason found himself chuckling, too, and it was a good day, he decided. He stayed and talked to Cass and Eli for a few, then made his excuses and retreated to his room to clean up. His hair was getting shaggy, he noticed, so he took his razor to it and cut it down to a buzz, just like he did back when he was in the navy. He shaved his jaw and then showered. Once dressed in a T-shirt and jeans, he threw on a jacket, grabbed Achilles's leash, and off they went into the truck to drive out to meet Sage at the office downtown. They'd ride over together.

He pulled up to the office as she was putting her coat on. Sage immediately flipped the CLOSED sign on the window as he parked. She shut the lights off, locked the door, and got into the truck with a smile and pat for Achilles, who sat next to him in the seat. "What a day."

"I hear you," Jason said, chuckling. But in his eyes, the day had just improved vastly. Had it been hard? Yes. Nothing about ranching was easy. But the day was over now, and she was here, and he just felt calm and relaxed and . . . happy. Huh. It had been a while since he realized what that felt like.

Happy. Carefree.

Relaxed.

Achilles wiggled in excitement at his side, and he automatically put an arm around the dog so he would give Sage room to put her seat belt on. She did, and then she stared at him in the darkness of the truck cab.

"What is it?" he asked.

"Your hair," she murmured. "You shaved it."

"I did. You hate it?"

"No. Can I touch?" She reached a hand out and then pulled back, hesitant.

"Of course." Jason leaned in her direction, giving her silent permission.

She reached out and brushed her fingers over his scalp, rubbing back and forth over the short bristles. Her touch immediately made his cock hard. "Rough," was all she said, but he could hear the smile in her voice.

"It's a lot easier to take care of this way. Used to wear it like this in the navy." He dragged his hand over his skull, feeling the bristles move, and then turned back to her. "If you hate it, I'll grow it out again."

"I didn't say that." She reached out and lightly touched him again, and he thought he would lose control right then and there. Even the smallest of Sage's touches just felt so damn right.

And they made him hard as a brick.

"So why was your day bad?" he asked, voice gruff as he tried to concentrate on anything but the aching length of his dick. "Too many Christmas cards? Unpaid water bills?"

She didn't laugh at his joke. "Greg and Becca broke up," Sage said, a worried look on her face. "The wedding was supposed to be tomorrow, and Becca just never showed up to work. I texted Greg to see if everything was all right, and . . . I guess it's not." The expression on her face was bewildered. "I feel so bad for Becca. She loves him and she's been looking forward to get married and starting a family."

The more Jason found out about Greg, the less he liked the guy. Seemed kind of like a piece of shit to him. He tried not to be jealous that Sage had texted Greg. They were friends, and he knew it was innocent on Sage's part even if he suspected it wasn't on Greg's. "People are terrible sometimes."

"They are," she said softly, then bit her lip. "You don't think it's my fault, do you?"

"Your fault?" He was shocked she'd even think such a thing. "Why would it be your fault?"

"Because I stopped being Greg's go-to buddy. I stopped making him lunch and cookies and picking up his dry cleaning. I've been spending all my time with you." She had that look on her face that told him she was blushing, even as she shyly reached up to run her fingers lightly over the side of his head again. "I've been avoiding him when he wanted to talk to me."

"None of that means this is your fault," Jason told her huskily, and it felt as if each brush of her fingertips was a brush over his whole body. The light, exploring way she touched his head made him ache. "He just wants to have all the toys and he can't. He needs to grow up."

"I guess so," she said softly. "Part of me feels bad, though, because I'm so happy and he's not."

It was about time the tables had turned, Jason thought, but he didn't say that out loud. Sage had a soft heart. "I need you to switch places with Achilles," he told her, then rubbed the dog's head as if in apology.

"You do?" Sage looked at the dog that sat between them inside the truck. "Why?"

"Because I need to kiss the hell out of you, and it's going to be mighty awkward with him in the middle."

She giggled, the sound light and joyous. "We can switch

to my Jeep if you want. You can drive. I have a back seat that's perfect for a good boy like him."

"Works for me." He cared less about who was driving and more about getting his arms around her quicker.

Sage opened her door, and he unharnessed Achilles while the dog licked his face. He couldn't even be mad about that, either. Silly dog was just too good-natured for Jason to get irritated with him. He rubbed the dog's ears, giving him attention until Sage signaled they should join her, and then they went out to the Jeep.

The moment they were inside, Achilles settling down on the blanket in the back seat, Jason slid the driver's seat back and pulled Sage into his arms. It was a little tight thanks to the bucket seat, but he tilted his chair back and wrapped his arms tight around her. "This is more like it."

"My backside is pressed against the steering wheel," she warned him.

"If we honk at someone, we'll blame it on the dog," he teased her, wrapping his fingers around one lock of her soft hair. "I missed you today."

Her eyes went soft with pleasure, and she slid her arms around his neck. "You did?"

"I did. Kept thinking about those dimples." He rubbed his knuckles lightly over her cheek. "That smile. The scent of your hair." He glanced down and couldn't help but grin. "That damn ugly sweater. What the hell is that thing?"

"Teddy bears, but they're supposed to be Krampus, who's a Christmas monster." She looked down proudly at the green-and-red monstrosity over her chest.

Well, it was certainly creative. Hideous, but creative. "All right, I guess I missed that, too. I mostly just missed you and hearing your voice."

She looked so damn soft and sweet as she leaned in

against him. "I missed you, too, Jason. So much. That's silly, isn't it? We've been apart less than a day, but I missed you." They'd gotten together repeatedly over the last week but it never felt like enough time.

"I don't think it's silly," he murmured. "Because I feel the same way." And he dragged his hand through her thick, glossy hair and then pulled her in for a kiss.

He always forgot just how good kissing Sage was. It was like the experience was so damn amazing that his brain couldn't possibly be remembering it correctly. But she always tasted sweet, and her little tongue danced along his with shy strokes. He loved the way she sank against him, her mouth open to his, as if she were giving him everything. This was what he'd been looking forward to all day, just the moments with her in his arms. The weight of her pressed against his thighs, pushing down against his cock, and he wanted to rip that denim off of her and sink deep inside her.

She moaned against him, breathless, and her fingers rasped over his scalp again, as if she couldn't get enough of the tactile sensation. He knew just how that felt, because her gorgeous hair kept sliding through his fingers, and he wanted to bury his face in it and just breathe in her, forever. "Sage," he murmured, flicking at her mouth. "You feel so good."

"I'm"—she kissed him again, her weight shifting on his lap, then continued—"not too heavy?"

Never. He liked the solid feel of her against him, and it didn't matter to him that she wasn't a stick-thin waif. She was strong and capable, and she felt real. He loved the way she felt. "Not at all." He kissed along her jaw and then moved toward her ear. "You're perfect."

Sage shuddered against him and then made an unholy

sound when he nipped her earlobe. He could feel her thighs clench in response, and her reaction made his cock ache even harder. God, she was sweet. "You like it when I nibble on your ear?" He flicked his tongue over her earring and felt her hands grip at his jacket. "Or are you just imagining me nibbling on other spots, instead?"

"Other . . . spots?" she managed, clinging to him and holding him against her as he licked and bit at her sweet ear. It sounded as if she were having a hard time concentrating, and he loved that. When he touched Sage, it felt like the rest of the world fell away, and he was gratified that it was the same for her.

"Like . . . your pretty breasts." He wanted to cup one desperately, but his girl was shy, and he knew this was all new for her, so he'd just talk about it for now. "Or maybe you'd like me to go lower."

Another moan escaped her. "Oh, Jason, the things you say make me feel . . . oh . . ." She sucked in a breath as he gently bit her earlobe again, and she squirmed on his lap. "Oh mercy."

"No mercy," he murmured, then gently licked the soft skin of her throat. Maybe he'd leave her a nice hickey here, so she could show the world that she belonged to him. He liked the thought of that. He liked it so much that he scraped his teeth over her throat and loved her shudder of response.

Her phone rang, a happy Christmas song blaring out into the quiet car.

Sage jerked against him, and the car horn blared in response.

The sound startled both of them, and the horn honked again, even as Sage crawled off of his lap. He didn't move, the sudden loud sound sending adrenaline rushing through his body. He could feel it creeping down his arms, making his skin prickle. He felt cold all over, but he knew he'd be sweating in a matter of moments. His head was spinning, like he was losing control. *Not again. Not again.*

"Sorry," Sage told him in the quiet of the car.

He nodded. Desperate not to let Sage know he was going to lose it, he dropped his hands to his sides and quietly clenched them in and out, trying to relax. Trying to chase off the feelings of another anxiety attack.

A warm tongue touched his fingers, and Achilles licked his hand, then pushed his head against Jason's palm. Absently, he touched the dog's head and stroked it, noting how calm Achilles was. The dog's peaceful nature helped ground him, calm him. There was nothing to worry about. He wasn't in Afghanistan. The street was quiet, but safe. Achilles would have reacted if they were under attack.

Or if there were chickens. The dog really hated chickens.

For some reason, that thought made him bite back a smile, and he scratched at Achilles's head more vigorously, fighting off the last vestiges of the panic that threatened to grip him. He tried to focus on Sage and noticed she hadn't answered her phone. She just stared at the lit-up screen and bit her lip, her brows furrowed with worry.

"Who is it?" he asked, voice hoarse as he kept stroking Achilles's head.

Sage looked over at him, worry and confusion in her eyes. "It's Greg. I didn't answer, so he just texted me. Jason, he's at my house and wants to talk to me. I told him I had a date, and I guess he decided to show up anyhow."

"You want me to go beat him up?" He was only half joking.

She took a shuddering breath, and he hated the pinched look of concern on her face. "I don't know what to do."

"Tell him you're out with me and you won't be home until late."

She nodded and started typing, worrying her lip as she wrote. When she was finished, she sighed and closed her eyes, leaning back against the headrest of the car seat. "Sorry."

"Why are you apologizing?"

"Because Greg's being pushy and I honked the horn and startled us both." Sage gave him a chagrined look. "Did I ruin your evening?"

"Nope, I'm fine." He meant it, too. Had he had a flare-up? Sure. But he was able to chase it back, just like when Truck was at his side. He kept petting Achilles's soft ears, thankful for the dog's reassuring weight against his side as Achilles scooted closer and closer. He liked this dog a lot, he realized. He'd been annoyed initially at having him foisted on him, but now . . . he was grateful.

"So what do we do about Greg? I don't want to go home yet."

He nodded at her phone. "Put that away, and let's go get a bite to eat at the restaurant. Maybe by the time we're done, he'll have gotten the hint and left. If not, I'll send him a few videos of me nibbling on your ear so he can see that he's got no chance."

And he loved her delighted giggle of relief.

Jason tried to keep her distracted all through dinner so she wouldn't think about Greg. He wanted to kick that asshole in the teeth for showing up at her house and making her worry. He knew Sage felt responsible, even though the idea was ludicrous. Her crush on Greg all those years had been entirely unrequited, and for Greg to decide to put the pressure on now was the height of selfishness. He hated the guy, and he hated how his sweet Sage somehow thought it was her fault. So he teased her and held her hand, rubbing little circles on her skin as they sat together. They ordered dessert because he'd learned she had a sweet tooth, and he fed her a few bites and loved the sight of her blush. They had a cup of coffee and lingered at the pub until he saw her yawn. Then Jason paid the bill and took her hand in his. "Let's get you home."

"But . . ."

"If he's still on your doorstep, I'll take care of him," he promised her.

Sage seemed uneasy but nodded. He walked her back to her Jeep and then got in his own truck so he could follow her to the ranch. As they drove out into the night, he kept close behind her, sending furious thoughts to Greg if the man had dared to stick around. Thankfully, when they got to Sage's ranch, there was no car in the driveway. She pulled up to the garage, parked, and then hopped out of her Jeep, and even from inside his truck, he could see the relief on her face.

"I think he's gone," she told him, coming up to his window. "You don't have to stay."

"Nonsense." He wouldn't relax until he'd checked the perimeter anyhow. This time it wasn't to appease his own senses, but to protect his woman. "You stay here, and I'll check the grounds." Not that he expected a whiner and manipulator like Greg to try something, but you never knew. So Jason took Achilles with him and circled the house and checked inside the barn. When he was sure no one was outside, he went into the house and checked all the rooms while Sage waited inside his truck, the heater on. When he was satisfied, he went outside to get her. "All clear."

"You don't think Greg would break into my house, do you?" she asked him, full of disbelief as she got out of the warm truck. "He's not the type."

"Was he the type to dump his fiancée on the day before the wedding?"

She was silent at that.

He put a hand to the small of her back and led her inside, and they immediately gravitated toward her comfortable sofa. Sage looked up at him, her hand going to his waist. "You want a drink? Something to eat?"

"Nah."

She bit her lip and then curled her fingers into his jacket. "Will you stay the night with me?"

He wanted to. He wanted to more than anything. "I wish I could, but I have to be up at dawn to help Eli."

"Oh, of course. I always forget that just because it's the weekend, the cows don't know that." Sage leaned against him, as if seeking comfort. "I just love having you here."

Jason loved being there. He wanted to stay all the time, too, but he felt a responsibility to Eli, and he needed to stay employed. "Just because I have to wake up early doesn't mean I have to leave right now. We can still spend some time together, you know."

She smiled up at him. "What did you have in mind? Did you want to watch something?"

Watching television was the last thing he wanted to do. He took her hand in his and led her to the couch, then pulled her jacket off her shoulders. He tossed it onto the nearest chair and then took his own off. Achilles settled himself in front of the quiet fireplace, and Jason sat on the end of the couch and held a hand out to her.

Sage's dimples showed as she took his hand and sat down carefully beside him. He could tell by the look on her face that she knew this wasn't about watching television. He could practically see her breathing harder, lips parted. Her gaze was utterly focused on him.

It was probably driving Greg crazy that she was here with Jason, that Jason was the one with her in his arms. That Jason was the one that got to kiss her. He knew guys like Greg back in the navy. They had a girl in every port and a sweetheart back home who needed to remain loyal and chaste, even if the rules didn't apply to the man. Sage deserved better than that.

She deserved better than him, too, but she seemed to want him, and he was going to be grateful for that every day he had her. Jason caressed her beautiful face lightly, and when she slid against him, her full breasts pressing to his chest, he put a hand to her waist and pulled her in for a hard, driving kiss. It was a possessive kiss, as if he could brand her as his and scorch Greg out of her mind and her worries entirely. Sage moaned against him, clinging to him even as her fingers sought the buzz of his hair, rubbing against it even as his tongue flicked against hers. Over and over they kissed, mouths working together, tongues dancing and teasing until the need for her threatened to overwhelm him. He ended the kiss and loved that she was panting, her eyes soft with arousal.

"How far have you gone in the past?" he asked.

"Gone?" Her brows furrowed. "Jason, you're my first boyfriend. I thought you knew that."

He knew that part, but it wasn't entirely what he meant. "I know. But you can pleasure yourself, too."

Her pretty pink mouth parted, and then her cheeks flushed. She ducked her head, burying it against his neck. "You're asking if I . . ."

"Yeah. You touch yourself, sweetheart?"

She gave a little moan, and he wasn't sure if it was embarrassment or arousal. Maybe both.

"There's no being ashamed between us," he murmured, lightly running his fingers through her thick hair. "You think I don't touch myself when I think of you?"

"You do?" She lifted her head to look at him. The expression on her face was no longer embarrassment but fascination.

"All the damn time. Every morning, in the shower. Every night, before I go to bed. I imagine my hand is your hand and it makes me come so damn hard."

Sage sucked in a breath. "Really?"

"Really." He traced a finger along the edge of her jaw. "Because you're so perfect and sweet I can't help it. I need you, even if it's only my imagination."

"Oh, I need you, too, Jason." Sage's words were an intense whisper as she pressed her breasts to his chest again. "So much."

"We'll take it slow, sweetheart, but that doesn't mean we aren't free to explore each other. You can touch me however you want, or I can touch you. You tell me which one makes you more comfortable. Which one arouses you."

She licked her lips. "Both."

Ah, that was his sweet girl. He chuckled. "You pick one, then."

He expected her to think about it, to duck her head and blush again. To his surprise, she leaned back and pulled her ugly sweater over her head in one fluid motion, revealing a pale pink bra. Jason stared, his mouth dry at the sight of her beautiful body. He hadn't been expecting that, and now he couldn't stop staring. She looked so damn soft, and her breasts were perfect, high handfuls against that demure bra with its tiny straps. Her belly curved, gently sloping, and he could see her navel peeking out just above the waistband of her jeans. Her skin was pale and silky looking, and she had a beauty mark on the slope of one perfect breast. He wanted to kiss it. Hell, he wanted to kiss all of her. "You're gorgeous." He reached out and rubbed his knuckles along the length of one arm. "That mean I can touch you?"

Sage took in a shuddering breath, closing her eyes. "Please, Jason."

He pulled her close again, tucking her against him as he claimed her mouth in another kiss. As he kissed her, he let one hand move over her arm and her back, touching her as much as he could to get her used to his caresses. He'd never been with someone as innocent as Sage, and even though his cock was aching for release, he had to go slow. He needed to make this good for her. So good. He wanted her trembling with need, not trembling with shyness.

With another deep kiss, he slid his fingers up her spine and loved the shiver of response that brought on. He swept up her back again and then teased at the clasp of her bra, testing her reactions. When she moaned against his mouth, he gently undid the clasp and brushed his fingers over the now-bared spot so she'd know exactly what came next.

She lifted her mouth from his, breaking the kiss with a little pant. "Do . . . do you want me to take my bra off?"

His brave, beautiful Sage. "I'll do it," he murmured, and slid one strap down a pale, perfect shoulder. "Damn, you're pretty."

She closed her eyes, shuddering as he eased it down one arm as far as it would go and then to the other arm. Then she leaned back, and he could see the molded cups of the bra clinging to her breasts by sheer gravity alone.

Her breath quick and nervous, Sage met his eyes and then lifted her shoulders, and her bra tumbled into his lap.

And . . . damn. She was beautiful. Her round, plump breasts were tipped by the palest pink nipples, tight little buds that seemed to grow even tighter as he stared. He couldn't resist touching one, rubbing his thumb over the peak, and loved her whimper of pleasure. "Oh mercy," she breathed, leaning forward to press her forehead against his shoulder. "That . . ."

"Shhh," he murmured, idly rubbing the nipple and loving the way she squirmed against him in response. "Too much?" At her choked whimper, he suggested, "Should I stop?"

"N-no."

Damn, he loved that. He loved how responsive she was. "I can't wait to put my mouth on these sweet little nipples," he murmured into her hair as she writhed against him. "I bet they taste so damn good."

Sage moaned, then her mouth went to his in another fierce kiss. This time, she was the aggressor, licking at his mouth as if his hand on her breast was making her crazy with need. He cupped the other, too, then he was teasing both nipples at once, and he could feel her shudder against him. Her frantic kiss turned into a little cry, and she shifted against him, restless.

"Sit up," he whispered into her mouth. "Feed one to me. Let me taste you."

She moaned again but did as she was told. She arched up against him, moving into his lap, and he put one hand on her plump backside, tugging her against him even as she panted, pressing her torso closer to his face.

With his lips, he captured one nipple and brushed his mouth over it in a tease, loving the frantic cry that escaped her. He licked it gently, then circled the peak before sucking lightly on it, trying to figure out the way she liked to be touched best. It all felt amazing to him, but he wanted to make Sage wild with need.

He wanted to see her lose control. To see her come with the force of her pleasure, to feel her cling to him as she lost control. Yeah, he liked the thought of that a lot.

So he coaxed and teased one breast, then moved to the other, lavishing it with attention until she was aching and whimpering against him. He could have stayed there forever, but her movements grew more and more restless, and his cock ached fiercely as it strained against his pants. He needed to slow down if he was going to take his time with her, to do this right. But he wanted to see her come, and come hard, so he claimed her mouth with his again, pulling her down until she straddled his lap. The feel of her pressing against him was exquisite, and he groaned into her soft mouth.

"Please, Jason," she whispered, digging her fingers into his shirt as if she wanted to tear it from his body. "Please."

"Please what?" he murmured, nipping at her mouth. God, she was gorgeous like this, all flushed and needy. "Do you need more, sweetheart?" At her eager nod, he touched the waistband of her jeans. "You want me to touch you everywhere?"

She gave a shuddering gasp, clinging to him.

"Do you need to come?"

Sage cried out, her mouth moving desperately to his again.

Oh yeah, she needed to come. With quick hands, he managed to undo the waistband of her jeans and slipped his fingers down the front. He felt the brush of curls between her thighs and then touched her folds.

And damn, she was soaked.

Sage clenched against him, panting. "Jason," she whispered. "Oh god, Jason."

"I've got you, sweetheart," he murmured, letting her press her forehead against his as she rocked against his hand. Her movements were jerky, her breathing erratic, and she wouldn't look at him. That was all right. He knew what she needed. With gentle fingers, he explored her folds, seeking out the button of her clit. And when he found it, she jolted against him. "Right there?" he murmured.

She gave a jerky nod, moaning.

"I've got you," he whispered again and then rubbed her gently, tracing little circles around her clit. She was so damn wet and so aroused that it was making him crazy. He was going to come in his pants if he didn't do something soon, but Sage's pleasure was more important. She rode his hand, pressing against his fingers as if she needed more but didn't know what. He let her lead, his focus entirely on her clit, and when she rocked against his fingers, sobbing out his name, he knew she was close. "I've got you," he told her over and over again. "I've got you, Sage."

Her entire body clenched and her thighs tightened around his hand as she came with a hard shudder, a swallowed moan, and a rush of wetness.

Beautiful. So beautiful. And she was his. He felt a possessive surge as she sagged against him, lost in the wake of her pleasure. He idly stroked her as she rode through the orgasm, and when she pulled away from his touch, he slid his hand out of her panties and kissed her brow. "You're gorgeous."

Sage gave him a shy look, kissing his mouth. She still seemed dazed and soft eyed as she gazed at him. "Did you . . ."

Jason shook his head. His needs seemed secondary to

hers. His cock ached with need, but he'd ignore it and jerk off to this later as he replayed it in his head. "I'm fine."

"Oh." She looked disappointed and then bit her lip. "Can I . . . touch you?"

He bit back a groan. She wanted to explore him? While he was this hard and aching? "It might not be a good idea." At her crushed look, he explained quickly, "You don't want me coming all over your hands."

"Why not?" she whispered, voice husky. "Don't you want to do that?"

He groaned again, pulling her in for a hot, hard kiss. "You sure about this, sweetheart?" When she nodded, he closed his eyes, trying to get together enough control to make this last. He feared the moment she touched him, he'd start shooting off like a rocket . . . but he was also craving her touch. So he helped her ease off his thighs, and then when she crouched in front of him on the floor, he nearly lost it. "God, you're so damn pretty, Sage. Not sure how I got so lucky."

She just smiled at him, looking like a goddess with her tits out and rosy from his ministrations, her hair tousled and falling over her shoulders. His fingers fumbled a little as he tried to get his damn zipper open, and then he eased his cock free and let out a heavy sigh as it strained into the air. Some of the pain of constriction left, but it took everything he had not to grasp it in his hand and start stroking at the sight of her.

Sage's eyes went wide as she gazed at his cock, and her cheeks flushed again. "It's so big and thick."

Well, that was flattering. "You want to touch it?"

She licked her lips, and he nearly came apart all over again. He wasn't going to last long at this rate, not with how tight his sac was, his need ready to boil over.

Sage leaned forward and ever so delicately put her finger-tips on his shaft. "Oh, you're so warm here. And your skin is so soft." She gripped him. "But you're as hard as iron."

His eyes nearly rolled back in his head when she squeezed him. He clenched a fist at his side, trying to retain control as she explored him, her hand moving up and down his length and tracing the thick veins. Her gaze went to the thick beads of pre-cum dotting the crown of his cock, and then she looked at him. "How do I make you come?"

He covered her hand with his and stroked. Once. Twice. Then he paused, watching her reaction, waiting to see if she wanted him to continue or if she wanted to stop. The look in her eyes was full of fascination, though, and when he released her hand she pumped him again. Jason gripped her hand again, and she looked up at him, her lips parted. It only took a few more pumps before he came with a low growl in his throat, his need exploding out of him and coat-ing both of their hands with his release.

Sage kept her hand on his cock, idly stroking him even as she moved up to kiss his mouth. "I'll get a towel."

He watched her as she covered her breasts with her free hand, then studied his seed on the back of her other hand as she left the room. He hoped she wasn't embarrassed, and when she returned a few moments later with a shirt on and freshly washed hands, he just smiled. He took the warm, damp towel she offered, cleaned himself off, and then pulled her against him for another round of kisses. She went into his arms happily, and he tugged her into his lap, nuzzling at the fall of her messy hair. "How do you feel?"

"Mmm," she responded, leaning her head on his shoul-der. "Languid."

Him, too. He hadn't come so hard in a long, long time. "That was amazing. You're amazing."

Sage chuckled and snuggled back against him. "You're not so bad yourself. Sure you can't stay tonight?"

If he did, he'd end up taking her virginity, and he knew that things were moving too fast just yet for that. He wanted her to have time to process things, to go over how she felt before he rushed her into bed. "I wish I could."

Soon, he told himself. Soon he'd stay overnight. Just not tonight.

CHAPTER SEVENTEEN

Days passed and everything was quiet. Sage didn't hear from Greg for another three days, and even then, it was just more of the same nonsense. He wanted to see her. He wanted to have lunch with her. She did everything she could to avoid answering his texts. She didn't see it, she'd lie. Then she'd use work as an excuse. Things were busy. She was helping the mayor finish up some last-minute projects before the office closed for Christmas week. She just didn't have the time to have lunch with a casual friend.

It wasn't entirely the truth, but what Greg didn't know wouldn't hurt him, she supposed.

The rumor mill kept running around town, though, thanks to Hannah's efforts. Becca returned to her salon that Monday, only took scheduled appointments, and quickly closed up shop the moment her last client left. Hannah took great delight in telling everyone how sad Becca was, how her heart had been ripped out of her chest.

Sage just mostly felt guilty. Becca deserved better than

that. Sage felt guilty because she suspected Greg was fixating on her . . . but mostly she felt guilty because she was so dang happy.

Jason was the one who made her happy. Being with him had brought a lightness to her heart that she hadn't felt since her father passed. She didn't feel alone anymore. She didn't feel sad or left out. Now her days were filled with text messages from her boyfriend—how much did her heart skip with joy at being able to call Jason her boyfriend? And their nights were spent together, making out on her sofa in front of the fireplace or taking Achilles on long walks in the snow.

She was thrilled to see that the dog went everywhere with him, and the more they were together, the more in sync they seemed to be. Achilles remained at Jason's side as if he were glued, and Jason looked at the dog with affection and constantly touched the yellow, furry head as if to ground himself. His PTSD flare-ups seemed to happen less often when Achilles was around. They didn't go away entirely, of course. The dog wasn't a magic cure, and neither was Sage's affection. But she noticed he was able to pull himself out of a bad spell quicker than he was before, and when the panic hit, it was far less immediate and violent.

He seemed happier, too.

And dating Jason? It was like a dream come true. Sage floated in a cloud of happiness everywhere she went. They kept their dates fairly close to town because Jason had to be back at the Price Ranch early, and they needed to go to places that would turn a blind eye to Achilles, who didn't wear service dog gear . . . because Jason wasn't supposed to know that he was an emotional support dog. He thought he was helping Achilles, when really, Achilles had been planted at his side to help him all along.

Sometimes she worried about that, and how Jason would react if he ever found out. But when she was with him, she was so happy, and he was, too, that she thought it wouldn't matter. At some point, she'd confess. For now, she was content to leave things as they were.

Sage did need a present for Jason for Christmas, though. She'd been racking her brain on small things that would mean something to him. Oatmeal raisin cookies, of course. She'd already bought the ingredients to make an absolutely enormous number of them for him, and the dog-shaped cookie jar to put them in. She wanted something more than just food, though. Something that would make him realize how much he meant to her. So she ran errands into Casper for work, and when she was there, she tried to shop and find things for Jason. She got him a tooled leather belt and an engraved pocketknife, but she didn't have the perfect gift for him. Not yet.

When she was at the mall, though, she passed a lingerie shop and stared at the bright red-and-white panties and bras.

Was she brave enough to do that? To wrap herself up as the present?

She hesitated for a moment and then went inside. An hour later, she walked out with a push-up bra in bright red edged with white lace and a pair of matching thong panties. The lady behind the counter had convinced her to get a pair of thigh-high red stockings, so she did and then headed toward the shoe store for a pair of ridiculously tall heels.

If she was going to do this, she'd do it right.

Jason scanned the horizon as the horse underneath him twitched and pranced. He held the reins loosely, because he'd learned the hard way that the more he tugged, the more the horse acted up. The weather was cold, the wind blowing hard from the west, and the distant mountains were covered in caps of snow. The sun was out, but the temperature was steadily dropping, which meant more work for him. Normally, that would irk Jason, but today, it was just kind of nice to be out in the fresh air and not feel that hunted sort of panic nipping at his heels. He glanced down at the side of his horse, and Achilles was walking close by, wearing a ridiculous doggy sweater and boots that Cass had made for him since it was damn cold and muddy. Achilles lifted his feet gingerly every time he took a step, which had made Jason snort with laughter all day long, and he'd sent a video to Sage so she could share in the amusement.

Eli rode up next to him, gazing out, too. "Well?" he asked, and Jason knew this was another test.

"Wind changed again," Jason told him. "So that storm is probably going to hit us. Since it's just you and me, we should keep the cattle in the pasture they're in and ride out the storm."

Eli stared at him with hard eyes under the brim of his cowboy hat. "Waterin' hole's kinda chewed up with mud, though." Not a question, just a statement.

Jason knew that was part of the test. "Yeah, but if it's cold enough the mud'll freeze up. I think it's smarter for us to keep them close instead of moving them out farther because we'll need to cake 'em with extra feed to keep them warm. Be less work for us if we keep 'em close and manage the mud instead of trying to wade through a snowbank to get to them."

There was a long pause, and then Eli grunted. "Good call. You ride along the fence one more time to make sure there's no breaks."

Jason nodded and flicked the reins, and his horse headed

out. Achilles got to his feet and trotted a safe distance away, and Jason held in his grin until he was far enough away that Eli wouldn't notice.

He felt like he'd just been tested . . . and passed. He might not know a ton about ranching, but he was proving that he could work hard and that he wasn't an idiot, and Eli gave him less shit as the days went by.

Sage would be proud of him.

And then she'd tell him to get back to work because cattle didn't wait for daydreams. He grinned to himself and rode forward, whistling for Achilles.

By the time the two men rode in that night and tended to the horses, the wind was blowing fiercely and the snow falling hard enough that visibility wasn't more than a few feet ahead. It wasn't Jason's favorite weather because it meant staying inside instead of visiting Sage, but he'd Face-Time her tonight and make sure she didn't feel neglected. He hated that she was out at that big, lonely ranch by herself. Someone like Sage should have been surrounded by love and celebration at Christmastime, not sitting alone on her couch and FaceTiming him. He wanted to invite her up to the Price Ranch for Christmas Eve, but he didn't think she'd abandon her cattle, so he'd have to go to her. That would mean staying late and waking up early, but he'd do it for her.

He was starting to realize he'd do just about anything for her. Sage just made him so damn happy, and he felt intensely protective of her at the same time. She was smart and capable about so many things, and so completely innocent about others.

Cass dished out big plates of a meaty casserole and put

her baby in his seat nearby. The dogs were curled up in the corner, watching them eat—all except Achilles, who remained at Jason's side, ever clingy. He didn't mind that, though. He never gave the dog scraps at the table; learned that with Truck. Dinner was pleasant enough, and Jason decided he'd ask a favor.

"You guys know I've been dating Sage Cooper for a short time," he began.

"Very short," Eli said.

Cass swatted him with her hand and beamed. "I think it's wonderful. Sage is a lovely girl and deserves to be happy. You should invite her over for dinner sometime."

"She'd love that," he told them, and he knew she would. "She's all alone at that big ranch, and I hate the thought of her spending Christmas by herself. I thought I'd run it past you two, see if I could spend Christmas Eve there with her and come back the next morning. I'd do all the morning chores here before heading out, and I'd be back here in time to do the rest, but I'd be handling things a little past the usual schedule."

Eli and his wife exchanged a look.

Eli shrugged. "It'll give me and Cass a chance to have some alone time."

Cass smiled.

He felt relieved. "I'll make sure to take care of my normal set of duties before I head out, and if something comes up, you can always call me."

"Oh, it'd have to be a real emergency for Eli to call you," Cass said, her mouth twitching with amusement. "You know how he feels about phones."

Eli just shot his merry wife a look, but Jason could have sworn that one corner of the man's hard mouth turned up in a smile.

"Did you get Sage something for Christmas?" Cass asked between bites. "Do you need ideas?"

"Babe," Eli murmured.

"I'm just curious," Cass said brightly. "It's just . . . you know Sage. She gets everyone something. She even bakes special cookies for the dogs."

He'd been thinking a lot about what to get her. Not that he'd had a lot of time to shop, but the idea had hit him when he'd been at her place, looking around at the big, empty house. "I've got most of an idea, but I still need to finalize a few things." He reached down and stroked Achilles's head, propped in its usual spot on his thigh. "Though if it falls through, I'll definitely need ideas."

Eli lifted his chin at Jason. "How's that dog? He bugging you?"

He could have sworn that Cass kicked Eli under the table. Odd. Did they think it was a sore spot because Annie had imposed on him? He'd been bitter about it the first day, but Achilles was such a calming presence that he didn't mind. In fact, he kind of looked forward to having the big yellow mutt at his side all the time. Jason rubbed Achilles's ears. "We get along pretty good, him and I." It was almost like having Truck back . . . almost. Achilles had a different personality than Truck had, of course. Achilles was more softhearted, more needy, whereas Truck had looked after Jason's every need as if he were doing his sworn duty and Jason was his to take care of. It was different . . . but it was still nice, and having a dog at his side constantly made the ache of Truck's loss bearable. "He's good company," he said, and glanced down at Achilles, who looked up at him with adoring eyes, as if Jason were his entire world.

Eli just grunted. "Be glad you're not a chicken."

Jason snorted with laughter.

* * *

Three days passed before the weather got any better. His bad leg ached, and he wasn't able to spend time with Sage because the roads were a mess of snow and ice, and then suddenly it was Christmas Eve. Since he hadn't been able to leave the ranch to go shopping for her, he'd made a few calls in to the local souvenir shop and spoken with Nelson, who'd handled his request and wrapped it up, and Jason just had to pick it up for her. So that was one problem solved. He woke up earlier than usual and got to work, cleaning the barn and feeding the horses. By the time dawn hit, he'd loaded the spooler with hay and was spreading it for the cattle. He was a man on a mission—to spend time with his woman—and he needed to get done quickly so he'd have that much more time with Sage in his arms.

At lunchtime, Eli clapped him on the back. "Get out of here. Tell Sage we said Merry Christmas."

He nodded at Eli and all but raced back into the barn to unsaddle and brush down his horse.

Even if the weather was bad, he was staying with Sage tonight, because he was not going to leave her alone for Christmas.

CHAPTER EIGHTEEN

S age hummed to herself as she put the finishing touches on the presents underneath her tiny tabletop Christmas tree. She had a ham cooking in the oven, with potatoes and stuffing and three kinds of Christmas cookies. She'd made treats for the dog and had even made a big batch of apple cider, since neither she nor Jason drank. The fireplace was full of wood, there were clean linens on the guest bed, fresh snow was on the ground, and she was just waiting for Jason to show up.

After the last few days of being apart, when he'd suggested staying overnight in her guest room so they could spend Christmas together, she'd jumped at the idea. Even though they had text messages and FaceTime to keep connected, she still missed him intensely and dreamed about his kisses . . . and more. In her mind, she'd replayed their last make-out session over and over again, his hands in her panties as he made her come, her hands on his cock as he growled his release.

She wanted to do so much more.

Well, she wanted to do all that again, too, because it had been amazing. The last three days had been the longest that she could recall. Other than the mail, the municipal office was closed for Christmas week, and even the mailman had offered to sort the few envelopes and catalogs that had come in. There was nothing for Sage to do, and for someone that liked to stay busy, it was a special kind of hell. She'd cleaned the house from top to bottom and had gone through her father's closet and maybe wept a little (okay, a lot) as she'd packed up clothing to donate. After all, if she was moving, she couldn't take it with her. That would just be silly, and she knew there were people out there who could use it.

Even if it did break her heart a little, it kept her busy. There was a lot to be done if she was truly going to sell the ranch in spring. Sage could think of a million ways to procrastinate, to wait until next fall, or the year after, or until Jason left . . . but her father would never want her to make her decisions around a man she'd only been dating for a short time. Even she knew that wasn't wise. So yes, she was still selling the ranch in the spring even if she was dating Jason.

If they were still together at that point, they'd figure out how to make it work. She wouldn't get too far ahead of herself.

After all, look at Becca.

She shuddered at the thought. Becca'd fallen in love, and it had ended disastrously, but at least she'd never given her business up for Greg. There was a lesson to be learned there.

The sound of tires on the gravel road touched her ears, and she jumped up from her chair in the kitchen, putting on her last-minute "Christmas bow" pin, her heart fluttering. She'd thought long and hard about how best to "wrap" Jason's biggest present of all—herself—but nothing sexy had come to mind. She'd fussed over her hair, curling the ends into soft ringlets, and put on a hint of makeup and perfume. She'd shaved everything—*everything*—and lotioned her skin until she smelled like roses. Underneath her plain white sweater, the red panties and bra itched against her skin, but she wasn't wearing them because they were comfortable. She wore the bow on her sweater, pinned over her heart, because, well, she was his present, too.

She just hoped he liked it.

Nervous, she turned down the Christmas music playing in the kitchen and headed to greet Jason. It had been days since she'd last seen him in person, and my goodness, three days had never seemed so very long. Would he greet her with a kiss? Just say hi? How did this work exactly? Biting her lip, Sage opened the door, a beaming smile on her face—

And was immediately swept into Jason's arms.

His mouth was on hers before she could even breathe his name. He dipped her low, as if they were dancing, kissed her hard, and then eased her back to her feet. "Missed you," he murmured, rubbing his nose against hers.

God, she loved him.

The thought struck her like a bolt of lightning, and Sage had to bite back a gasp.

No, absolutely not. She couldn't be in love with him, not that fast. Sure, he was so gorgeous he made her heart skip, and he was thoughtful and kind and protective, yet somehow vulnerable and . . . oh no. She had it so bad.

She loved Jason Clements. And it wasn't the same as the love she'd thought she'd had for Greg. That was a childish crush, the envy of wanting something you couldn't have, and just sheer loneliness. The love she had for Jason? It was overwhelming. It made her chest hurt at the thought of leaving him.

And it made her ache deep inside at the thought of being his forever.

"You all right? You have a funny look on your face."

"I'm fine," she told him quickly. Sage smiled at him. "Long time no see, stranger." When he gave her another curious stare, she impulsively flung her arms around his neck and kissed him, hard. "I'm so happy to see you."

He chuckled, his arms going to her waist. "Merry Christmas. I'm glad we're going to spend it together."

Oh, she was glad, too. So glad. She'd never told anyone, but she was dreading this Christmas. It was her favorite holiday, and she loved making the magic happen for the town, but her father had died last fall, and her first Christmas alone had been . . . so lonely. She'd never felt so lost. Depressed. As if she'd never be happy again. Maybe that was why she'd thrown herself into the Christmas celebration in Painted Barrel this year—she was trying not to think about another lonely Christmas by herself.

Jason was an answer to all her prayers.

She kissed him again, suddenly fiercely thankful for her gorgeous cowboy.

"Is there mistletoe above me?" he murmured between kisses, his hands sliding to her butt and cupping it.

"No," she breathed. "I just like kissing you."

"Mmm, me too." He pulled her against him, dragging her hips against his front, and she felt the steel length of his erection pressing against her stomach. Oh. He was hard with need, and suddenly Christmas was full of all kinds of things to look forward to.

Something butted against their legs, and Jason chuckled as Achilles shoved past them. "He's not a real big fan of the snow, it seems."

"It seems not," she echoed, licking her lips. She could taste him on her mouth, and she wanted more kisses . . . oh, but she was getting greedy. "Come on inside."

He gave her one more quick kiss. "I will, but I need to get your present out of the car."

Her . . . present? A giddy rush of excitement coursed through her. "You got me a gift?"

Jason's brows furrowed. "Well, yeah. It's Christmas, sweetheart. It's not much, but I wanted to get you something. Wait here, all right?" He winked at her and then crunched back out to the car. Snow was starting to drift down from the clouds, but she didn't care. Let it snow all night long, because Jason was going to be here with her. She hugged her arms to her chest and felt the press of the lace and underwire of her bra, and remembered that she'd gotten Jason a little something special, too.

Oh, except her shoes were upstairs. She had her thigh-highs on underneath her jeans, and she was wearing slippers. Whoops. Her toes curled. Maybe she'd be able to slip away and put on the stilettos that she'd bought for such an occasion.

To her surprise, Jason came to the door with a large, flat box. It had been wrapped in plain brown paper, a twine bow at the front. "It's not a fancy wrapping job," he told her, dusting the snow off his shoulders as he stepped inside. "But I hope you like it anyhow."

Her lips parted and she took the package from him. "You didn't have to do this." She was so touched that tears threatened to overflow and ruin her careful eye makeup. "Jason, just having you here with me has made this the best Christmas, truly. You didn't have to get me anything—"

"Sweetheart, I got you this because I wanted to. Because

you're amazing and you think of everyone except yourself, and I wanted you to realize that someone out there thought you needed a little Christmas cheer directed your way." He cupped her face and leaned in and kissed her while she hugged the box to her chest. "Open it now, though. I want to see if you like it."

Shyly, she tugged at the bow on the front of his gift. "I got you a few things, too. Just small things, though. Nothing big." She hoped he hadn't spent too much on her, because suddenly, wearing lingerie and getting him a belt seemed like the lamest Christmas gifts ever. Sage pulled off the twine and then tugged at the wrapping paper. Whatever it was was inside a large, plain white box that was no taller than an inch or two, and she wondered about it. Did he get her . . . a clock for the wall? A calendar? What?

Nothing could have prepared her for what was inside the box. Sage sucked in a breath as she pulled the picture out, and then a hot, choked sob erupted from her throat.

It was a picture of her daddy.

Winston Edward Cooper stared out at her from the old newsprint photograph that had been framed. He was young in the picture, maybe thirty-five or forty. He had a bridle in his hand and stood next to a horse, and an enormous cowboy hat was perched atop her father's head. The ranch spread was in the background, and her father wore a brilliant, dimpled smile.

She'd never seen this photo before. Oh, her heart hurt at the sight of it.

"I know you mentioned you're going to leave in the spring, and I wanted you to have a little something to remember this place by, so I called and talked to Nelson at the souvenir shop, and he said there was an old newspaper article about the Cooper Ranch, and he was able to get me a copy . . . Are you crying, sweetheart?"

"No," she sobbed, her nose running. She swiped at her face, smearing makeup all over it, but she didn't care. "Jason . . . this is the nicest thing anyone's ever done for me. Ever." It was like he'd given her back a little bit of her father this day, and she ached with missing her daddy, even as much as she loved the photo. She couldn't stop touching the glass covering it, or crying.

"It's all right," Jason murmured, and pulled her into his arms. "I'm sorry it made you sad—"

"It's wonderful," she sobbed, curling up against him. "I love it. I just . . . miss him so much."

"I know." He stroked her hair. "I should have told you that you looked real pretty today. You still do, just ah . . . a bit messy."

Sage choked on a giggle and sniffled, wiping at her tears with her sleeve. Oh, her pale, pretty white sweater was covered in makeup and mascara. "I'm sorry. This probably wasn't what you wanted to see today."

"All I wanted to see was your dimples," he told her, hugging her close. "I don't care if you wear a bit of makeup or if you wear heaps of it. I just like seeing your smile."

She leaned back and smiled up at him through her tears. "You're the most wonderful person I've ever met, Jason Clements."

"You stole my line," he murmured, wiping away her tears. "Don't cry, sweetheart."

"It's a good cry," she promised him. "Though I feel guilty, because what I got you isn't nearly as awesome." Sage wiped the corners of her eyes and grimaced when her fingertips came away coated in mascara. "Ugh."

He cupped her face and rubbed his thumb over her lower lip. "If you want to clean up, I should probably take Achilles's snow boots off before he chews them up."

"Give me five minutes," she promised and then headed upstairs to repair the damage.

Sage grimaced at the sight in her bathroom mirror. She looked dreadful. Not only were her eyes red and swollen, but her makeup was smeared under her eyes and all over her face. She looked like a sad clown. She scrubbed all of her makeup off, put in eye drops, and then changed her now-ruined sweater. She'd picked out the soft, clingy white top just because it made her feel sexy, and she hunted in her closet for something similar. Not finding anything, she went for a plain white T-shirt and then fastened her bow corsage on it once more. It wasn't ideal, but she doubted Jason would care. It was what was underneath that counted, right?

And what she was wearing underneath was impressive . . . she hoped.

She headed back downstairs with her stilettos and paused in the doorway at the sight of Jason lying on the rug with Achilles. The dog's jacket and booties had been discarded, and Jason was spread out in front of the fire, a hand tucked behind his head. Achilles lay alongside him, leaning on Jason's chest, eyes closed as Jason stroked his head. They looked so peaceful and sweet that her heart squeezed with love. She carefully tiptoed to the kitchen, determined not to disturb them. She knew from Jason's texts that he'd been working hard over the last few days, and ranching wasn't easy work even with a full staff. With Dustin gone for the next two weeks, he was going to have his hands full just trying to keep up with Eli, but he hadn't complained. He never would.

Sage sat in the kitchen and drank a cup of coffee while Jason dozed in front of the fire with his dog. She regarded the picture of her father thoughtfully. He'd been so handsome back then, and so happy. He'd always been a happy man, even after the death of her mother. Maybe she'd been too little to see him grieving, but she remembered his brilliant smile and how much everyone in Painted Barrel had loved him. She'd always wanted to be like him, a cornerstone of the community, there for everyone to depend on and always able to extend a helping hand. She thought of the stream of cowboys and ranchers who had worked on the Cooper Ranch over the years—some had questionable histories, some were just desperate for work, and her father had never asked questions. If they needed help, he helped them. If they needed a job, he gave them one. The ranch had been a special place growing up, and even though it was just her and her father and an endless merry-go-round of ranch hands, she'd always felt loved. Special.

That was one of the things she loved most about Jason. He made her feel special, too, but in different ways. Her father would have liked him a lot.

She stared at the picture of her father as an uneasy realization occurred to her. He would have liked Jason . . . but he wouldn't have liked that she was going to sell the ranch. That she'd sold off the livestock and was busy denuding the walls of memories so she could move in the spring. He'd worked hard to establish this place. He'd sunk his entire savings into the land and had built the house himself with a bit of help. He wouldn't understand her loneliness or her need to leave and start over.

The thought was a sobering one. She wasn't even sure she wanted to start over anymore, not when things were finally feeling as if they'd slid into place with Jason at her side. Why did life make things so hard? Why was Jason coming into her world just after she'd decided to let Greg put the ranch up for sale in the spring?

Inwardly, she grimaced at the thought of Greg. Her father would hate that she was using him as her Realtor, too. He'd liked Greg—he liked everyone—but he'd also always, always told her that she could do better than a "lazy boy" like that. And maybe Greg was lazy at times, but it was her ranch and she would keep control of the sale. She wouldn't let Greg ruin things, and he needed a win in his column for his real estate business. Really, it was just more helping people out, and wouldn't her father have approved of that?

But she couldn't shake the feeling that he wouldn't. She knew what he would say. *You stay in Painted Barrel. You stay where you're at home. You stay with your people. If things aren't the way they should be, you make the changes.*

But how could you possibly change being lonely? Even her father had never remarried after her mother's death. He'd said it was because he didn't have time, but what if it was because there just hadn't been anyone to date? What if he'd been fighting a loneliness as deep and soul swallowing as the one that threatened her before she'd met Jason?

She got to her feet and put her coffee cup in the sink. Popping a mint into her mouth to freshen her breath, she went back into the living room and gazed at Jason's sleeping form.

He opened his eyes as she approached and rubbed them, sitting up. "I must have dozed off."

"It's all right. I don't mind. I was just having a cup of coffee and straightening up the kitchen." Sort of. Mostly she'd been lost in thought.

Jason gave her a gorgeous, sleepy smile. "Merry Christmas. Some company I am, right?"

"You're the best company," she told him, and meant it. She'd been so touched when he'd offered to sleep over in the guest room just so she wouldn't be alone on the holiday. He knew how lonely she got. Of course he did. He understood her better than anyone. Achilles sat up and thumped his tail at her excitedly but remained at Jason's side. Already, it was clear that the dog utterly adored Jason. He never left him, and even when they were together, Achilles hovered within a handspan's distance, as if he needed to make sure Jason was near for his sake, too. "Oh, before I forget, I got Achilles a small Christmas present, too, but I didn't wrap it." She went to the kitchen to retrieve it.

She could hear Jason moving behind her, and she heard his soft chuckle. "Is it covered in peanut butter? Because sometimes I think that's the only thing he cares about."

"Not exactly." She retrieved the small gift and held it out to Jason. It was a dog kerchief, bright red and sturdy. On the edges, she'd embroidered ACHILLES in bold lettering, and on the underside, she'd put the address for the Price Ranch and a phone number. She'd wanted to put Jason's name on there, too, or that Achilles was an emotional support animal, but she wasn't supposed to know that he belonged to Jason. Jason didn't even know that yet.

Even such a small lie was becoming harder and harder to maintain. Wordlessly, she held the scarf out to him.

He laughed, throwing his head back in delight and making her heart pitter-patter. "You didn't have to do this. You're too good, Sage."

His reaction filled her with warmth. "I figured everyone should have a gift for Christmas."

"Yeah, but he didn't get you anything."

"Oh, that's all right. I get things for everyone and most of the time they don't give anything back. I'm used to it."

She tilted her head and kept her words light. "Sometimes I think you're the only one that knows I'm alive."

Jason's smile dimmed. For a moment, he looked . . . sad. For her? "Is that why you're dating me?"

"No," she whispered. "I'm dating you because I like you." She loved him, actually, but it was too soon for that secret, as well.

He smiled again, then moved forward and touched the back of her neck, pulling her close and kissing her. "I speak for Achilles when I say he loves it."

"I'm glad." She put a hand on his chest, mostly because she wanted to touch him. Oh mercy, how she wanted to touch him. "When do you want to open your presents?"

That boyish smile returned full force, and if he heard the note of nervousness in her voice, he didn't acknowledge it. "I'd love to now."

"All right." She gestured at the small packages under her miniature tree. Each one had a bright red oversize bow, just like the one she'd pinned to her top. "Everything with a bow is yours."

And she held her breath, wondering if he'd realize the significance of that statement.

Jason grinned, then picked up the first package, turning it over in his hands. "There a particular order I should open these in?"

"Nope. Just unwrap everything you feel like." God, she was terrible at being sexy, wasn't she? She leaned slightly over one of the dining chairs across from him as he sat down and began to unwrap the first present. Her breasts were practically in her face with this silly push-up bra, but he hadn't noticed it, or the big, dumb bow on her shoulder.

"Sunglasses. Perfect." He chuckled and put them on his

face, testing them out. "I didn't realize how much the glare on the snow would bother me. Thank you, Sage."

"Of course." She kept smiling as he unwrapped more of her silly, practical gifts. The leather belt emblazoned with his name. Thick gloves with good hand grips. Extra-thick, wooly socks. An insulated mug. They were all small things, practical things that a cowboy who spent his time outside in the winter could use, but they weren't really special gifts . . . not like the one he'd given her. Suddenly, buying lingerie didn't seem like enough. She wished she'd done more. This was her first Christmas with a boyfriend, and already she was failing at this. Miserable, she bit her lip as he set aside the last wrapped present and smiled at her.

"You're too thoughtful, sweetheart. It's all great." He reached a hand out to her, and when she slipped her fingers into his, he squeezed them. "Thank you, Sage."

"You haven't finished unwrapping your gifts," she whispered, a nervous knot choking her throat.

He glanced back at the small tree, at the sea of discarded wrapping paper under it, his brows furrowing.

Obviously, she was going to have to help him out. "Everything with a bow on it," she repeated, and squeezed his hand.

He turned those creased brows to her and opened his mouth. She saw the moment his gaze focused on the bow pinned to her plain T-shirt—the same bow that had been pinned to her sweater earlier. And she saw the moment he realized what she meant. His eyes grew hooded, sultry, and the look he gave her made her shiver with need.

Mouth dry, Sage pulled her hand from his and then tugged her shirt over her head, revealing her festive red-and-white lace bra with the teeny tiny straps and delicate snowflake bow tucked in the valley of her breasts.

Jason groaned at the sight. His gaze searched hers. "Sweetheart, are you sure?"

"I'm sure. Merry Christmas, Jason." And before her nervousness could take over, she undid her jeans and dropped them to the floor, too, kicking off her stilettos. Now she stood in front of him in nothing but her Christmas lingerie, her toes wiggling in the red thigh-high stockings that had seemed so impractical at first and now made her feel sexy.

He made a sound in his throat again, and one hand immediately slid to the front of his jeans, pressing against his erection as if to calm himself. "You're the most beautiful thing I've ever seen." He held a hand out for her, and she put hers into it again. "Turn for me so I can see all of you, sweetheart."

She did, her movements slow, her cheeks hot as she did a circle, knowing that her butt was practically revealed in her thong. She hoped he liked it. "Is this a good present?" she asked nervously.

"Too good," Jason told her, voice gruff. "I'm about to spill in my pants at the sight of you."

Well, she liked the sound of that. Turning to face him again, she admitted, "I wanted to give you something special . . . so you'd know how much you mean to me."

"You're amazing," he murmured and then pulled her against him. She thought he'd tug her into his arms and kiss her, but instead, he backed them up to one of her kitchen counters, put his hands on her waist, and then lifted her atop it. Her bottom hit the cool surface, and she wriggled, even as he pushed between her thighs. "I didn't get to unwrap this one."

Oh. She supposed she'd been the one doing the unwrapping. "Sorry."

"Don't be sorry. I'll finish the job." He grinned up at her. "But I'm going to enjoy the sight of you first."

CHAPTER NINETEEN

Damn, but you're beautiful." Jason couldn't believe the loveliness seated on the counter in front of him. Sage, looking vulnerable and gorgeous, her long legs encased in sheer red stockings, her body covered in nothing but a skimpy pair of bright red panties and matching bra. She'd done this for him.

She wanted to be his present. She wanted to seduce him.

He was the luckiest man alive.

But he knew she was a virgin, knew that when he touched her, he was the first one to caress her breasts, the first one to slide a finger between her sweet folds, and he'd be the first one to sink deep inside her and claim her. So he had to go slow.

Really, really slow.

He leaned in and kissed her, tasting her sweet lips. She was coffee and mint and nerves, he could tell, because she trembled against him even as she leaned into his embrace. He'd make this good for her, though. It would be his present to her, to make her come so hard that she'd see stars. So he cupped the back of her neck and licked into her mouth, plunging deep and conquering it with hard, intense strokes that mimicked what he'd soon do between her thighs. She moaned into him, the tension easing from her body, and he kept kissing her, making love to her lips and tongue, showing her how much he desired her, how much he needed her. He could kiss her forever, but his cock had other ideas. So even as he kissed her, he eased one hand down her back, caressing her soft skin and getting her used to his touch. Her little responsive shivers and the tiny noises she made as he touched her told him she liked it, and slowly, her legs locked around his waist, holding him against her.

And damn, he loved that.

"Jason," she moaned between kisses, her hand moving up and down the front of his shirt as she petted him through his clothing. "Can you take this off? I want to feel your skin against mine."

Okay, maybe he didn't have to go as slow as he'd thought. Sage was new to this, but she was eager, and it made his heart hurt with how perfect she was. He grinned at her and tugged his shirt over his head, loving the way her eyes widened with appreciation.

She immediately reached for him again, and her palms skated up and down his front. "Oh wow. Look at you." She paused over one of his scars. "From Afghanistan?"

A hard knot formed in his throat, and for a moment, he was back there, lying in his own blood, listening to the snipers pick off his friends and unable to get the strength to call for help. He didn't remember how long he'd lain near death next to their overturned vehicle, just that it had seemed like an eternity. He'd thought he'd died a dozen times, only to wake up in blistering pain. And then, finally, he'd woken up in the hospital. "Yeah."

The sympathy in her eyes bothered him. He didn't want to think about Afghanistan right now. Not when she was so pretty and nearly naked. So he leaned in and took her mouth in another kiss, this one frantic and hard-edged as if he could kiss the bad memories away with her touch. And while they didn't fade entirely, kissing Sage became its own pleasure again, and when her hands fluttered over his shoulders, he enjoyed it. He needed to be with her, in that moment, because she needed him.

And he could do that for her.

Jason sank a hand into her glossy hair and tugged on it lightly, forcing her to arch her neck. Sage did as he asked, gasping as he leaned in and nipped at her throat. She made aroused little noises, her legs clenching around his hips every time he kissed her throat, and he liked the sound of that so much that it wasn't long before her entire neck was covered in love bites. He was branding her with his mouth, and that possessive, feral part of his brain loved it. "My Sage," he told her. "My Christmas present."

Her thighs tightened around him. "All yours."

Hell, he liked that, too. He swept a hand down her side, running his fingers along her skin, and felt her jerk and tense, as if she expected him to rip her clothes off and maul her. He only kissed her again until her mouth was soft and compliant once more and then slowly slid one hand up to cup her breast.

Her bra was thick, the material making it impossible to feel her nipple through it, and he immediately hated the damn thing. She'd worked so hard to be pretty for him, though, that he couldn't say that aloud. Instead, he slid one strap down her arm and then tugged her breast free of one cup, and he loved the gasping sounds she made as he leaned in and claimed that pert, pale pink nipple with his mouth.

Sage moaned in arousal, clinging to him as he tongued her nipple, teasing the peak with licks and nips until she was writhing against him. He pressed hot, frantic kisses to her skin and then moved to her other breast, freeing it, then taking the other nipple into his mouth as he teased the other with his fingers, rolling the pink tip between his thumb and forefinger. Her little cries grew wilder, her movements more erratic, and he wanted to give her even more, to tease her beyond her limits.

He wanted to taste her everywhere.

Jason reached behind her and undid the clasp of her bra, then slid it off her arms. Her pretty breasts were at eye level and made his mouth water at the sight of them. He wanted to pull her back into his arms, to tease those perfect little buds until she was clawing his back, but his need for her was becoming overwhelming. The more he thought about tasting her, the more he needed it. Craved it.

"Put your arms around me, sweetheart," he murmured, pulling her against him.

A flash of confusion showed in her eyes, but she immediately complied, trusting him. She wrapped her arms around his neck, and he lifted her off the counter, then tugged at the tiny panties.

She gasped, her legs tightening around his hips. "Jason?"

"Just unwrapping the rest of my present," he murmured, nuzzling at her neck. "You want me to stop?"

"No," Sage breathed.

Good, because he didn't want to stop, either. He tugged the panties down her thighs and then slipped them off her legs as she sat on the counter once more.

And stared.

She'd shaved between her legs. Her mound was completely bare, the pink lips peeking out between her thighs. Sage shifted uncomfortably on the counter and tried to cross her legs, but Jason put a hand on her knee. "Let me look at you, sweetheart. You're gorgeous." She gave a shuddering breath, and he knew she was feeling shy.

But holy hell, she was magnificent. Her long, strong thighs were spread atop the counter and he could see the wetness gleaming from her folds. He wanted to put his mouth there, to taste her. Jason looked up into her eyes and saw her face was pink, her expression uncertain. He reached up and kissed her to show her that he thought she was beautiful. That she was utterly gorgeous and all his. As he kissed her, he stroked up and down her body, caressing her breasts, her thighs, her stomach, teasing her with touches until she started to arch against him, a silent request for more.

When he pulled his mouth from hers, their eyes met and he saw she was soft with need, her mouth parted and her nipples taut.

"Can I taste you, Sage?" he rasped, his hands on her hips.

His sweet, innocent girl leaned forward to give him her mouth.

"No, sweetheart," he murmured. "I want to taste between your thighs."

A little whimper escaped her.

"If it makes you uncomfortable, I won't—"

"No," she said quickly. "No, I want it. Please, Jason." Her fingers flexed on his shoulders. "Please."

He grinned, pulling her close and burying his face against her breasts. Then he began to slowly kiss downward, loving the way she wiggled and squirmed against him. He kissed her stomach, then down to her navel, and he could feel her trembling. "I've got you, Sage," he murmured and then gently put a hand to her shoulder. "Lean back and let me taste all of you."

She swallowed and then nodded, leaning back against the cabinet behind her. It angled her body, presenting her lap to him as he snagged a chair from the nearby table and pulled it toward him. He sat down and then grabbed one of her long legs and eased it over his shoulder. Seated in front of her like this, her gorgeous sex was right there. Oh yeah, that was more like it. "Look at how beautiful you are, sweetheart. I bet you taste incredible."

"I hope so," she said, shyness and uncertainty in her voice. Her hand pressed up against the cabinet behind her, and she moaned as he leaned in and rubbed his jaw along the inside of one soft thigh. "Oh god, Jason."

"I've got you," he told her again. "But if it's too much, we can stop."

She shook her head, biting her lip.

He lowered his head again, then licked and nibbled a path along the inside of her thigh, heading slowly toward his destination. He could feel her trembling, could feel her body tensing and her back arching as he moved toward the vee between her thighs. He put one hand on her ass, gently tugging her forward, and then pressed a kiss to the mound of her sex.

Her breath exploded out of her in a gasp. "Oh."

He could smell the scent of her arousal and gripped her hips even tighter. She was hot and wet here, the tops of her thighs damp. Jason leaned in and brushed his mouth over her folds, and her hands flew to his head. She held them there for a moment, flexing, and then let go. "No," he told her. "Hold on to me, love."

Sage's hands went back to his head. "A-are you sure?"

Oh, he was sure. He was also sure he wasn't going to lift his head until she came. With another brush of his lips over her mound, he went lower, licking the seam of her sex.

She made a throaty sound he'd never heard before, and her hands clenched on the buzz of his hair again. Oh yeah. He liked that. "You taste beautiful, love." When she just made another soft noise, he took one thumb and gently parted her lower lips, admiring the sight of her. She was all pink softness, pretty and delicate as a flower.

He explored her with the pad of one thumb, pressing small kisses to the inside of her thigh as he teased a circle around her clit, loving how she shuddered against him. She moaned when he carefully pressed into the hot well of her core, feeling her tight walls suck his finger. It would be her first time and he'd have to prepare her. She was wet, but she definitely wasn't ready. Not yet. That was fine, because now that he had his mouth buried between her thighs, he wasn't going anywhere anytime soon. So he pressed kisses and teased her with little flicks of his tongue, all designed to make her squirm with impatience. He didn't go in for her clit right away after that first touch. He knew that was her hot spot, the place that would make her come the hardest, and he wanted to build up to that. Instead, he kissed the top of her mound and traced his tongue down the length of her slit. He flicked it against the core of her, lapping at her wet heat, and then skated away again to lick and tease the inside of her thigh. She arched and moaned against him, squirming, but her hands rested easily atop his head. He'd wait until she pushed at his head, demanding more from him.

Sage's little cries became more insistent, her thighs clenching every time he nipped at her skin. She was moving constantly on the countertop now, unable to stay still, and her breathing was coming in shallow pants. Closer, but not quite where he wanted her. Jason teased a finger up and down the seam of her sex and then pressed it into her core, loving her cry of response. "Does that hurt, sweetheart?"

"N-no," she panted, her fingers flexing on his head. "I'm o-okay."

She sounded dazed, lost in her need, and he kept going because her responses were making him utterly crazy with his own need. His cock felt as if it were going to punch a hole in his jeans, he was so damn hard. But Sage came first. He pushed deeper into her with his finger, feeling the tight clench of her around him. He gently pushed a second finger into her but met with resistance. She was tight.

It was time to get her relaxed, then.

With his fingers still lodged inside her, Jason parted her lower lips with his other hand, then leaned in and brushed his mouth over her clit. She cried out, arching against him. Her hands dug at his scalp. "Jason," she panted. "Oh . . ."

"I'm here," he murmured and then flicked his tongue over her clit again. Another shuddering, restless cry arose from her throat. "You like that?" he murmured, licking the sensitive nub and then blowing cool air across it. "Or should I stop?"

"No!" she cried out immediately, and her hands jerked on his head. "No, don't stop."

And there it was, the subtle pull of her hands on his head as she tugged him down, trying to guide him toward the apex of her hips. She pushed her back against the cabinet, trying to arch against his mouth as he went down again for another quick taste, and when her tight passage clenched around his fingers again, he began to work them, pumping slowly in and out of her channel even as he teased her clit with his mouth.

It didn't take long before he figured out which touches, which flicks of his tongue and where, got her off. Sage pushed at his head, silently guiding him even as she panted, and her little cries did the rest. He sucked on her clit, teasing the sensitive flesh as he continued to pound into her tight channel until she was utterly slick with arousal. He added a third finger, pushing into her, and when she arched with pleasure, he nearly lost control himself.

She was so damn beautiful, so responsive. She made all kinds of noises as he worked her delicate flesh, determined to bring her to orgasm. "Look at how wet you are," he told her, and thrust his fingers into her again, the sound of her slick heat audible. "You're going to clutch my cock like you're clutching at my fingers, aren't you, sweetheart?"

Her response was incoherent, but her insistent hands pushed at his head, driving him back toward her clit.

Jason chuckled and lavished more attention on it. She wanted less talking and more tongue? He could give her that. He redoubled his efforts, licking and sucking at the small nub and letting her push his head forward until she was practically grinding against his face, her breath coming in short, raspy pants.

"Jason," she cried out and then just as quickly panted his name again. "Jason. Jason!" Her voice was insistent, her thighs trembling, and he knew she was close. "Oh. Oh. I need—" She gasped, arching against his mouth. "I need—"

He ignored her wild cries, continuing to work the side of her clit with his tongue, rubbing it in a slow, steady motion that she'd shown she loved.

"Right. There!" She made a choked sound and then shuddered against him. Her channel convulsed on his fingers, shuddering, and her release rippled through her body. Her sex grew impossibly wet, and he kept pumping into her wet heat with his fingers, biting back his own growl of pleasure as she took thrust after thrust and kept coming, her thighs jerking against his shoulders.

With a little whimper, she sagged back, letting out a gusty sigh as she continued to shudder. He gave her sweetness one last lick and then slowly pulled his fingers free from her body. He immediately moved them to his mouth, tasting her arousal, and she watched him with heavy-lidded eyes, her sated body sprawled above him on the counter.

"Oh," was all she said.

He stood up and pulled her into his arms. He wanted to drag her over to the table and put her face down on it, pushing into her from behind and taking her so hard that she screamed . . . but this was her first time. She needed a bed, and she needed intimacy. Jason kissed her cheeks and jaw, peppering her face with small nips as he struggled to ignore the aching weight of his cock in his jeans. "I'm taking my present up to your room," he murmured. "Hold on to me."

Sage immediately put her arms around his shoulders and buried her face against his neck. He loved that she sagged against him, as if utterly exhausted and boneless with pleasure. He couldn't resist skimming his hands over the rounded curves of her bottom before gripping them and hauling her against him.

He carried her out of the kitchen and through the living room. Achilles got to his feet, tail wagging, and looked expectantly at Jason. "Stay," Jason murmured, and was relieved when the dog immediately sat back down in front of the fire again. He made a mental note to get something to occupy Achilles next time—because there would definitely be a next time—and took his woman upstairs.

Jason knew which bedroom was hers even if he'd never

been inside it. He managed to open the door and then pushed inside, noting the pale green decor. Sage, like her name.

It suited her, as did the simple watercolors of prairie scenes and the fluffy quilt on the bed. He was glad to see it was a king-sized bed and not a single. That meant they'd be sleeping together tonight. He gently set her down atop the blankets. She clung to him, not letting go of his neck, and her legs locked around his waist. "Stay, Jason."

"I'm not going anywhere, sweetheart." He kissed her fiercely to prove it. She gave a little sigh, rubbing her foot against his thigh even as he loomed over her on the bed. His jeans felt as if they were constricting his blood flow, they were so tight across his cock. "Let me undress, love."

"Hurry," she whispered, her eyes shining up at him.

Oh, he planned on it.

Jason tore at his jeans the moment he straightened. He'd never managed to pull his clothing off so fast, and the moment his jeans were on the floor, he immediately had to pull them back up to fish out his wallet. Condom. He needed a condom. He found one tucked in a side pocket and then tore the package open, rolling it on as quickly as possible. He needed to touch Sage again. He couldn't stand being apart from her, even for this brief moment. He needed to sink deep inside her, to feel her envelop him, to feel her thighs clasp around his hips again.

He needed her.

Once the condom was on, he looked up and saw her gazing at him. Her eyes were wide and fascinated, but she didn't seem scared. If anything, she seemed more turned on than ever before. He moved onto the bed, covering her body with his, and she immediately wrapped herself around him, holding him close. "Jason," she breathed, as if his name were a benediction. "My Jason."

"Yours," he agreed, and it felt right. He was most definitely hers, in every sense of the word.

Sage kissed him, and as she did, her hands roamed all over his torso, as if she didn't know where to touch him first. Her hands finally settled on his hips, and then lower, and she gripped his ass in her hands and pulled him down against her, until his cock was settled against her mound. He rocked against her, getting her used to the feel of him, and when she opened her legs wider, he shifted his weight and pressed the head of his cock to the entrance of her core.

She sucked in a breath, tensing.

"Don't be afraid," he murmured. "I have you."

She nodded, and he kissed her again to distract her. It didn't take long before she was moaning underneath him again, her body moving against his and pushing back against the cock he had wedged against her entrance. Every time she squirmed against him, he nearly lost control. He'd give her what she wanted so badly, then. He pushed into her, just a little, and found the clasp of her body tight but not unforgiving. Inch by inch, he pumped into her, easing his way in with intense kisses and teasing her breasts. When he was halfway into her, he had to pause to control himself. It took everything he had not to thrust deep and claim her right in that moment, but she was enjoying herself, making little sounds of pleasure against him and digging her nails into his shoulders. He wouldn't trade that for anything.

He was pretty sure he'd be eligible for sainthood if this took much longer, though. "How do you feel, sweetheart?"

"More," she told him, breathless.

Jason groaned. "I'm trying to go slow for you, love—"

"I know. But I want more. Give me everything," she told him, her eyes full of need. She arched her hips up against him and he sucked in a breath. "Please, Jason. Don't go slow anymore. I can handle it."

He pressed his forehead to hers, holding her close . . . and sank deep.

She sucked in a breath and shifted uncomfortably under him for a moment. He remained perfectly still, because if he moved, he was going to drive into her so hard they'd push across the bed. "That wasn't so bad," she whispered, patting his side.

Well, there was faint praise. Jason bit back a chuckle. He knew she was trying to make him feel better, but "wasn't so bad" hurt his ego. He clearly needed to make her lose her mind with another orgasm, then. He kissed her gently, tugging on her lower lip with his teeth and then worrying away the bite with a flick of his tongue. "Do you hurt?"

"No," she told him honestly. "It feels different and . . . tight, but not bad." And she shifted her hips again as if to prove it to herself.

He pulled back and sank into her again, and when she gasped and held on to his ass, encouraging him to do it again, he couldn't stop. He began to thrust into her, picking up a rhythm. She tried to meet him, lifting her hips clumsily to match his until she moaned, and another shudder rippled through her. "Oh."

Aha. Jason couldn't help but grin even as he thrust into her again. Was she enjoying this part finally? He kept going, trying to keep as steady a rhythm as possible, even as he reached between them in search of her clit. When he found it, she cried out, arching against him.

"Oh god! Jason!"

"I know," he murmured, and stole her mouth in another hard kiss even as he rubbed her clit. He wanted her to come, and come hard. Her movements were jerky, almost as if she were trying to bear down on his cock, so he pushed deeper, pumping hard into her, and he could feel her shudder against him. She whimpered as he rocked into her over and over again, her hips coming off the bed, and he could feel the tension building in her. It was building in him, too, his balls drawing up tight and the need roaring through him like a freight train.

And then she was coming with a little scream of his name, her nails digging into his back, her head thrown back as she arched, her tight channel squeezing him with clench after clench of her release—and then he came, too. With a roar, he let go, his release flooding out of him in one last rough thrust before he collapsed atop her.

Within the space of a few breaths, he propped up on his elbows, shifting his weight so he didn't crush her, and waited for the spots to leave his vision. He'd come so hard he'd practically felt the earth shift, and he knew she'd come just as hard, because he could feel her muscles twitching with little aftershocks of her release. Leaning down, he pressed a light kiss to her mouth. "You okay, sweetheart?"

"Mmm, Merry Christmas," she told him, her voice dazed. A dreamy smile curved her mouth.

He couldn't help but chuckle at the satisfied expression on her face. "Best present I ever had," he told her, and meant it. Sage was special. He could see himself growing old with a girl like her, and for once, the prospect of another fifty or sixty years on this earth didn't fill him with dread. It made him feel utterly content.

With one last kiss, he slid off of her. "I'll get a towel."

In contrast to the rest of the house, her bathroom was messy with makeup and hair products littering the counter, and he grinned to himself at the sight, digging around in a cabinet before he found her hand towels. He peeled his condom off, cleaned himself, then wet another towel with warm water and went to tend to his woman.

Sage gave him shy looks as he insisted on taking care of her, but when he was done and lay back down on the bed, she immediately curled up against him. He pulled her into his arms and tucked her body against his, loving how she fit against him. She felt perfect against him.

Hell, she was perfect, full stop.

When he was with her, he didn't feel like a broken man that had somehow been put back together. She'd never judged him, never made him feel like less even when he showed up on her doorstep in a near panic. Having Achilles around was helping—he knew the dog's calm presence was beneficial even if it wasn't a service dog. Maybe at some point he'd talk to Annie about letting him keep Achilles for his own. But even so, it didn't mean he was fixed. He'd probably always struggle with his memories, with feeling just a little shattered in certain parts of his mind. And he wasn't sure if he should saddle Sage with someone like that. She deserved all the happiness in the world.

Then again, the thought of her being in any other man's arms like this made him feel downright murderous. He pulled her tight against him and pressed a kiss to her temple.

"Hi," she said with a breathless chuckle, patting his chest.

"Hi," he murmured. "How do you feel?"

"I'm fine." He could practically feel her blushing. It was amusing how she was sprawled against him, totally naked, and five minutes ago she'd been panting his name and screaming for more . . . and now she was embarrassed?

"I didn't hurt you, did I?"

"No, it was wonderful." Her hand smoothed down the front of his chest. "Thank you."

"Why are you thanking me?"

"Because it was supposed to be your gift but I feel like the one who ended up with the present," she admitted. "I love you, Jason."

His throat went dry.

"You don't have to say anything," she told him, still rubbing his chest with her fingertips. "I know it's fast, and I probably sound like a crazy person, but I wanted to say it. And even if this never goes anywhere, I'm glad we had this moment."

"That is . . . astonishingly mature," he managed.

Sage laughed. "I'm a virgin, not a moron." She ducked her head against him, nestling close to his neck. "You just make me happy and I wanted to share it. Don't worry. I'm still leaving in the spring."

And he was still a broken mess. When her fingers skated over one of his old scars, he could feel her hesitate, and then she kept going, as if nothing was out of the ordinary. He'd noticed, though. He knew she was trying not to make a big deal out of it, but as long as he held on to those scars and those memories, he probably wasn't the right guy for her.

And didn't that make him feel like shit. She was happy, and beautiful, and when she sold the ranch, she'd be well off. What did he have to offer her? Questionable employment, anxiety attacks, and a half dozen nearly maxed credit cards that he'd lived off of between jobs.

"You're thinking too hard," she murmured, her hand moving to his belly button, and then lower. "I'm supposed to be the one freaking out."

"I just . . . think you can do better than me, Sage."

"Fuck you," she told him, and he looked over at her in surprise. Sage just grinned. "You let me decide what's best for me, all right?"

He didn't know what to say to make that better, so he deflected. "Potty mouth," he teased, amused at her swearing.

"Damn right," she said fiercely, and propped up on one elbow so she could look at him, her hair cascading over her shoulders. "You may think whatever you want about yourself, but do you know what I see when I look at you?"

Jason remained quiet.

"I see a man who knows the value of hard work. I see a man who's kind, generous, funny, and does the best job he can every day. I see a man who's responsible and good with animals. I see a man who realized he'd taken on a job that he knew nothing about and decided to make the very best of it. I see a man who has never made me feel small or stupid. I see a man who makes me feel beautiful every day, and makes me realize that I deserve someone better than Greg. I see a man who makes me wonder how I got so lucky as to have him smile at me." Her hand stilled over his heart. "I don't see Afghanistan. I don't see PTSD. Because you might have PTSD, but that doesn't mean it's who you are. You're Jason Clements, and you're wonderful."

He cupped her cheek, staring up at her shining eyes. She was too pure for this world. He knew she saw him with rose-colored glasses. She saw him as a hard worker, and he saw himself as desperate. Afraid of another dead-end career that led to nowhere. Afraid of letting down more people in his life. Afraid of letting down her.

Damn, but he was tired of being afraid.

He rubbed his thumb over her cheek. "I don't think I'm

the best man for you, Sage," he told her, because he thought she deserved honesty if nothing else. "But I'm going to try to be that man anyhow."

And the smile she beamed at him was one of pure and utter joy.

CHAPTER TWENTY

Sage woke up early the next morning, curled against Jason. Her heart flooded with happiness as she listened to him breathe. She'd never felt so content. Last night had been a dream. They'd made love, curled up by the fire and munched on cookies, made love again, and she'd fallen asleep in his arms. For someone who imagined growing old alone, the sheer joy she felt right now was staggering. She kept worrying that she'd wake up and it would all be a dream. That she'd imagined everything. That this was happening to someone else, not lonely Sage Cooper.

She eased out of bed after a few minutes and pulled on a robe. It was before dawn, but she was used to waking up early. Coffee was needed, and then she'd start making breakfast, and when Jason woke up, they'd take care of the animals together. She stroked Achilles's head as she left the bedroom, but the dog didn't follow her out. He remained at Jason's side, as if he knew his master needed him nearby at all times.

She puttered around in the kitchen, still daydreaming about Jason's mouth and all the places he'd kissed her last night. Oh mercy, but he'd kissed her in places she'd only dreamed of a man touching her, and she'd come so hard that she'd thought her body would explode into a thousand pieces. But he'd held her tightly as she'd come, speaking words of love, and that was almost better than the orgasm. Almost.

Over on the counter, her phone buzzed with an incoming text.

Sage's stomach clenched. She was starting to dread her phone. Who texted on Christmas morning before dawn? The only person she wanted to hear from was upstairs in bed sleeping. Reluctantly, she picked up her phone.

GREG: Merry Christmas.

That seemed . . . benign enough. She didn't respond, though. That would just be encouraging him to text her again. She set the phone back down and returned to making bacon and pancakes. Jason would have to leave soon to go start the morning chores over at the Price Ranch, and she wanted him to have a full belly when he went. Lost in her thoughts, she almost missed when her phone chimed with another unfamiliar sound a few minutes later.

Frowning, she turned back to it. The screen was lit up, and when she picked it up, she recognized the name of the app that had sent her a notification.

It was one of the dating apps.

Ugh.

She'd been so wrapped up in Jason and their developing relationship that she'd forgotten all about the apps. Her profiles had never gotten hits in the past, and it seemed ironic that she'd get attention now, when she didn't want it. She opened the app to disable her profile and frowned at the message on her screen.

DATES4DAYS: You have matched with GREG!

Was . . . that a coincidence? It had to be a coincidence. Her stomach churning, Sage clicked on his profile.

It was Greg all right. The picture was of him in the bathroom mirror, holding up a sign: GO OUT WITH ME, SAGE. Definitely targeting her and only her. Instead of finding it charming, she was annoyed as hell. How many times had he laughed that she could never get a hit? How many times had she complained to her friend that her profile was gathering dust and he'd just teased her about it? Since she'd been avoiding his texts, he'd obviously decided to push things a little further.

He wasn't going to go away quietly. She needed to do something. With a scowl, she deactivated her profile and then deleted the app, and all the other dating apps she had on her phone, just in case. She would talk to Greg about things, explain to him that she was happy. That she was in love with Jason, and that he needed to get over this fixation he had on Sage and get back together with Becca, who truly loved him.

"That's an angry look," Jason murmured, stepping into the kitchen. "Everything all right?" He moved to her side and pulled her close even as she set her phone down on the counter and went back to her bacon.

"Just Greg being his usual annoying self," she admitted as Jason stole a piece of bacon and then caressed her butt through the robe. It was hard to stay mad at Greg when Jason put his chin on her shoulder and wrapped his arms around her from behind.

Heck, it was hard to think of Greg at all.

"You want me to handle it?"

"No. I need to talk to him and make him realize it's not going to happen. I don't know if he'll believe it if it comes from you."

Jason leaned in and nuzzled her neck. "I don't know if he'll believe it if it comes from you, either. He doesn't seem to be good with reality."

He had a point. "We've been friends for a long time, and I think he's just struggling with figuring out who he is. I really do think it's cold feet to do with the wedding and not about me, but maybe I'm wrong. But I'll tell him to meet me in town so we can talk it out." She almost felt sorry for Greg. Almost. It was clear he was having a crisis, and she'd been his friend for so long that it was hard to not jump in to try to help . . . except that he was trying to ruin the best thing that had ever happened to her. So, no, she was going to put her foot down and that was final.

"You tell me if he gives you any grief or makes you uncomfortable," Jason said, holding her closer. "Some men think it's just playing hard to get, and I don't want you thinking you have to handle this on your own. I'll put him in his place if it needs doing."

She tilted her head back and smiled at him. "I know you would. I'm sure it's nothing, though. I'll just chat with him the next time I'm in the office." When he leaned down to kiss her, she slid away, laughing. "If we start making out, I'm going to burn the bacon."

"You're making me choose? Cruel woman." But he moved the pan off the burner quickly and then approached her again, pinning her against the wall and kissing her until they were both breathless.

It seemed Sage won out over bacon, which was gratifying.

The next day, she headed into town, determined to have her talk with Greg. She went into the office, greeted the mailman and mayor, sent out a few customer emails, checked in library books, and kept herself busy until midmorning. Then she sent a text to Greg.

SAGE: You wanted to talk to me?

The answer came immediately.

GREG: Yes! Can we do lunch?

SAGE: Do you promise not to make it weird?

GREG: Oh, come on. We've been friends for forever. You know I won't make it weird.

She didn't know that. And because she'd known him since childhood, she knew how he tended to act when he didn't get something he wanted. Still, she had to put this to bed. She didn't want it hanging over her head like a cloud, marring her happiness with Jason. Greg needed to realize that she'd moved on from her silly crush, and he needed to move on from her.

SAGE: All right. I'll meet you at the pub. Noon?

GREG: You don't want to go somewhere else?

SAGE: Nope. It's there or nowhere. I have to be back at work this afternoon. There's lots of paperwork that has to be filed for the end of the month.

GREG: All right, pub it is.

GREG: See you soon.

Even though she did have a fair amount of billing work to do, Sage couldn't concentrate. It wasn't just the upcoming confrontation with Greg, but Jason, too. He'd come over late last night and they'd made love, practically devouring one another the moment he stepped through the door. Then he'd had to leave again, but not before thoroughly kissing the heck out of her and promising to come back again tonight. She knew he was running himself ragged between his job ranching and spending time with her. All the driving back and forth cut into his sleep, but he said he didn't mind. Something would have to give at some point. Maybe she needed to look at selling off her poor old cattle—or her ranch—sooner, that way she and Jason could figure out better sleeping arrangements. If she was in town instead of on a ranch a half hour in the opposite direction, he'd save a lot of driving time. Of course, it was early to plan that sort of thing yet but . . . she still thought about it.

And she doodled his name linked with hers in a notebook like a teenager, just because.

Jason's texts were less frequent this morning, but he'd started with an apology. There was a lot to do without Dustin on hand to help out, and Cass had a cold, so Eli was playing nursemaid and supervising Jason, which meant everyone was short on time. So she sent him happy messages and pictures to take up the slack, since she knew that even if he didn't have time to respond, he'd like the entertainment.

Then it was noon, and she closed the office for lunch, put on her jacket, and headed down Main Street toward the pub. She tried not to look over at Hannah's window at the inn, where the woman was sure to be watching people come and go and speculating on everything. She also avoided looking at Becca's salon, as if that would somehow assuage her guilt at meeting with Greg. Greg and Sage had been friends for ten years, though. Friends could have lunch with friends and have it not be anything weird, right?

Of course, every other time they'd had lunch together, Greg hadn't just dumped his fiancée without explanation. But Sage wanted to have lunch in the middle of town deliberately—because she knew it was public and people would talk, and she wanted them to realize there was nothing to see.

Greg was waiting inside the pub as she entered, and she gave him a bright smile of greeting. "Hey, stranger."

"Here," he said, rushing forward to meet her. "Let me take your coat for you."

"I've got it," she told him quickly, shrugging it off before he could help. "Where are we sitting, the bar?"

"I got a table in the corner," he told her, and tried to put a hand on her back. She immediately sidestepped and headed toward the table in question. Ugh, it was the dating table. It was the table everyone joked that people sat at when they wanted privacy. Not that there was any privacy in this town . . .

She sat down with a thump and dumped her coat and purse onto the chair next to her so he couldn't sit at her side. "How was your Christmas?" Sage kept her voice bright and cheery.

"Sad," Greg said, sitting across from her and wearing his most hangdog expression. "Lonely."

Sage fought the urge to roll her eyes at his drama. "You didn't spend time with your parents? Didn't call Becca?"

"Becca won't talk to me, and I didn't want her anyhow." He gave Sage a morose look. "The person I wanted to talk to most wouldn't text me back."

She wasn't falling for the guilt dogpile. She knew that trick. "If you're talking about me, I had plans. And my Christmas was lovely, thank you for asking." And because she was thinking about Jason, she couldn't help but smile.

"Well, hello, you two," Wade said, coming up to the table. "How are we doing today?"

Sage beamed up at him. "Hey, Wade. How was your Christmas? How are Gloria and the kids?"

Wade chuckled, putting a hand on her shoulder. "They're great. Kids got a couple of mini piglets for Christmas. Cutest little buggers, but I heard they don't stay small. It's a good thing we know a lot of people with farms." He shook his head. "You're positively glowing, though. Your holiday must have been delightful."

"It really was." She blushed, but she wasn't embarrassed. Rather, she was thrilled that someone else realized how happy she was. "Jason got me the most wonderful gift, a picture of my father I'd never seen before."

"That boy's very thoughtful. I've seen the way he looks at you," Wade said, giving her a nod of approval. "Glad you finally found someone who realized what a gem you are." He gave her shoulder a pat, and then she could have sworn he frowned at Greg like a disapproving father. "And you? How was your holiday?"

"Fine." Greg sounded like he was sulking. "Can I get a coffee and a burger?"

"Of course." Wade winked at Sage. "Your usual lunch sandwich, darlin'?"

"Yes, please." Oh, she'd miss the people in this town when she left. Why did she always think she was never seen when there were people like Wade who doted on her like a favorite uncle? Or the mayor, who staunchly defended her even when she messed up? Or Hannah, who loved to talk gossip about anyone and everyone in town, but would be the first one to open her doors if someone needed a place to stay? Her throat grew tight. Painted Barrel was a small, sometimes claustrophobic community, but it was a community . . . and she'd miss it.

Greg just shot a sour look at Wade as he walked away. "You'd think I'd shot his dog with the way he's acting. I'm allowed to have lunch with you."

"You wanted to talk about something?" Sage prompted. "What's troubling you?"

He reached across the table, waiting for her to put her hand in his.

She deliberately ignored the gesture, keeping her hands in her lap.

Greg sighed. "Sage . . . I feel like I've messed up."

"About Becca?"

"No. I realized I should have never gotten engaged to Becca in the first place." He looked woefully sad. "That there was someone else who had been waiting all along for me to notice them, and I was too blind to see it. Someone perfect, and giving, and kind, and right under my nose, and I want her to know that I finally see her."

Oh lord. "Are you talking about me? Because if you are, just come out and say it, Greg."

"I am. Sage, I can't marry Becca, because I have feelings for you."

Ugh. Her stomach churned uncomfortably. "Greg, no." She kept her voice gentle even though she wanted to smack him upside the head. "I did have a crush on you for a long time, that's true. But when you got engaged to Becca, I realized that we were just friends. I was truly happy for you, that you found love, and I'm sad you've dumped Becca because you have cold feet."

"I don't have cold feet, Sage. Even when we were engaged, I kept feeling like something was wrong." He put his hand on the table again, as if he wanted to snatch hers up . . . except she wasn't offering it. "Becca never looked at me like you do."

"Like we're friends?"

"No, like I'm amazing. And she never makes me cookies, or helps me out, and you've always been there for me in the past." He shook his head, bewildered. "I don't understand why you're being so cruel now. I'm pouring my heart out to you."

"Greg, I'm not trying to be cruel. I'm trying to get you to wake up." She crossed her arms over her chest. "It was wrong of me to keep letting you walk all over me. I shouldn't have made you cookies or picked up your laundry from the dry cleaner. I definitely shouldn't have paid your water bill for you. I realize now you were using me and I was too sad and lonely to realize it. Becca won't do those things for you because you're an adult, not a child. I shouldn't have done them for you, either." She shook her head. "And I'm not in love with you. I'm dating Jason."

He'd been frowning at her through the whole conversation, but when Jason's name was brought up, he scowled. "That junkie cowboy? You're serious about him?"

"He's not a junkie," she snapped, growing defensive. She wanted to tell him the truth, desperately, but Jason would hate that. So she bit her lip and stewed on the secret. "And Jason is wonderful. He's thoughtful and kind and he has always seen me."

"So you're dating him to take revenge on me because my timing was off?" Greg sat back, shocked. "I had no idea you were so petty, Sage."

How was he turning this around to make it her fault? "You're being a spoiled brat, Greg. You can't have your cake and eat it, too. Go back to Becca and apologize, see if she'll take you back." She got to her feet. "I'm sorry that we were friends for so long, because obviously it's painted a strange picture in your head of who I really am. I'm not going to be your girlfriend, so stop texting me when you want sympathy, and quit following me on dating apps. It's not going to happen."

"It would have happened if—"

"No," she said, cutting him off before he could finish that statement. "Enjoy your lunch, but I think I'm going to take mine to go."

A moment later, Wade was there with her sandwich, brown-bagged and ready to go. "I heard the conversation and thought lunch might be ending early," he murmured as he handed the meal over to her. "So I took the liberty of bagging things up for you."

At least one man in this pub had sense. She gave Greg another disappointed look and then paid her bill and left.

Greg was just going to have to figure this out on his own.

CHAPTER TWENTY-ONE

Two Weeks Later

No man had a right to be this happy in terrible weather, Jason figured, but he was. The wind was downright awful, the snow was melting to a sleety crust that was hell for the horses and cattle, and that meant extra work for Eli and Jason. It also meant Dustin's return had been put off several days, as he didn't want to risk driving through the icy mountains with his wife and baby in the car. Once, Jason might have griped about that, but he was surprisingly content. It made it feel like Christmas had been held over for a few more weeks, and there was nothing wrong with that.

"You're grinning to yourself again," Eli told him. "Wasn't aware you were having that much fun."

"Just thinking about Sage."

Eli rolled his eyes. "I could have guessed. Plans tonight? Roads are nasty."

"It's not a bad drive," Jason protested. It wasn't a great drive in this weather, but if the difference was staying home or going to see his woman, he'd take his chances on the road. "She wanted to know if you and Cass liked the jams she sent over."

Eli clucked at his horse, easing it forward as they rode along the gently rolling hills, checking the fences. One of the cows had been slipping away from the herd on the regular, and they couldn't figure out how she was getting out, which meant checking everything. It was a cold, blustery day, but Jason had finally come to an understanding with his horse, Buster, and it no longer felt like the damn thing was trying to buck him every time he sat in the saddle. Sage said it was because he'd had more practice and was no longer so stiff. Jason suspected it was the extra carrots and apples he slipped to the surly beast. Whatever it was, he was getting the hang of this cowboy stuff.

"Cass liked 'em all right. Caught her spreading the jam on crackers at three in the morning last night. Scared the dickens out of me because I thought she was pregnant again and having those crazy cravings she used to get. Nope. Turns out she just wanted to eat my share and hers." A hint of a smile tugged at his hard face. "I told her she could have mine. I ain't interested in peach jalapeño jam. Jam shouldn't be spicy. Cass is addicted to the stuff, though."

"That'll make Sage happy. I'll have her send more over. It gives me an excuse to go spend time with her." Like he needed an excuse. Plus, the baking and cooking and canning were things Sage liked to do on the weekends, which meant she spent a lot of time in the kitchen . . . which meant there was a lot of time to distract her. He'd made love to her on every surface of that kitchen, and then she'd gone crazy cleaning everything with her cheeks bright red in a blush . . . so he'd had to help her dirty it up again. Naturally. She was always game, though, and he was starting to wonder if all the cooking projects she took on regularly were part of a silent tug-of-war. She'd deliberately pick projects in the kitchen knowing he'd distract her with sex.

Well, that was all right with Jason.

"Pay attention," Eli told him. "You're so busy grinning to yourself that you're riding right past all the fences without even lookin' at 'em."

"Got it." Jason chuckled. Once, Eli's surly manner had irked him, but he was used to it now. As long as you worked as hard as he did, Eli didn't much care otherwise. He knew he worked hard enough to please Eli—Cass had mentioned several times how happy she was that Jason was around, and that made him feel good. Like he had a place.

Like he belonged. Weird for an adult man to need to belong so badly, but after the last few years, he craved the belonging like he craved nothing else.

Well, except for Sage. He craved her all the time.

Two weeks after their first time, he still couldn't get enough of her. Kissing Sage, caressing her, making her come? It all raced through his mind a dozen times a day. And while she'd declared her love for him—and usually declared it again every time he was balls-deep inside her—he'd held back the words. Maybe he needed to prove to himself that he wasn't as broken as he thought, so he kept telling himself that if he went a week without an anxiety flare-up, then he'd tell her.

It was getting harder not to say the words, but he didn't want to trap her into a relationship with him. Not yet.

Thinking about his nerves always made his anxiety ratchet up. It was like actually focusing on his problems summoned them, so he scanned the slushy ground, looking for Achilles. The dog was nearby, tail wagging as he followed behind two of the ranch dogs, Bandit and Jim. He wore the silly bright-blue sweater and booties Cass had given him, and the red neckerchief Sage got him. Dog wore more damn clothes than he did, but he was also wading through the snow, and Jason didn't want him to get cold.

He loved that damn dog.

Achilles was the most attentive creature he'd ever met. Truck had been loyal to a fault and utterly competent, and Jason still couldn't think of his old friend without a knot in his throat. Achilles was a different sort of creature entirely, though. Truck had been fierce and determined, and Achilles was less of a warrior than his name implied. He was a happy dog, gentle and easygoing, with a silly streak that showed up from time to time. More than that, though, he was utterly devoted to Jason. The dog followed him everywhere—even to the bathroom—and liked sleeping at his feet. At first he hadn't known what to think of it, just because having Achilles nearby felt like a betrayal to Truck and his memory, but now he couldn't imagine a day without Achilles at his side. The dog loved Sage, too, and she didn't even mind when the dog crawled into bed with them . . . though he made sure to put the dog in the bathroom when he was going to make love to her. Achilles's clinginess was oddly comforting. It was like the dog needed him as much as he needed the dog, and having him around helped ease Jason's mind from the near-constant anxiety attacks that had plagued him after Truck's passing.

He was getting better, day by day, and he knew Achilles helped. He needed to talk to Annie about keeping him. Achilles got along with all the other ranch dogs, so that wouldn't be a problem. He wasn't much of a herder, but Annie had a white Boston terrier, so it wasn't like pets were forbidden. If they gave him a hard time about it, he'd just tell them he'd fallen in love with his buddy and Achilles needed him.

No one had to know his secret.

They weren't able to find the hole in the fence, much to

Eli's consternation, but eventually they went in. As they rode up to the ranch, Jason saw Dustin's truck in the driveway. That meant the others were back from their trip. Heading into the barn, they dismounted and Jason was surprised when Eli grabbed Buster's reins. "I'll rub him down. You go inside and clean up so you can head out. It'll be dark soon and you'll want to be careful on the roads."

That was nice of him. "I'll trade and do yours this weekend," Jason said, then headed toward the house. He entered the mudroom quietly, carefully shutting the door behind Achilles as gently as he could. It tended to slam in the wind and woke the babies—and triggered him—so he made sure to ease it shut quietly and then started to remove his boots.

He was bent over, pulling off one boot when he heard Annie's voice. "So it went well? No problems? He didn't suspect anything?"

"No. At least, I don't think so. They get along great. Achilles goes everywhere with him." Cass's voice.

They were talking about him? Jason paused. He straightened and leaned in, listening.

"Oh good," Annie said. "I was worried he wouldn't take to the dog. Is it helping?"

"From what I can tell. He's been less nervous lately, but I think some of that has to do with Sage, too. You know they're in love?"

"Good. She deserves someone who makes her happy." Annie paused. "So how should we play this?"

"Mmm, I'm not sure. Did you register him as an emotional support animal yet?"

"No, not yet. It needs to be his idea. Achilles has the right personality, but he's still untrained. If Jason wants to go through with it, he'll need to take the final steps on his own. If I do it, it'll seem too obvious."

Hot anger rushed through him as he realized what they were talking about. Achilles wasn't a dog that Annie had rescued because he had attachment issues. They'd gotten Achilles deliberately to place with him on the sly. Which meant they'd known he had PTSD. It didn't make sense, though. He'd only told one other person . . .

His anger was quickly followed by betrayal.

Sage had told them? But she'd sworn to keep his secret from everyone. She knew how it bothered him . . . but she'd never been surprised to see Achilles, had she? Even when he'd shown up with the dog in tow the first time, she'd taken it in stride. She never complained that the dog had to be with him, always.

The answer was obvious—it was because she'd known the whole time.

Furious, he snagged his keys off the hook and slammed back out of the house. Achilles trotted after him, still in his ridiculous dog booties and jacket, and for a moment, Jason wanted to send him inside to be with Annie. He dropped to the ground, and Achilles automatically went into his arms, expecting petting. Some of his anger softened. Even if the dog was a trick, Achilles didn't know it. He was a damn good dog, loyal and loving. He didn't deserve to suffer just because Jason was furious at Sage and her betrayal. "Come on, boy," he murmured to the dog, rubbing his head. "I think you and I have both been played by a pretty pair of dimples."

And he needed the truth. Because if Sage didn't respect him, how could he trust her with anything ever again?

Sage checked her phone for messages from Jason and then put the pan of homemade enchiladas back in the oven to warm. Normally, if he was running late, he'd send her a text, but she hadn't heard anything for hours. A twinge of worry hit her, but the weather had been bad and that was likely keeping him at work longer. He was probably just out arm-deep in the mud retrieving a stray heifer or something. Well, she'd keep dinner warm for him. Sage drifted in and out of the kitchen, her thoughts on Jason and the few hours of time they'd have together tonight. He always came to see her, but lately, the stolen moments after work and on weekends didn't feel like enough. It always made her sad when he left, and she always craved more.

Was a month of dating enough time before you asked someone to move in with you? Actually, it hadn't even been a month. It had been three weeks . . . but she was so comfortable with Jason she didn't care. The amount of time didn't matter. She loved him and trusted him, and she wanted to be with him always. Maybe it was time to sell the ranch after all and stop stalling. She could get an apartment in town and be that much closer . . . but the thought made her heart hurt. This was her home. Her father had loved this place with every ounce of his being. It made no sense to sell it just to move a half hour closer to town . . . but it also made no sense to have this big ranch and not use it.

But while she was here, she still felt close to her father. And Sage wasn't ready to give that up just yet. She touched the framed picture Jason had given her for Christmas, in its place of honor in the front hallway, and then drifted back toward the kitchen.

The doorbell rang, and her heart leapt with excitement. That would be Jason. Turning around, she raced for the door and threw it open. There was Jason, his gorgeous frame filling up her doorway, Achilles at his feet. She beamed at him and wanted to fling herself forward for a kiss in greeting . . .

Except he wasn't smiling. In fact, he wasn't happy at all. His face was grim, the lines of his mouth hard as he stared down at her. Instinctively, she knew something was wrong. "Jason . . . what is it?"

"Did you tell Annie and Cass that I'm fucked-up?"

She winced at the harsh tone of his voice, at the choice of his words. "I would never say such a thing—"

"Did you," he continued, enunciating slowly, "tell them I have PTSD?"

The knot forming in her stomach seemed to go directly to her throat. "Jason . . . it's not what it looks like."

"Really?" She'd never seen him so angry. His hands clenched at his side, and he paced back and forth on the porch, as if unwilling to enter her house. "Because it looks like you're working with them to try and 'fix' me. Is that what this is? You decided I'm broken enough for a new project and took me on, Sage?"

"No," she said quickly. "Jason, I'm just trying to help—"

"So you helped by telling everyone what a mess I am? How a loud noise will turn me into a shivering mess? How I'm messed up and need to keep my job out of pity? Is that why they never fired me?" He laughed, the sound hard and bitter. "Here I thought it was because I worked my ass off. Nope, turns out it was all for pity." His jaw clenched and he stood still, as if trying to compose himself. "How could you, Sage? I trusted you."

Tears pricked her eyes. "Jason, I wasn't trying to hurt you."

"Well, you did. How long have they known? How long has everyone known behind my back?"

Her heart hurt. "Since your second day."

He just stared at her, and she felt ashamed. "I'm so sorry."

"I trusted you, Sage. More than I've trusted anyone in years." He shook his head. "I can't be with you if I can't trust you."

"Jason," she sobbed. "I'm sorry—"

But he turned around and left. She watched in silence as he stormed back out to his truck, Achilles at his heels, his tail waving uncertainly, as if he didn't know what to make of his master's mood. Sage watched his stiff back as he retreated, waiting for him to turn around, to say how angry he was but that he forgave her, that he still loved her and wanted to make things work . . .

He didn't turn around, though. He got back into his truck and left, disappearing into the snow.

Sage sank to her knees and wept. Was the world ending? Because her heart felt like it was. The only thing he'd ever asked of her was to keep his secret . . . and she'd spilled that quick enough, hadn't she? She'd conspired against him.

He was right to hate her, and she sobbed in misery.

CHAPTER TWENTY-TWO

She slept on the couch, her phone next to her head, and stared at the front door, hoping vainly that he'd show up and tell her that he'd forgiven her. That he understood why she'd done it. That she'd been trying to protect him and he got it.

Instead, she woke up with a crick in her neck, and the world went on around her. Miserable, Sage fed Lucy and Ethel, cried, showered, cried, got dressed, cried some more, and went in to work. She wept all over the outgoing mail. She wept on the mayor's shoulder. She went through an entire box of tissues until her nose was red and her eyes swollen, and she still couldn't stop crying.

When she'd dreamed of being in love with Jason, she'd never thought she'd lose him so soon. That he'd reject her like this and make her feel as if the world had ended when he'd walked out the door. It hadn't ended, of course. Life went on, and Sage did, too. But it hurt. Oh, it hurt. And she didn't know if she'd ever get over this hurt. Her heart felt like a hollowed-out shell.

Hannah showed up at the office to pick up her mail, took one look at Sage's red eyes, and immediately pulled her in for a hug. "Oh, sweetheart," she said, her voice gentle. "I hate to see you hurt. There's no one kinder than you, and it pains me to see you crying."

And because that was so nice, Sage sobbed on her shoulder as Hannah rubbed her back and told her about how hard it had been for her to go on after her first husband died. It was *not* the right story to tell at the moment, but Sage knew Hannah was trying, and she appreciated it even if the tale just made her feel worse.

"I just love him so much, Hannah," Sage said in a wobbly voice, balling up her tissue in her hand.

"He loves you, too," Hannah replied, and Sage's heart skipped a beat. How did she know? But Hannah went on, patting her back. "I'm sure he had a reason for breaking your heart." The woman watched her closely.

Sage just nodded. There was a reason, and Sage couldn't fault it . . . but she also wouldn't tell Hannah what it was. "I messed up," she said simply.

"Well, no relationship is without mistakes. He'll come to his senses, or you'll move on. You're the sweetest girl, Sage, and so pretty. You'll find someone else."

"Thanks, Hannah."

The old woman beamed at her. "Maybe you rebound with Greg, hmm? Maybe it's fate that you're both single again after all these years."

All these years? As if Sage hadn't been single this entire time, waiting for Greg, only for him to ignore her? Again, she managed to keep smiling, somehow. "I appreciate the pep talk."

"Of course. If you need me, just holler. I'll be across the street." She took her mail . . . and instead of heading back to her hotel, she went down the street to the salon, no doubt so she could tell everyone the gossip of the day. Sage bit back a sigh. Even tigers didn't change their stripes.

That was all right. She'd manage.

Somehow.

You could still function with a broken heart, right? Her dad had done it all those years . . . but he'd had Sage.

She had no one.

She pulled out another handful of tissues and mopped her eyes miserably.

After a few more days of silence from Jason, Sage's misery compounded. She knew what she had to do. That change she'd been putting off for so long? It was time to make the leap. Her heart utterly heavy, she texted Greg.

SAGE: Hey. I know we talked about putting the ranch up for sale in the spring when the market was best, but I think I need to sell it now.

GREG: I am absolutely ready to help you—but what made you change your mind?

SAGE: Long story. What do you need from me to start the listing?

GREG: I'll send you some paperwork, but let's get together and start the ball rolling. Can I come to your place? Say, tomorrow night? We'll do a walk-through and I'll take a few preliminary pictures.

SAGE: Sure. 7 p.m. okay?

GREG: Great. Shall I bring dinner?

SAGE: No, it's okay. My appetite hasn't been much lately.

GREG: Everything okay???

SAGE: Just fine. I just need to make a change.

She wasn't going to tell him that her heart was broken. Everyone in town already knew that anyhow. Sage had been given so many sympathetic looks over the last few days. She kept hoping the rumors to turn, that people would say, "Oh, but what do you expect? It's Sage Cooper." But they never did. Everyone was kind and gracious to her, and that made things worse.

So yeah, it was time to start fresh. To finally clean the slate like she'd talked about for so long. To start a new life in a completely different place.

She wasn't looking forward to it in the slightest, but maybe in time it would be a good thing. Maybe.

Jason was in a foul mood.

That was nothing new. He'd been in a foul mood ever since he'd found out the truth. He was angry at Cass and Annie, angry at Eli and Dustin, angry at Sage . . . angry at the world. He went through work with a scowl on his face and said nothing to anyone. He knew Dustin and Eli suspected something was up, but they didn't ask, and that was just fine, because he wasn't volunteering it. He took on chores that meant he could avoid conversations, and he spent most of his days stabbing at hay with pitchforks because that helped ease his anger. He did his work, but he wasn't pleasant about it, and he made sure the others knew how he felt. The only one he trusted was Achilles, and that was because the dog was too innocent to know what he'd been pulled into.

He was irritated with Cass and the others for prying into his business, but he expected it. People always gave him weird looks when they found out he had post-traumatic stress. They always treated him differently, acted strangely. Forcing a dog on him to try and calm him—even if it had worked—was irritating and typical. At least they hadn't tried to force him into therapy or pushed essential oils on him as if sniffing lavender would fix his brain.

What hurt the most was Sage's betrayal. He'd trusted her. He'd let her in and gotten closer to her than he had any other human being. He'd opened himself up . . . and she'd immediately gone behind his back and tried to fix him despite claiming that he wasn't broken in her eyes. That was what hurt the worst. That she said one thing and did another.

After a few days of Jason's surliness, though, Eli and Dustin confronted him in the barn. "What's chapping your ass?" Dustin asked, arms crossed. "You've been pissy ever since I got back."

Jason just tried to step past them. "I'm not in the mood for chitchat."

Eli put a hand on his shoulder, stopping Jason before he could storm away. "You need to speak up, because you're making everyone miserable."

Was he making everyone miserable? Good. He glared at both of them.

"Heard you and Sage are done," Dustin continued. "That why you're so pissy? She dumped you?"

Hearing her name made him ache. Not just because he felt betrayed . . . but because he still missed her. Part of the reason his mood was so foul was that he felt as if something he cherished had been snatched from him. Sage was his home, and now his home was destroyed. He missed her, he missed her kisses, her smile, her dimples, her sunny outlook . . . but he couldn't get past the part where she lied. How she thought he was broken and needed fixing.

That still hurt, and it was going to take more than a few nights' sleep to get over. "Don't talk to me about Sage," he told them. "That's private."

"You're new to this town, so I'm gonna let you in on a secret—not much is private around Painted Barrel," Dustin said with a wry grin. "Might wanna get used to that."

"You mean like the part where someone set me up with an emotional support dog without my knowledge?" he lashed out.

"Ah," said Dustin.

"That why you and Sage broke up?" Eli asked, frowning at him.

"I can't be with someone I can't trust. Someone that doesn't have my back," Jason said.

"You dumbass." Eli gave Jason an incredulous look. "That's why you're both so miserable?" He shook his head. "That's just plain stupid. She's a great girl."

"And she's always had your back," Dustin added, glaring at Jason as if he were the one in the wrong.

"Nice try," Jason said, hating that his heart ached. "It's pretty clear to me that Sage means well, but it doesn't mean her actions don't have consequences. I wanted to take this job so no one knew I had PTSD."

"You dumbass," Eli said again. "She's the only reason you still have this job. When you got here on day one it was obvious you didn't know what the hell you were doing."

"And that you'd never sat on a horse before," Dustin added.

"You were sweating like a pig and got all nervous every time someone said something. Kept looking around like you expected an attack. We thought you were on something and were about to give you the boot, but Cass felt sorry for you and went to talk to Sage, instead. Sage refused to tell her anything about you. She wouldn't betray you and she had your back. It was only when Cass said that you were gonna get fired that she mentioned what the real problem was."

Dustin nodded. "Cass twisted her arm. We haven't said anything to anyone else in town, either. Sage was heartbroken to spill your secret, but she also didn't want you to lose your job. She just was in a bad position."

Jason swallowed hard. Sage . . . hadn't wanted to betray him?

"And I'm not gonna apologize for what my wife did," Eli said gruffly. "We have babies in the house and have to think of their safety. We thought you might be dangerous, especially with the sneaking out and circling the house. Look at it from our perspective."

He knew what they were saying was the truth. Hadn't he been fired from other jobs in the past because he'd made other workers nervous with his obsessive patrolling? He knew he got nervous and sweaty when he was in the throes of stress. It was hard to look at it from the outside and realize maybe, just maybe, his anger was misplaced. "I see."

"You probably don't wanna hear this right now," Dustin said, "but Sage is a good girl. Everything she's done for you, she's done probably because she genuinely wants you to succeed. I've never met someone with such a big heart, and I just don't think you should throw her away."

Eli nodded.

They didn't know the half of it, either. They didn't know how she'd worked with him that entire first weekend, determined to teach him as much as she could about working on a ranch. They didn't know how many times she'd quietly steered him out of a situation that made his anxiety flare. She'd always been there for him . . . which was why her betrayal had cut so deep.

But if Cass had basically forced her to choose between his keeping his job and sharing his secret . . . he supposed she chose the right thing. "I need to think about this for a while."

"If you don't want to work here, that's fine," Eli said. "If you don't want Achilles, that's fine, too. We'll find him a home. But Sage deserves better than this."

"I'm keeping Achilles," Jason said gruffly, and he scowled when Dustin just grinned as if pleased. "And I'd like to stay on here, if you'd have me."

"You can't ride for shit but you work hard," Eli said flatly. "We've made cowboys out of worse."

Jason snorted, biting back a laugh. "Thanks, I think."

Dustin just shook his head, smiling. "You think about what we said . . . just don't think too hard or wait too long, because you know that Greg asshole is just waiting to make a move."

He knew Dustin was right . . . and he didn't like it. Sage was amazing and kind, but she also had a big blind spot when it came to Greg.

And Greg was a damn user. He'd see this as an opportunity to get "his" woman back.

Jason would just have to go over and talk to her. See if they could work this out between them, because even though he hurt and felt betrayed . . . he still loved her. And the thought of Greg muscling in and stealing her away made him crazy.

Sage was his. It had taken a hard talk from Dustin and Eli to make him realize that . . . Now he needed to make her realize that, too.

CHAPTER TWENTY-THREE

When a vehicle pulled up to Sage's house an hour before she was supposed to meet with Greg, her heart skipped a beat.

Please be Jason. Please be Jason.

Maybe it was just a fantasy that she hoped he would show up, flowers in his arms, telling her that he loved her and he forgave her for not keeping his secret. That he couldn't live without her. That everything was meaningless unless she was in his arms. Smoothing her hair, she rushed to the door, hope brimming in every pore.

But the truck that pulled up was Greg's flashy yellow oversize pickup, not Jason's plain gray compact truck. She sagged with defeat, fighting back the tears that threatened.

It had been a nice fantasy for the brief moment it existed. Ah well.

Greg hopped out of the truck and strode up to her house, and Sage couldn't help but notice that he was wearing a button-up shirt and jacket, and instead of approaching, he went to the far side of his truck and opened the door, then pulled out an enormous bouquet. When he came closer, she could smell his cologne.

Oh no. Her fantasy was quickly turning into a nightmare. "Hi, Greg," she managed, giving him a faint, watery smile. "Come on in. The flowers will look great in the main dining if you're taking pictures tonight." She'd been cleaning all day in preparation for this, but now that it was here, she just ached. Soon her home wouldn't be her home anymore.

"The flowers are for you, beautiful," Greg said, thrusting them into her arms. He frowned at the sight of her face. "Why is your nose so red? And your eyes are all puffy, too."

So much for the "beautiful." Sage would have laughed if she wasn't so danged sad. "That's what happens when you cry." Her nose was raw and she was clogged up from all the tears. It definitely wasn't her sexiest moment, but then again, she hadn't invited Greg over for that anyhow. She just wanted to get the house up for sale, finish her business here in Painted Barrel, and lick her wounds somewhere else. Maybe Seattle. Maybe Boston. Maybe Tampa. Who knew?

"Don't be sad," Greg told her, moving in for a hug.

She held the flowers between them, blocking him off. "You're not here to hit on me, are you?"

"Sage," he said, exasperated. "You and I are friends."

Her shoulders eased a little at that. "You're right. Sorry."

"But it doesn't mean we can't be more. I know you're hurting right now, but I want to tell you . . . I'll wait." He put his hands on her shoulders. "I'll wait, Sage."

Oh brother. She shrugged his hands off. "Greg. You and I are never happening—"

"But Becca and I are done. And since you and Jason are done, this seems like fate, doesn't it?"

No, it just seemed like the world's most awful irony. "I'm selling the ranch and leaving Wyoming, Greg. For good."

His brows furrowed. "But . . . I can't leave Wyoming. My real estate license is here."

You weren't invited, she wanted to say, but she just shook her head. "I'm going to start over fresh somewhere else. This is just about the house, Greg. It's not about me looking for a rebound."

"It's not?" He really did sound surprised. "I thought . . ."

"No."

"But . . ."

"No."

"Sage . . ."

"Still no."

Greg sighed. "I broke up with Becca for you, Sage."

"No." She kept her voice firm. "You broke up with Becca for you. Don't pin that shit on me."

His eyes widened. "I've never heard you cuss."

"It's something I'm working on." Jason would have been proud of her salty mouth . . . and that just made her feel like crying all over again. "So what do I need to fill out for the ranch sale?"

Greg looked embarrassed. "Ah, I didn't really think that was why you were inviting me over, so I didn't bring the paperwork."

What? "But you said you were bringing it."

"I thought it was a ploy to get me to your place so we could have some alone time."

Ugh. Flowers or not, she was suddenly sick of him. "You know what, Greg? This isn't working for me. You're clearly not taking this seriously, so maybe I'll find someone else." She thrust the flowers onto the nearest surface and went back to the door. "I'll see you around town."

"No, Sage, wait—"

Screw waiting. She opened the door, intending to show him out—

And there was Jason on her porch, his cowboy hat dusted with snow. Achilles was at his feet, wearing his red bandana, and Jason was leaning in, one hand up as if about to knock.

"Hi," he said softly.

Oh. She sagged against the door, so full of longing that her entire body felt heavy with it. "Jason . . . what are you doing here?"

"I wanted to talk to you," he said quietly. "Is this a bad time?" He looked over her shoulder, and then his eyes narrowed.

She turned and saw Greg standing behind her, his arms crossed. Oh no. Oh no, he was going to think she was replacing him with her old crush. Oh god, this was a nightmare that just never ended. "Greg was just leaving," she blurted.

"Sage," Greg whined again.

"No, you're leaving. We can talk about the ranch some other time." Her voice was firm as she gestured at the door. Jason's expression changed to one of relief, and a hint of a smile curved his mouth. He stepped to the side as Greg shoved his hands in his pockets and stormed out the door.

She almost felt bad. Almost.

Jason remained quiet until Greg got in his truck and drove away. He glanced over at her. "Did I smell cologne on him?"

"Unfortunately." She sighed. "That did not go as I planned."

Jason's gaze grew intense as he watched her. "I saw him here and thought for a moment that maybe you'd already moved on from me."

Sage wanted to weep all over again. It did look like that, didn't it? "I called him here because I told him I wanted to put the ranch on the market now."

"You do? I thought things were slow in the winter?"

"There's no reason for me to stay," she whispered, her voice breaking. It was difficult to have a normal conversation with him, especially when he was so damn gorgeous looming over her, all lean and hard and sexy.

"I don't want you to go," Jason said suddenly. He reached out and caressed her cheek, brushing his fingers over her face. "Sage, talk to me first. Let's work this out before you make any decisions, all right?"

"You want to work things out?" Her lips parted in surprise. "With me?"

"Well, yeah." His throat worked. "I love you, Sage."

She sagged against the door, her knees unable to support her.

He reached out and put a hand to her waist, holding her steady. "Come here, sweetheart," he murmured, pulling her against him. He pressed a kiss to her brow and held her close. "I'm sorry."

Hot tears flooded her eyes for what felt like the millionth time. "Why are you sorry? I'm the one who betrayed your trust—"

"But I should have known you'd have a good reason. That you wouldn't try to fix me. I should have had more faith in you." Jason pressed another kiss to her brow, then another. "I need to explain—"

"It's okay," she said quickly. She was just so relieved that he didn't hate her.

"It's not okay. I need to tell you this so you understand." He cupped her face and tilted her gaze up to meet his eyes. "I was just so mad at the world I couldn't see straight. It was like I was losing everything I had all over again and I was powerless to stop it. I was going to lose my job and lose my woman, and then I'd lose everything." She shook her head, but he continued before she could speak. "I always react out of fear. It's fight or flight with post-traumatic stress, and I went too quickly to 'fight.' I talked to Dustin and Eli, and they warned me that I was going to lose you, and I realized that I didn't care about any of that as long as I had you in my life. That you were the only person who had always believed in me and that you'd supported me even in my worst moments. I still think of that first time I saw you in the municipal office. I showed up on your doorstep sweating and in a panic, and you just made me feel like that sort of thing happened to everyone. That I wasn't a weirdo."

"You're not weird—"

"Not to you. Never to you. That's just one of many reasons why I fell in love with you. Even if you can't forgive me, don't go back to Greg. You deserve better than him, sweetheart."

"I don't want anyone but you, Jason. I love you. That hasn't changed. I'm just so sorry I hurt you."

He pulled her close in a tight hug. "Eli told me that Cass forced you to speak up because she threatened my job. I can't hold that against you. You were trying to protect me."

"I don't think you're broken," she told him softly, holding on as if she never wanted to let go. "I just didn't want you to lose your job over something that's not your fault. Because you know this isn't, right? It's not something you can help. No one would choose this. You're braver than anyone I've ever met because you fight it every day and get through it." She buried her face against his chest, and he put a hand to her hair, holding her against him. "Don't you ever think badly of yourself ever again."

"Are you really selling the house?" Jason asked softly, stroking her hair.

Her breath caught in her throat. "I can't be here without you," she admitted.

"Then be here with me. Just don't leave me."

Her fantasy was coming true after all. "Tell me this is real. That you're really here." She closed her eyes. If she was dreaming, she didn't want to wake up.

"I'm here," he said softly. "Somewhat cranky at Greg, somewhat mad at myself for all these days apart. And wondering what I need to do to make it up to you."

"You don't have to make anything up to me," she protested, lifting her head.

"Nothing? But I hurt you."

She'd hurt him, too, but they were moving past that. She bit her lip and suddenly felt like teasing him. "Kissing, maybe."

His mouth tugged up at the corner. "Kissing, you say?"

"A few kisses for forgiveness," Sage agreed, hoping he'd realize she was being playful. "And then perhaps other things."

"I'm very open to forgiveness," he murmured. "Very. So are you the one doing the forgiving kisses or me?"

Did it have to be just one of them? She pretended to consider. "Perhaps I'll start and you can finish. I think we're both in need of kisses, I mean, forgiveness."

"I like where this is going." To her surprise, he leaned down, put an arm behind her legs, and then picked her up in his arms, princess style. He smiled down at her and Sage's heart fluttered.

God, how she loved this man.

Her emotions must have shown in her eyes. His smile faded and he gazed down at her. "I love you, Sage. Meeting you was the best thing to ever happen to me."

"I love you, too. So much, Jason."

He carried her toward the sofa, their normal make-out spot of choice. "If you want to leave Wyoming, I still understand. It'll be harder to carry on a long-distance relationship, but I'm willing to make it work if you are."

Sage stared up at him, dumbfounded. He wanted her even if she left? "Jason, I don't want to go anywhere if you're here. I only wanted to leave because I was lonely. With you here, my life is perfect."

"I'd ask you to move in with me, but I'm afraid there's not much room at the Price Ranch," he admitted. "But if you don't mind waiting a few months for me to save some money up, I want to be with you."

Her heart skipped a beat, and then pure joy coursed through her. "You can stay here with me. Now. Forever."

"It won't make you sad to stay here?"

"It'll make me sadder to leave." She looked around at the house, at its oh-so-familiar furnishings. "My father loved this place with every breath in his body. I want my children to love it just as much."

"Our children," he told her, and her chest filled with love.

"Ours," she agreed, her arms going around his neck.

Jason gave her a crooked smile. "Hope you like dogs. I'm gonna keep Achilles."

She gasped with pleasure. "You are?"

He nodded. "Gonna get him registered as my emotional support animal. It's not the same as a service dog, but he's a good boy, and he needs me as much as I need him." He glanced down at the floor, where Achilles was squirming with puppylike joy. "Even if it wasn't my idea at first, it's still a good one."

"I'm glad," Sage told him. "And lucky for you, I love dogs. But not as much as kisses."

"Then I'll just have to make sure to give you lots of kisses," he murmured, setting her down gently on the sofa. The moment he did, she pushed their bodies forward until she was lying atop him, her arms around his neck.

She kissed him with all the love in her heart, and neither one of them got up for a very, very long time.

EPILOGUE

Two Years Later

Sage rubbed her aching back and got up from her chair in her office. It was too darn warm for the middle of December, and the heater was going full blast. With a hand to support her heavy, pregnant belly, she waddled out of her office and into the main part of the municipal building.

"Good morning, Mayor!" her new assistant said brightly. Charlotte was a sweet girl, freshly graduated from Painted Barrel's schools and eager to take over the library and other municipal duties now that Sage had been elected to replace the mayor. "How's the baby kicking this morning?"

"Hard, as usual." She smiled at Charlotte. "He hears the Christmas music and likes to dance along with it."

Charlotte giggled and shook her head as she sorted the mail. "Now I can't stop picturing a dancing baby in there."

That made two of them. Ever since Sage had felt the first flutter of her son in her belly, the child had been rambunctious and active. He did flips, he shifted his weight, he kicked her bladder at three in the morning—you name it,

and that baby did it. Not that Sage minded. He was just re-
minding his mother that he was getting ready to come out.
She hoped he'd stay in through the holidays, though. Sage
still had the Christmas festival to finish planning
and presents to buy, and . . . she shook her head. Even if the
baby showed up on Christmas Eve, she'd be thrilled, because
it would mean their little family was finally complete.

"Have you seen Jason?" she asked Charlotte. He always
came by in the morning and brought her a fresh cup of
coffee. She was in the office by seven every weekday because there was so much to be done, but Jason stayed
around the Slanted C Ranch in the morning to tend to
the herd. They had two cowboys living in the cabins out
behind the barn—old ex-navy friends of Jason's who were
greenhorns—getting their feet wet and learning ranching.
The herd was small at less than a hundred cattle, but more
than enough for her busy husband and their two greenhorns. She didn't know if they also suffered from PTSD.
She didn't ask. She just knew they needed jobs and that was
enough. Jason split his time between their ranch and helping out at the Price Ranch, where he and Dustin and Eli ran
the much larger herd. He didn't have to work there, but he
loved it, so she didn't complain, even when it kept him out
late. He liked being part of the community.

She knew what that was like.

"Oh, there's your husband," Charlotte said just as Sage
started to waddle away again. Sage turned, and sure enough,
there was her gorgeous cowboy in the windows as he headed
up the walk. She drank in the sight of him greedily, as hungry for him after nearly two years of marriage as she was
that first night he kissed her. He wore his cowboy hat easily
now, the brim battered with seasons of use. His shirt was a
dark blue plaid with a quilted vest over it to keep him warm,

and he wore jeans that outlined his lanky frame. And boots. Always boots. At his side, Achilles trotted in his bright red service harness, ever present. Her husband had a cup of coffee in one hand and a bag of donuts in the other, and Sage wanted to swoon with how thoughtful he was.

She'd woken up last night craving fresh donuts, and he'd laughed even as he'd rubbed her swollen feet so she could go back to sleep. He'd remembered her craving this morning, though, and that made him the sexiest man on the planet. "My two favorite men," she greeted him and Achilles as they entered the office.

"Brought you some decaf, sweetheart." He leaned down and gave her a soft kiss of greeting. "How's my baby?"

Sage put her hands on her belly. "Tap-dancing as usual."

He grinned at her and held up the bag. "I brought my other baby some donuts."

"I see that." She held her hands out and made a grabby motion. "Gimme."

Jason handed the bag over, and she took a bite out of a soft, melt-in-your-mouth-fresh donut, her eyes closing with pleasure. God, he was a good man.

"Hmm," Jason said, drawing her attention. He glanced around the office and tapped his chin while Charlotte giggled behind the counter. "Something's missing."

"It is?" Sage asked, swallowing her bite. She looked at the festive office—there was a Christmas tree with presents underneath it in one corner, festive bows on every surface possible, and the windows were covered in frosted snowflakes. The office was so cluttered with Christmas decorations that it was practically screaming with holiday cheer. Maybe Sage had overdone it, but this was her first Christmas as mayor of Painted Barrel, and she was going to go all out. "What are we missing?"

Jason snapped his fingers and pulled something out of his pocket. "This needs to hang over your office door."

She looked down at the mistletoe in surprise, then laughed. "Why mistletoe?"

"Because that was where we kissed for the second time." He smiled down at her. "And that was where I fell in love with you."

What a romantic. Sage sighed happily and pointed at the maintenance closet. "There's a stepladder in there."

Five minutes later, her husband had the mistletoe hung in front of her door, and he pulled her under it. He tugged her into his arms, rubbed a hand down one side of her bulging belly, and grinned at her. "Now you need to avoid everyone that comes in here trying to steal kisses from you. I'm the only man the mayor kisses."

She snorted with amusement. "Remember who you're talking to?"

"Oh, I remember. Sage Cooper-Clements, prettiest woman in Painted Barrel, my lovely wife, and the mother of my baby." He pulled her close and gave her a kiss full of promise. "Merry Christmas, my love."

"Merry Christmas," she whispered back. He didn't even have to joke about her kissing other men—she'd never wanted anyone but him, and she never would.

Jason was everything.

Keep reading for a sneak peek
at the next Wyoming Cowboy romance

THE COWBOY MEETS
HIS MATCH

Coming soon from Jove!

S ometimes it was hard to live in a town like Painted Barrel. While the community was small and intimate and supportive, it was also impossible to have secrets. Worse than that, everyone seemed to think they knew what was best for you, even if you didn't agree.

Which meant Becca heard a lot of well-meaning advice daily, no matter how many times she tried to escape it.

"You really should get out there and start dating again," Mrs. Williams told her for the seventh time in the last hour. "A pretty thing like you? You don't want all your good years going to waste. If you want to start a family, you need to move fast."

And wasn't that just depressing? Becca did her best to smile as she plucked foils off Mrs. Williams's head, as if the woman's kind words weren't stabbing her in the heart. "I'm not sure I'm ready to date. I'll know when I meet the right person."

Her customer *tsked*. "Like I said, don't wait too long.

You don't want to be the oldest mother at the PTA meetings." She nodded into the mirror at her reflection as if this was the worst thing in the world to happen. "It's very difficult for the children."

"I'll keep that in mind," Becca murmured as she pulled off the last of the foils. "Let's rinse now, shall we?"

The good thing about rinsing was that because the water was going, it meant Becca didn't have to talk—or listen to Mrs. Williams talk. Thank goodness for that rinse, because she needed a few minutes to compose herself. Becca had always thought that two years would be enough time to mend her broken heart. Two years surely should have been enough time to get over the man who left her on the eve of their wedding. It should have been enough time to get over the bitterness that swallowed her up every time she paid the credit card bills that she still had from the wedding that never happened.

Instead, it all seemed to just irritate her more and more.

It didn't help that everyone in Painted Barrel still asked about The Wedding That Wasn't. Of course they did. Becca being left at the altar (well, practically) was the biggest scandal that Painted Barrel had in all of the town's uninspiring history. She'd always been popular around town. She was moderately cute, tried her best to be friendly to everyone, ran her own local business, and for ten years, she'd dated the ex-captain of the local football team: handsome, blond Greg Wallace.

Oh, Greg.

Greg was not good at making decisions about what he wanted in life. It had taken her ten years to figure out that particular tidbit of information, but now that she had, it explained so much. It explained why Greg never finished college, or why he'd never held down a job for longer than a year or two. It explained why he'd gone back and forth on their relationship, first wanting to see other people, then wanting Becca back, then getting engaged, calling it off, getting engaged again, and then deciding a few days before the wedding that he'd changed his mind and was in love with another woman.

She'd been a damned idiot for far too long.

Becca scrubbed at Mrs. Williams's hair, then shampooed it, asking about the woman's grandchildren without listening to the answer. Her thoughts were still on Greg. Why had she wasted so much time with him? Was she truly that stupid?

But no, she supposed it wasn't stupidity as much as it was a soft heart, a fear of being alone, and the fact that Greg was a terrible decision maker but a great apologizer. He'd been so sweet every time he'd come crawling back that she'd felt like the world's worst person if she said no. So she said yes . . . and yes, and yes . . .

And now look where she was. Becca Loftis still had her salon in Painted Barrel, but she was turning 30, utterly single, and now she was being warned that her womb was aging with every day that passed.

For someone who had always said she didn't want to turn into her mother, she sure was doing a terrible job of breaking that pattern. Heck, according to Mrs. Williamson, she was failing children she hadn't even had yet and—

"Too hot," the woman under the water cried out. "Too hot, Becca!"

"Sorry," Becca said quickly, turning the water cooler and trying not to feel too ashamed. Even now, Greg was ruining her life, wasn't he? "You were saying it was Jimmy's sixth birthday last week?" She was relieved when Mrs. Williamson settled back down in the salon chair and began to talk once more.

Enough about Greg. She had customers to take care of, unlike him.

Becca was sweeping up underneath the chair after her last appointment of the day when the door to the salon chimed. She looked up, and inwardly felt a little stab of emotion when Sage Cooper-Clements waddled in. The new mayor was the nicest woman, and once upon a time, Becca had thought she was the loveliest, most giving person, sweet and shy and eternally single.

Then Greg had decided he'd wanted Sage instead of Becca.

Then Sage had turned around and married some tall cowboy and immediately gotten pregnant.

Now Sage was the mayor of Painted Barrel and the new "darling" of the small town. Everyone loved her. Everyone touched her belly when she walked in, and asked about her new husband. They asked about her family's ranch. They gave her advice and doted on her.

And Becca didn't hate her. Not really. It wasn't Sage's fault that Greg had bailed on Becca because he'd thought he was in love with Sage.

It was just that . . . it was hard not to be envious of someone who suddenly had everything you'd always wanted. Not the mayor thing, of course, but a loving husband and a baby? God, Becca had wanted so badly to be in her shoes.

She gave Sage a wistful smile. "Hey, Sage. How can I help you?"

Sage beamed at her and lumbered forward, all pregnancy belly and long, loose dress. She thrust a flier toward Becca. "I just wanted to let you know that we're having a Small Business Summit next month to promote local tradesmen.

All the shops in Painted Barrel and the neighboring towns can rent booths in the gym and we're going to make a big festival of it. There'll be food and drinks, and everyone can sell goods from their booths. I wanted to invite you personally since you're on Main Street and one of this town's mainstays."

The pregnant mayor smiled at her, and Becca did her best to take the flyer with a modicum of enthusiasm. It was just as Sage said, a festival featuring small businesses. "I'm not sure if I can do a hair cutting booth," she admitted. At Sage's crestfallen look, she hastily amended, "But I'm sure I'll think of something! Maybe quickie manicures?"

"Wonderful! Just fill out the form on the back and turn it in at city hall and I'll make sure we save you a booth, okay?" Sage glanced around the hair salon awkwardly, her hand on her belly. She looked uncomfortable, and Becca kept smiling, even though it felt frozen on her face. They'd been friends before The Wedding That Wasn't, and now it was a little tricky finding the right footing once more.

They smiled at each other for a moment longer, and silence fell.

Please don't say anything about Greg, Becca thought. Please don't—

"I'm really sorry about how things turned out, Becca," Sage said softly. She bit her lip, her hand running up and down the large bulge of baby belly under her dress. "You know I had no idea that he was going to do that."

Becca somehow found it in her to keep smiling. "Don't apologize, Sage. It was all him, okay? No one should have to make excuses for Greg." That big, walking human turd Greg. "He's a grown man."

"Yeah, but I feel responsible—"

"You're not." She cut the other woman off, just wanting

the conversation to end. Couldn't Sage see that this was the last thing that Becca wanted to talk about? With anyone? Certainly not with the happy, glowing pregnant woman that Greg thought he was in love with? "Please. Let's just not bring it up ever again, okay?"

"Okay, so, uh, I'm going to go," Sage said, thumbing a gesture at the door.

Becca held up the flyer. "I'll make sure to get this filled out, I promise."

"Great. Awesome." Sage turned toward the door, waving. "I'll talk to you later!"

"Bye." She stayed in place, clutching the broom handle in one hand, the flyer in the other, until Sage headed out of the salon and down the sidewalk of quaint Main Street. Once the other woman disappeared, Becca returned to calmly sweeping . . .

For all of a minute. Her hands were shaking and she gave up, setting the broom down and then walking to her small office at the back of the salon, where she kept her bookkeeping items and the tiny refrigerator with her lunch. She shut the door behind her, thumped down on a stool, and took a long, steeling breath.

She would not cry.

She would NOT cry.

Greg didn't deserve her tears. He'd had ten years of her life, keeping her on hold and promising her that they'd get married soon, soon, soon, and then soon finally had a date . . . a date he'd never gone along with. She'd given him enough of her time and energy. She wanted to move on.

Why wouldn't anyone let her freaking move *on*?

She swiped at the corners of her eyes carefully, proud that there were only a few stray tears instead of the normal deluge. Good. That meant she wouldn't have to go to extremes to fix her makeup, just a little touch-up here and there. She could end the day on a high note, in case she had any walk-ins. Of course, if she did have one, they'd probably just ask her about Greg again . . .

Her lip wobbled. Damn it.

Becca sniffed hard, and even as she did, the door opened in the main area of the salon, the bell chiming. Crap. Sage had probably come back to apologize again, and that would make Becca cry even harder, and it was going to ruin her evening. She'd just have to somehow tell the well-meaning pregnant woman that really, truly, she was fine and really, HONESTLY, she did not want to talk about it. Gritting her teeth, she forced a bright smile to her face, pinched her cheeks so the rosiness there would hopefully distract from her red eyes, and opened the door to face Sage.

Except . . . it wasn't Sage.

The hulking man who stood in the doorway wasn't anything like the mayor. In fact, Becca had never seen this man in her life. That was something interesting in itself, considering that Painted Barrel was a small town nestled in the less populated north of Wyoming, and most of the people that lived here tended to be lifers. Becca had grown up here, her family was still here, and she knew everyone in the small town. It was both comfort and annoyance—and lately it had been far more of the latter.

This man was a stranger, though. She stared at him, doing her best not to gape. He wore a faded black and red checked shirt, and it seemed almost too tight for the massive breadth of his shoulders. He was tall, maybe six and a half feet, but more intimidating than that were his arms, which seemed like tree trunks, and his black beard, which seemed like something out of a Paul Bunyan storybook. He wore jeans and big muddy work boots, and a dark cowboy hat covered longish, unkempt hair.

He really did seem like Paul Bunyan come to life if Paul Bunyan had been a cowboy, but wasn't Paul Bunyan friendly? This man had a massive scowl on his face as if he hated the world around him.

Becca blinked and tried to size up the man, thinking fast. There weren't many outsiders in this part of town right now. Either he'd gotten lost and needed directions or he was one of the new ranch hands. Not at Sage's ranch, because she'd met those nice gentlemen—former soldiers looking to start a new life. The only other "outsiders" in the area were the three new ranch hands at Swinging C up in the mountains, and those were Doc Parson's nephews. She hadn't met any of them, but rumor had it that they were from the wilds of Alaska, here to help out for a season.

This man definitely fit the Alaska stereotype. He didn't look like a typical customer. Heck, he didn't even look like he'd ever been to a salon. That beard was untamed and so was the hair under the hat. She'd bet his nailbeds were rough and his hands were covered in calluses.

It was a mystery why he'd shown up in her salon. Becca was just about to open her mouth and ask if he was lost when something behind his massive jeans-clad thighs moved.

Then, she saw the little girl.

The big cowboy was holding the hand of the tiniest, daintiest little creature. Becca's heart melted as the small face peeped around his leg and her thumb went into her mouth. The girl watched Becca with big eyes, not moving out from behind her protector's leg.

Well. This must be the daddy. It was clear he wasn't here

for himself, but for his little girl. That did something to her heart. For all that he was slightly terrifying, Paul Bunyan was a dad and this little one wasn't scared of him. That meant he was the best kind of dad.

"Hi, there," Becca said brightly to the two of them. "What can I help you with?"

The man just gazed at her with dark eyes. He said nothing, and after a long moment, he tugged on the hand of the little girl, leading her forward a step.

All right, he wasn't much of a talker. Ranching took all kinds, and she wasn't surprised that this one was a silent type. It would be kind of ironic if he was related to Doc Parsons, though, because that veterinarian was the nicest man but definitely a talker. She studied the little girl, who stood in front of her enormous father, sucking her thumb. Her cheeks were fat and rosy, and she wore the most adorable little pink dress and striped pink and white leggings. In contrast, the soft golden curls atop her head looked haphazard, pulled into a high, tight knot.

"What can I help you with?" Becca asked, crouching to get eye level with the little one.

The girl just stared at Becca, intimidated.

"Gum."

Becca looked up in surprise. The big, silent behemoth had spoken. "Gum?" She echoed.

He nodded and nudged the little girl forward again.

The thumb popped out of her mouth and the girl spoke. "I ate all of Grampa's gum and went to sleep and when I woke up my gum was all gone."

Oh. And she was here at a hairdresser. That wasn't a good sign. But Becca kept the smile on her face and put her hand out. "I bet I know where it is. Shall we take a look?"

The small, adorable creature put her hand in Becca's and

gave her a triumphant look. "It's in my HAIR! And Daddy said you'd be able to get it out."

Eek, did he say that? Becca cast the man an awkward look. "Well, let's see what we can do, then." She led the little girl over to the salon chair and lifted her into it. "What's your name, sweetheart?"

"Libby." She looked on eagerly as Becca pulled out a bright pink cape and tied it under her chin.

"How old are you, Libby?"

"Four."

"Three," corrected the man gruffly.

"Three," agreed Libby, kicking her feet under the cape.

"I see," Becca said as the man sat down in the other salon chair next to Libby's, his big legs sprawling out in front of him. "Three is a great age. That means you're a big girl." She reached for the ponytail holder to pull it out of the girl's topknot, only to realize the gum was twisted into it as well. Oh dear. Normally, she'd pick through the loose hair to check for lice—because you never knew with kids—but this was going to be . . . interesting. She touched a few strands, trying to determine how it had happened. Gum really was everywhere. Long strings of it seemed to be melted into the delicate curls, and all of it was mixed in with the hair tie. The entire thing seemed to be glued together with a light brown substance she couldn't figure out. After a moment, she sniffed. "Is this . . . peanut butter?"

She looked over at the big man, but his jaw clenched and he remained silent. After a long moment, he shrugged.

"Daddy tried to help," Libby said brightly. "But I didn't tell him about the gum for two days and he said that was bad."

Two days? Well, that explained the rancid knot atop Libby's little head. "I see."

"Late night," the man said in a gruff voice. "Sick cattle."

"I wasn't judging," Becca replied gently. She moved to the counter and grabbed a large bottle of hair oil. "Sometimes it's hard to get away from work. Trust me, I know." She crooked a smile at him, trying to put him at ease. "Emergencies come up, even at a hair salon." And she gestured to his little daughter.

He just stared at her.

Right. Okay, so that was awkward. She turned back to Libby. "Daddy was off to a good start with the peanut butter," she told the little girl. "We're going to put more oil in your hair and see if we can't work some more of this gum out, all right?"

"Okay," Libby said brightly.

"Why don't you tell me about you," Becca continued, dousing the girl's head with oil and trying not to worry about how the heck she was going to salvage this little one's hair without shaving it down to the scalp. "You're a big girl of three. Do you have any brothers or sisters?"

"I have two uncles! They're big and hairy like Daddy."

"Two uncles," Becca repeated, grinning. This was definitely one of Doc Parson's nephews. From the rumors around town, all three had come down from Alaska. "What about your Mommy?"

"I don't have a mommy." Libby said, kicking her legs some more. "It's just Daddy and Uncle Caleb and Uncle Jack and Grampa Curtis."

"I see." She discreetly glanced over at the girl's father, but the man didn't make eye contact with her. Kept his gaze on his daughter as Becca tried to work the hair tie free. Her heart squeezed with sympathy, just a little. A single dad with a young daughter? No wonder he hadn't noticed the gum in her hair until it was a disaster. She imagined that raising a child alone was hard, and with no other women to lean on? He was doing a great job.

Libby rattled on and on as Becca picked and fussed at the knot on her head. Long minutes passed, but Libby wasn't much of a squirmer compared to some of the other kids Becca got in her chair, which was a good thing. She was content to talk and talk, asking about all the hair products on Becca's counter and if she liked cartoons and flowers and everything under the sun.

"Is this your daddy's shop?" Libby asked as Becca's oily fingers worked out another strand of hair.

"No, it's my shop. I started it myself."

"So you can play with people's hair all day?"

She chuckled. "Yes, that's right. I like playing with hair. Especially little girls' hair."

"Do you have a little girl?"

Her heart squeezed. "No."

"A little boy?"

"I don't have any family," she said brightly. "No kids, no husband."

"Daddy doesn't have a wife either."

"Libby," the man growled.

Becca chuckled. "It's fine." Her cheeks were heating, though. She peeked at the man again. He was big and brawny, and under that crazy beard, he just might be handsome. Not that it really mattered all that much—she hadn't paid attention to any man but Greg for the last while, so her radar was off. This particular guy wasn't much of a talker, but maybe he was just shy. He did have a cute daughter, though.

Maybe . . . maybe this was a step in the right direction. Maybe she should take the bull by the horns and rustle herself up a date. Then everyone would realize she was over Greg, they weren't getting back together, and they'd stop treating her like the bastion of lonely spinsterhood. She could show everyone she'd moved on.

All it would take was one date. They wouldn't even have to have chemistry. It just had to be dinner, enough to show that she'd continued on with her life and everyone should forget about The Wedding That Wasn't.

She didn't jump on the idea right away, though. She needed time to mull over it, and working on Libby's hair was the perfect distraction. The gum was so entangled that she'd spent a good half hour on the child's hair and was just now starting to work the hair tie out of the knot. She was pretty confident she could get this done, but it would take a while.

Unless he'd rather shave her head and be done with the mess.

Pursing her lips, Becca wiped her hands on a towel. "Can I talk to you for a minute, Mr. . . ."

He didn't offer his name, just got to his feet and followed her as she headed to the far end of the salon, by the front door. It was getting dark outside, and it was long past time for her to close up shop. She kept wiping her hands on the towel, her thoughts all over the place.

The man just kept watching her, waiting.

Okay, she was clearly going to have to carry the conversation. "I think I can get most of the gum out of Libby's hair, but it's going to take a while."

He grunted.

"Like, hours. I have to go slow because her hair's very fine and I don't want to pull on it. The other option is to shave her head, but I'm not sure how you feel about that."

The big cowboy looked over at his little girl again, then back at Becca. He rubbed his bearded jaw. "She won't like it shaved."

"Well . . . I have time if you have time." She gave him a bright smile.

He paused. "Is . . . this an inconvenience?" The words seemed like they were being dragged out of him.

"No, like I told Libby, I don't have anyone waiting at home for me. It wasn't how I planned on spending my evening, but that's all right."

The big man grunted again. "Appreciated."

They both paused, and Becca took in a steeling breath. This was her moment. This was the chance she should take. She could ask him out on a date, and shake off the specter of Greg and The Wedding That Wasn't once and for all. So she toyed with a lock of her highlighted hair and hoped he found her reasonably attractive. "Is it true what Libby said? That you're not married?"

The dark eyes narrowed on her. Intense. Scrutinizing. He glanced at her, up and down, as if sizing her up.

Becca flushed. She charged ahead. It wasn't about this guy in particular. It was any guy, just to change how the town viewed her. She needed to change the conversation, period. "I know I'm being forward. I hope you don't mind. But . . . I figure now's as good a time as any to ask. Want to go on a date?"

He stared at her, up and down again. There was a long, awkward pause. Then he spoke one single word.

"No."

Ready to find
your next great read?

Let us help.

Visit prh.com/nextread